An Absence of Artificers

Emma Bradley

For all of us who are still fighting
for the freedom to choose,
with hopes of a better tomorrow.

The citadel is vast and full of spies,
but with your wits you should be okay.

Oh, and watch out for Talie.
Rumour has it she bites.

CHAPTER ONE

The middle-aged woman slumped crying over her desk definitely didn't abduct her husband.

Molly Acorn was almost sure of that, even from her hidden perch high up on a neighbouring rooftop. The patchwork stone lane laid out below was silent in the pre-dawn darkness, but she could see into the crying woman's living room easily enough by the lamp on the table.

From her vantage point nestled next to the central core of the citadel tower she lived in, she could see the great citadel of Faerie sprawling above and below, a seemingly endless hive of different levels. The citadel was formed of five towers that rose into the clouds, with walkways of metal running between them and archways of wood expanding to vast walls of glass that domed the entire structure inside.

Down below, the woman wiped her eyes and switched off the lamp. Molly rubbed a stab of pity from her chest and wished she could offer some comfort, even though she couldn't get involved. It was the first rule of the Menagerie: no emotional entanglements, even well-meaning ones. She glanced at the silver scar on the back of her wrist, a tiny tattoo of a spiralling cage cast in glimmering silver. It was the sign of her service to the Menagerie, mainly useful because it stopped the boots hassling her. As the law enforcement office of the citadel, the boots tried to keep order over the upper levels, but anyone in the know knew that the Menagerie pulled their strings.

Molly groaned quietly to her feet. She couldn't do much about any of it at fifteen, too busy trying to keep on top of the small workshop she'd inherited from her guardians as well as her Menagerie duties at night. It all kept the bills on the workshop paid, and one thing she'd learned young in the citadel was that nobody would be coming to save her, and anyone who offered to was after something.

She glanced up at the stretch of sky visible between the metal and wood of the level above, each level a continuing part of the endless spiralling lane going up and down. Rumour had it that nobility lived at the base of the citadel, but Molly was closer to the 'survive or don't get out alive' levels nearer the tower-tops.

With one last look at the sun rising above the citadel, she took off at a jog across the rooftops. As she headed toward the Menagerie offices, she shook away the usual daydreams of venturing to the more prestigious lower levels and venturing out to the wild forests beyond the glass. Up on her level, the windows were smaller and showed the wide expanse of sky, the forest far below a vast carpet of tiny fibres, but it was enough to feed a dream.

Not that she had any desire to swill in the bejewelled luxury the rumours said the lower levels had. She liked her modest neighbourhood as the lanes were mostly clean and the people honest enough about their dishonesty.

Dawn broke fast through the glass, the twinge of purple on an inky sky becoming a riotous blaze of gold and pinks as the scent of horse and the odd rattle of carriage wheels drifted up from below. She stepped carefully along one of the narrower metal beams with roofs below her feet. The Menagerie utilised the network of beams and girders between the levels, hiding amid the chimney stacks, flues and support pillars, and she had no fear of being seen.

At the end of the beam she climbed the pillar, already dreaming of her bed. Grooves and handholds had been harrowed in over the years to make the process of climbing easier for Menagerie spies, and she scaled up two levels with only minimal muscle ache, edging sideways until she reached the rooftop next to the Menagerie.

Sprawling through several rambling stone buildings, the Menagerie had two entrances, the respectable front doors from the lane outside, and the second floor window that was always open, accessible only from the roof. Molly dropped through the window, her steps soundless on the immaculate blue carpet, and padded toward the double doors at the far end of the hall.

Marcus, the owner of the Menagerie, prized punctuality and presentation above all things, other than loyalty, and he'd asked her to report in after her shift so here she was. She ran a rough hand through her hair, several blonde strands in need of brushing following her fingers. Unable to do anything about her threadbare cotton trousers or her t-shirt with the hole in the hem, she knocked on the door.

"Enter."

She pushed the door open and stepped inside. The office had several intriguing instruments set on wooden stands at either chest of head height. They formed a lopsided circle around the desk in the middle, but Molly had never been in a close enough position to Marcus, socially or hierarchically, to ask what they were. A large circle of dark blue glass swirled like herb-oil in water on his desk, and next to that the surface of a mirror flickered with the odd hint of movement. The mirror was lying down with its surface facing the ceiling, but a quick glance up and she couldn't see any sign of movement reflected up there.

Behind the desk, Marcus sat with his dark hair neatly combed and his severe gaze fixed on her.

"You were observing the latest missing artificer's family?" he prompted.

He wasn't one for small talk and Molly could appreciate that, even if his firm tone and permanently narrowed brow often gave her the jitters.

"Yes. Nothing specific to report. His wife went about her routine alone until the early hours, writing some letters. I had a quick look but they were all full of worry."

"You had a quick look?" he asked, his tone sharp.

She nodded. "Only through the window when she left the room. She was muttering about tea so I assumed it would take her longer than a moment or few."

"So, nothing yet. Which one was he?"

Molly frowned. Of the few Fae that had gone missing recently, one had been a member of the boots and one was a cobbler from a lower level. Then there was one from the Artificer's guild, where the more arcane Fae experimented with gift lore and the magic connections all Fae had inside them.

The fourth missing man, whose wife she'd spent the night watching, was the second man from the Artificer's guild to go missing.

"Another artificer," she said.

Marcus frowned. "Fine, you can go. Are you working on the same tomorrow?"

"Yes, unless there's something else?"

"No."

He dropped his gaze to papers on his desk and picked up his pen, so Molly tiptoed out of the office and shut the door behind her. She wouldn't normally let someone like Marcus rattle her, but as her employer he held her future in his hands.

She strode along the corridor back toward the window to the roof.

I only have two more years and my debt will be paid off. She let that thought soothe her weariness. *No need to think about how unlikely it is they'll let me go skipping off at the end of it.*

"Molly?"

Her name echoed out through an open doorway as she passed it, and she doubled back with a weary smile.

Celeste eased herself out of her office chair and padded closer. Old enough to be her mother, or much older sister at least, Celeste managed the more social side of the Menagerie. Although the place called itself a circumstantial employment service, it acted as a hub for more devious requirements. As far as Molly could work out, Celeste handled the legitimate business and Marcus the underhanded side. But Celeste was kind and full of smiles, always ready to stop and have a quick word.

"All done for the night, dearest?" Celeste asked, halfway through braiding her long sandy hair.

Molly nodded. "Yeah, no joy but I'll be going back tomorrow night."

"Less I know the better," Celeste chuckled. "But here, take this and go get yourself some sleep."

Molly held her hand out automatically so Celeste could drop a pesana and a boiled sweet onto her palm. She'd given up insisting it wasn't necessary, especially as pesanas were the only currency the upper levels of the citadel recognised and she needed all she could get. Celeste also liked to spoil all of the waifs and strays who ended up in dubious amounts of debt to the Menagerie.

"Thanks."

She pocketed the gifts and nodded a quick farewell.

The sun was rising fast over the citadel as she passed through the Menagerie's opulent entrance hall and vast front doors. She turned her face toward it for a few moments, then set off up the lane.

Her workshop was only four levels up from the Menagerie, and she lowered her hood as she neared home. To all those who knew her during the day, she was one of them, a local who bought their wares and fixed things for them when they needed it. Nobody knew she was a spy by night and she intended to keep it that way.

Her workshop was down a short side-alley off the main lane, and she checked over her shoulder and above her head before unlocking the front door. She would need to throw it open soon in case anyone came needing her services, but there were a few short hours left for sleeping first.

Exactly as she'd left it, the workshop was one square room with items strewn all over the place in organised chaos. There were a few woodwork projects she had to finish that were laid out neatly on the large wooden table in the centre of the room, mostly broken items people had asked her to fix and a few creative efforts she had to make as gifts for others. At the back she had her kitchenette in the far right corner, the tiny box of a bathroom in the middle that had a sketchy agreement with intermittent hot water, and her bed behind a screen to the left.

A loud rapping echoed on the door before she could even make it across the room. She inhaled deeply and fixed a smile on her face.

I need every pesana. I can't turn away work.

She swung the door open and eyed the woman leaning with one hand pinned against the doorframe.

"Hi, we just moved in next door," the woman announced.

Her cheeks were bright pink and she sounded out of breath, but that wasn't what Molly was focused on. The woman was ridiculously pregnant, like about-to-spill full of baby.

"Um, hi?"

The woman huffed. "Yeah. What's your name?"

"I- Molly, but are you okay?"

"I'm carrying half a cow, does it look like I'm okay?"

"Er... no?"

The woman wiped a hand through her bright purple hair as someone jogged up behind her. Molly tensed as the man put hands on the woman's shoulders and gave her a wry grimace.

"We said we'd come introduce ourselves together," he chided, clearly either completely dim or really stupidly brave. "It's also really, *really* early."

The woman glared at him and pointed at her stomach.

"Don't you think you've done enough?"

He grinned at Molly as she tried to discreetly shuffle backwards quickly enough to get the door shut.

"Sorry, she has hormones." He ducked the hand that flew at his head. "This is Beryl and I'm Harvey. It's lovely to meet- *ow* don't punch!"

Molly stared in horror as the woman managed to get not only a punch angled right into the man's gut but also a slap to the back of his head before she relented.

Note to me, don't piss off the pregnant woman.

"Well, welcome," she said, her hand firm on the door. "I need to start working but if you need anything, I'm here during the day."

Beryl nodded. "No problem. You won't even notice we're here."

Molly doubted that but mumbled a quick goodbye before retreating into her room. The moment the sound of squabbling receded, she crossed the room and sagged onto her chair. The couple likely wouldn't give her much trouble with a new baby, and she didn't have to justify herself to them anyway.

Pulling herself closer to the table so she could begin fixing the mechanism on Sable Copperblossom's automated grain dispenser, she glanced around at her room. It wasn't much, full of strategically placed clutter, but she'd learned early that most things could be fixed with a random assortment of other things, and you never knew when an unexpected item would be just the thing you needed.

It also helped keep her respectable and regular which hid her servitude to the Menagerie, and she enjoyed fixing and creating things. Her reputation was growing too. Not that she was low down the citadel enough for noble folk with their fancy percat money, but then she didn't need their patronage. Being born in the well-off half of the citadel didn't make you special. It made you lucky.

"Got you a bun."

Molly found a smile beneath her exhaustion, lifting her head to find Ru looming in the doorway and blocking out the murky morning light. His dark brown hair was rumpled, the deep blue eyes hooded from his own night on Menagerie business. Broad and strong but with a certain lethal grace, he was her best friend. Or as best a friend she could get in a place where safety was a luxury and trust was more like fantasy. She was so pleased to see the bun he was holding, she didn't even grumble at him opening the door without knocking.

"Thanks." She held her hand out without getting up. "Is it oia berry?"

He nodded and crossed the short distance between the door and her desk to set a brown paper bag in front of her.

"Yep, blue one as well. You know Merry only gives me the blue ones because of you."

Molly grinned and hauled out the pastry, which was spilling dark blue jam from one end.

"What you been up to?" Ru asked, rescuing the bag and pulling out a second pastry.

Molly gulped down her first mouthful. "Can't tell you that. You?"

"Can't tell you that," he echoed, his eyes dancing with wickedness. "These disappearances are getting weird though, we can say that for free."

"Two servants to two different lords and ladies, a cobbler from a lower level than here and one of the boots, who was so old they probably only kept him on to stop him blabbing secrets. Then the artificer most recently."

Ru chuckled, his pastry already gone. "There'll be a link, there always is."

"Ah, but what is it?" Molly leaned back in her chair. "That's the important question."

CHAPTER TWO

Molly realised the next evening that the link between all the missing Fae wasn't as important as figuring out why the missing artificer, whose wife she'd been spying on for the Menagerie, was currently sitting in his living room drinking a glass of *Beast*.

Sat on the high-up metal girder above his house, she couldn't see any immediate signs of him being dishevelled, bruised or even emotionally shaken. No, despite the quiet hunt for him over the past two days by various Menagerie employees, there he was lounging in an armchair as though nothing remarkable had happened.

It had taken her extra time to slip away as well because the new neighbours insisted on collaring her as she passed. One of the main rules the Menagerie insisted on was politeness at all times, because a person gained less attention that way. To all the realm Molly was a young woman working her way through life and going out to see friends in her spare time.

"Seymour, you can't just act like nothing's happened!"

The previously missing artificer's wife was rightly frantic as it floated out of their open window. Relieved she wouldn't have to resort to lip-reading, Molly relaxed her twingling muscles.

The woman clutched one hand in her hair with the other waving wildly enough to sweep an entire stack of magazines off a varnished table.

Seymour lifted his head and Molly craned her neck, one hand on the cold girder as she leaned forward to make out the baffled expression on his face.

"Well, nothing has happened," he said. "I went to Frankie's, lost track of time."

"You've been gone for three days! I went to Frankie's two days ago and he hadn't seen you."

Seymour rubbed his chin. "Are you sure you had the right Frankie? There's Frankie, then there's Frank."

His wife stared at him, her lips forming words she couldn't quite voice. Seymour stood up and patted her shoulder.

"I'll go see them, sort it all out. Then perhaps we can take a brief holiday to a lower level. You've been working so hard."

"I am not the one going mad!" She slapped a palm against his chest.

"I'll sort this out," he insisted. "Not to worry."

She called after him but they disappeared into the house and Molly lost sight of them. Rubbing a hand over her eyes, she contemplated the quickest way back to the Menagerie. The man's behaviour was weird by anyone's standards, not because he'd disappeared from his wife, but from everyone. Usually when the Menagerie were called in by someone worried for their significant other, there was a quick trail to an affair partner, a secret child, or in one case Molly remembered fondly a group of men hiding their equivalent of a stitch and bitch session. But a man who disappeared even from the Menagerie, then returned with no apparent recollection of ever having been away, that was odd even by Fae standards.

Molly eased out of her crouch with a grunt, freezing when a quiet thud filled the air. It was dark, most in their beds or at least in the cosiness of their own homes, and Molly only had a handful of hours before she had to be up and visible as her daytime self.

Down below, Seymour left his house while still pulling on his coat, heading along the lane going upward.

Molly bit her lip. She wasn't qualified for following yet and the Menagerie had strict rules about sticking to your role. Hers was watching and reporting.

But if I follow him, I'm technically still watching, just in an unexpected location.

It wasn't a justifiable excuse by any standards, but she was already moving. Her shoes made no sound on the metal underfoot, her fingertips brushing the pillars she passed and eased around.

She followed Seymour up eight levels, her insides grumbling as she passed over the alley that led to home. Seymour moved from shadow to shadow, his head turning as he checked every side lane.

Molly frowned as he dipped into a random alley. They weren't on a level that had much of note, just a range of warehouses and hardly any residential areas. The girder she crept along disappeared into a solid concrete wall and she paused with her attention tilted downward.

Seymour glanced around before lifting his hand to knock on a random door. From her vantage point, Molly couldn't see it, but a brief muttering echoed and Seymour disappeared from view.

Temptation warred with self-preservation. She should take everything back to Marcus, but he wouldn't exactly be forgiving if she admitted to following someone. His rules were clear and final about not overstepping clearance.

Molly looked up, searching the walls. She'd learned young that buildings could be a playground, the core of each level built the same. No matter how many exits or entrances there were at ground level, most had a smoke-flue or small window hatch higher up.

She spied a dark patch and pushed aside her doubts.

I'll just have the quickest look. If something weird is going on, we should be aware.

With a soft breath of resolve, she reached high up the nearest beam and started climbing. Her legging-grips needed re-surfacing but her muscles were strong enough to compensate, and she clambered up to the small hatch in the wall with confident movements.

The hatch appeared in front of her and she balanced on the wide ledge beneath it to look at the network of beams inside, a sure sign she was looking into a warehouse. With a small smile, she slipped through the hatch, one hand out to steady herself as she dropped onto the inside beam.

Voices echoed below and she dipped into a crouch, keeping to the wall. In the rare event someone saw her, she would be all hood and cloak hidden in the shadows.

Molly balanced a hand on a nearby beam, easing her foot around a lump of white fabric and a tangle of rope, no doubt some old banner or guard against the rain.

Down below, Seymour shuffled across the bare warehouse floor toward a table and two chairs.

"I sit here?" he asked, glancing back over his shoulder.

A low hum replied but Molly didn't catch the words or see who spoke.

Seymour took a seat, his hands twisting in his lap. Molly bit her lip and inched her foot backwards as doubt rippled through her chest. Only the middle levels seemed to have a misapprehension about the seedier goings on throughout the citadel, too comfortable to understand the struggle that drove crime but not yet avaricious enough to take advantage of it.

A loud slam echoed through the warehouse and she jumped back a step, her hand pushing hard into the beam to hold her balance.

"You again."

The voice sounded young and feminine, but with a sharp bite that hinted at regular snapping. Molly leaned forward to peer down as a girl of a similar age to her took a seat opposite Seymour.

Long-limbed with tumbling black hair, the girl's rumpled dark jeans looked so worn that the knees were going grey while her baggy navy cardigan exposed narrow wrists and long fingers decorated with bands of black and silver.

"You were the girl who told me about the spiked drink," Seymour announced.

The girl nodded. "Yeah, the party. What brings you back here? We told you everything that happened already."

"I remember strange memories." Seymour scratched his neck. "My wife is adamant I used to have a heat gift but I can't seem to find it, can't really recall. Did I… was there some kind of substance at this party?"

Molly leaned forward, gaze flicking over the girl's impassive expression.

"There might well have been, but we've not had any reports. Have you had any headaches, dizziness?"

Seymour shook his head. "No, just this strange nagging feeling in the back of my head that I'm forgetting something. From what I remember, it wasn't a particularly impressive party. No balloons, not many people."

"Oh, well we do try. What brings you back here?"

Seymour turned, looking around. Molly flinched behind the pillar as his head twisted up in her direction.

"Oh, um…" His voice faltered. "I thought… I'm not sure."

The touch of confusion in his voice overrode the uneasiness, as though he really couldn't remember the answer.

"They did say you drank a fair amount," the girl said. "Might be worth taking a quick holiday. I have heard of gifts becoming dormant a while, so maybe the drink has knocked it a bit."

She stared at Seymour with dismissive expectation until he rose from the chair.

"Right, yes you're probably right. Sorry."

The girl stood and shunted her chair under the table with

a loud clang.

"Go take a rest," she suggested again. "Focus on your family. You could have drunk far too much more, so I'd count yourself lucky."

Seymour nodded. "Yes, absolutely."

He stepped away from the table as an ear-shattering bang blasted through the air. Molly flinched back, her hand sliding along the beam in an attempt to catch and keep her balance. She steadied, breathing deeply with her heart thudding as she stepped forward to grab the beam again.

Her foot swung forward and caught on the abandoned piece of fabric.

She threw her arms out, her balance shot to nothing as the motion kicked the bulk of the fabric over the edge.

Molly teetered on one leg, her arms splayed like the rope walkers who had to fix the string lighting over the lower levels, the accursed fabric dangling from her outstretched foot.

The girl must have gone to see what the fuss was about as she came storming back to Seymour moments later, muttering under her breath.

Molly gritted her jaw as the fabric began to slip. No matter how much she lifted her foot or her leg, the weight of the fabric was too powerful and intent on going downwards.

Inching her knee into a bend, she tried to turn in time to get the middle of it sideways so it would fall over the beam.

So close to achieving it, she almost missed the subtle blur of darkness swiping in front of her face.

Almost.

Realisation dawned, fear exploding a second later. The bird settled like a behemoth of old in front of her feet, it's mottled brown head tilted up at her. She could see the sharply curved beak and each individual talon.

Don't do it, don't. She froze, aware of the slipping fabric.

The bird hopped forward.

Molly fought every natural instinct but an almighty shudder wracked her shoulders. It shook through her entire body as she battled the fearful scream burning up her throat.

It's just a bird. It's just a bird.

The mantra her guardian had taught her when they found out she was petrified of birds didn't help. Her mind twisted as her foot slipped, the fabric wrapping around her ankle.

With a startled yelp she couldn't gulp down in time, she tumbled downward.

CHAPTER THREE

Air rushed past Molly's face in a kaleidoscope of greyish brown, and she braced for a bone-shattering crash.

A violent jolt shot through her leg, but there wasn't any head or shoulder pain. Squinting up past a sea of dirty white, she eyed the rope attached to the fabric but also the beam high up on the other end, her foot tangled in between.

An orbing loading bay. She grimaced.

Falling tangled up in a huge loading sack was a small mercy, and she was only dangling a couple of feet above the ground, but she still had to find a way out without being seen.

"What in the levels..."

The girl's voice was guarded and worryingly nearby.

Keeping one hand on her head to secure her hood, Molly wriggled her foot free and thudded to the floor in a heap. Lifting her head with the hood clamped tight, she eyed a pile of sturdy wooden boxes against the wall, then the service ladder. From there it wouldn't be too much hardship to vault over onto the lower beam structure and back up to the hatch.

"It's a body!" Seymour shouted.

"What's all this noise?" A third voice, deep and

masculine demanded. "Talie, what's going on?"

Talie. The girl's name no doubt, but not something Molly needed to focus on right now. She eased her legs free of the fabric. Sure she had a clean break, she twisted onto her knees and used her free hand to launch to her feet, the other still clamped to her hood.

"Hey!" the girl, Talie, shouted.

Molly ran. Head down, she vaulted up the pile of boxes and shot up the service ladder. Gritting her teeth at the ache in her limbs from the fall, she twisted and leapt, hands outstretched.

It wasn't her most elegant jump, her forearms slamming onto the beam, legs flailing under her. Her hood slipped as she swung herself up with all her might and dashed with her arms out toward the hatch.

"I'll find you," Talie yelled. "Whoever you are, I'll track you down."

Molly squeezed through the hatch with her nerves jangling and ran the whole way to her level, across the rooftops and down into her lane. She dropped in front of her door and fumbled for the key she kept around her neck, shaking almost too much to get it into the lock.

Falling into her room, she shut the door behind her and stumbled to the chair behind her cluttered desk.

"It's okay, it's going to be okay," she muttered. "She has no idea who I am. I'll lay low, stick to my usual scouting assignments. Nobody has to know."

She grabbed a leftover mug of *offke* and gulped a huge mouthful of the tangy liquid.

A loud hammering on the door almost had her throwing

the mug.

Her insides jittered as she put it down and rose to her feet, inching toward the door with her mind a tangle.

Should I have a weapon in case? What can she accuse me of, spying? Marcus will be angry but I was technically over-performing my job.

It wouldn't matter to Lord Stickler of Rules Marcus, but she could try. She fixed her expression into a look of tired bewilderment and stood weaponless to swing the door open.

"I- oh, hi Ru." She sagged, her muscles dribbling to jelly.

He frowned. "Expecting someone else?"

"No?" She cleared her throat to get rid of the unexpected squeak. "Why would I be?"

She stepped back and he stepped in, closing the door behind him.

"Do you want some leftover *offke*?" she asked.

He leaned his back against the door and folded his brawny arms across his chest. His sweatshirt sleeves were rolled up, a sign he'd probably spent the night on Menagerie business.

"You're being weird."

"I'm always weird."

"No, weird for you. Squirrely. What's going on, Mol?"

She hesitated. Ru was her friend, her best friend. He was also her liaison at the Menagerie. If she told him what she'd done and seen, he might tell Marcus.

Unless I convince him otherwise.

He'd learned to navigate her charm gift so it didn't work

on him much now, she wasn't sure how, but nobody knew about her compulsion gift. Not even him. Compulsion gifts were sought after by many, and she'd learned young that Fae often wanted to control those who could easily manipulate others.

Temptation warred with wariness as she pulled her Fae connection to the fore, the familiar warmth of it tingling over her skin.

Ru's suspicious expression twisted before she could find a way to word-tangle the idea of her 'squirrely' behaviour out of his head. He raised a hand to rub at his chin, the hints of stubble emerging after a long night.

"Never mind." He sighed. "I'm tetchy because... well, anyway, it doesn't matter."

She forced her gift back with a frown, wondering immediately what had caused his mood, and his sudden desire to drop things he'd usually go for the throat over.

"I'll tell you mine if you tell me yours," she said.

Fae couldn't lie. She'd heard the frightening tales growing up, of humans in some far-flung other realm who could lie at will, but Fae had to be far more artful in their deception. It wouldn't even be deception technically if she only told him a tiny part of the truth.

Ru hesitated, a slow grin breaking over his face. With his forearms folded over his chest, he tilted his head back against the door.

"You first then."

She stepped back until she hit the edge of her desk, almost dislodging an orb mount she'd been fixing.

"I was watching over someone tonight, last night

anyway, as it's almost morning now." She wrapped both hands around the back of her neck. "I might have kind of followed him."

Ru's jaw dropped. "How far?"

"Only a couple of levels-"

"Up or down?" he demanded.

"Up two. He went into some warehouse, not entirely sure why. I came back here."

Ru seethed through his teeth.

"You're not usually a rule breaker, Molly. What brought this on? And what exactly did you see?"

He sounded properly worried and a tiny flutter lit in her gut.

He's my liaison and my friend, that's all.

"Intuition," she snipped back at him, ignoring his final question. "Now, what about your secret? What's got you all squirrely?"

He looked her up and down, inhaling sharply in a way that definitely didn't look like he was going to say 'oh, alright then'.

"Molly-*aah*!"

He stumbled forward, arms flying out wide. The good thing to do was to reach out and cushion his fall into her table. With a grimace and a fleeting thought for the organised chaos on her desk, she stepped aside and closed her eyes at the almighty clatter and pained grunt that followed.

"Only me, I wanted to borrow some *offke* if you have some. Cravings. Oh, have I interrupted?"

A flash of purple filled the doorway, joined by a wicked

grin that intimated all sorts.

Molly scratched the dusty recesses of her brain, finely tuned for useful knowledge but a scant thimble-size for things like names of random new neighbours she only met once.

"I- Cheryl, isn't it?" She tried without much hope. "I have some *offke* left, hang on."

"It's Beryl actually."

"Oh, sor-"

"Cheryl's my sister. You'll meet her soon enough."

Can't wait.

Molly grabbed the nearest packet of *offke* granules and hurried past a still recovering Ru to hand them over.

Beryl swiped them up and leaned against the door frame with no apparent sign of leaving again.

"Cheers. Still getting the hang of the place. Sent Harvey to the shop and he came back with a box of *Beast Lite*. That was the craving two whole days ago! Oh, have you heard the news?"

Molly blinked, blindsided by the constant stream of chatter. Ru appeared beside her.

"What news?" he asked.

Beryl frowned. "Who are you?"

"He's a friend," Molly offered. "But what news is this?"

Beryl wiped a hand over her pink cheeks and huffed a weary breath.

"Two more artificers have gone missing!"

CHAPTER FOUR

Molly scanned the communal park, picking out various faces in the crowd and mentally discarding them. No warehouses on the park level, which was one below her own, just thick metal pillars covered with worn, weatherproofed wood for the aesthetic, and an abundance of slim-trunked trees dotted around the grassy space. Every single inch of her ached from a combination of her fall in the early hours and the continual lack of proper sleep, but she'd promised Merry that she'd help at the park's food kiosk for the evening and didn't want to let her down.

"I'm taking five Molly, back in a bit," Merry said.

Molly nodded and plastered on her usual smile as a girl approached the counter, her black braids tied in a ponytail and her torso clad with what looked like two pink sweatshirts.

"Two meat pockets please."

Molly nodded and turned away to package the order.

"So, your name is Molly?" the girl asked.

She frowned at the grill. "Yeah, why?"

"You know my sister."

"I do?"

She glanced back over her shoulder in time to see the

girl nod.

"Yeah, I'm Sammy. Talie's my sister."

Molly froze over the grill. She'd heard Talie's name during her idiotic fall in the mysterious warehouse, but she hadn't given her own. Now Talie would find out her name, could even trace her back to her shop. She might not be able to trace her back to the Menagerie, but Molly fought to contain her smile as nerves burst in her chest.

She couldn't lie and say she didn't know who Talie was, but she was so rattled by the revelation that her ability to word-tangle fled.

"Talie?"

"Uh-huh." The girl, Sammy, grinned wide. "She comes home this morning going on about this annoying girl who ruined her night's work. Then we come down here, and here you are like magic. First face she spotted pretty much. I said I'd come over and find out about you because she's shy."

Molly had nothing to say to that, nothing useful anyway, but she had to try.

"Are you sure she's not confusing me for someone else?"

A question was as good as a lie if phrased properly. She waited, unable to turn around as the meat pockets crisped and the cheese oozed properly.

"She never forgets a face."

Molly shrugged. "Maybe someone has been glamouring as me, I really couldn't say."

The idea that someone had been glamouring as her for some unknown reason was technically a possibility, so it wasn't a lie. She really couldn't say why that might have been necessary for anyone either, not without betraying the oaths she took to the Menagerie.

"What's taking you so long?"

Molly scowled, even though she recognised the voice from that morning, and the implication she was holding things up gave her enough indignation to spring into action.

"Won't be a moment," she called out through clenched teeth.

"Don't worry, it's not you," Sammy said cheerfully. "She's always grumpy like this."

"I am not!"

Molly turned around with the two meat pockets wrapped in brown paper bags, both splurging over with cheese.

Talie narrowed her gaze as her eyes met Molly's. Her short dark hair was tucked loose behind her ears, and she was wearing the same jeans and baggy sweatshirt as before, along with the same hostile expression.

"She's still not entirely sure if she can trust people," Sammy announced, as if that explained everything. "It makes trying to get her a date all but impossible."

It was entirely gratifying to see Talie grinding her teeth but Molly only nodded.

"Fair enough, and you?"

Sammy pulled a face. "I'm still on my 'everyone is icky' phase with no plans to change my mind, so no trying to set me up with pointless dates."

Molly hesitated at the witheringly vehement tone, but

Sammy's gaze was fixed on Talie, who grimaced.

"I did that once! And it was because you insisted."

"And that was more than enough. Eww."

Bewildered, Molly realised there was nothing left to do for them but pay, yet neither of them were making any attempt to do it.

Knowing my luck they're here to distract me.

The thought sent cold dread splashing through her. If Talie was part of whatever weird deviancy Molly had stumbled onto by following Seymour the mysterious returning artificer, that might not be too far from the truth.

"That's three pesanas," she prompted.

She lifted her gaze past the two of them and bit her lip. Seymour was still at his table, still staring into his mug. Not that she should be following him, not that she technically was, but him turning up at the park acting like nothing was wrong seemed odd.

Sammy eyed Talie until she grudgingly pulled out the necessary coins and tapped them onto the counter.

Molly didn't even get a chance to thank her. She froze as Talie swiped up her meat pocket and leaned closer.

"What were you doing?"

Molly tensed all her muscles in preparation for an argument.

"Serving food?"

Talie rolled her eyes. "Last night. You fell into our warehouse and legged it back up the wall like a spider, I saw you."

Molly fussed with the sauces on the counter, averting her gaze.

"Are you sure you have the right person? I think I'd remember if I was falling into warehouses."

It was a poor attempt by any standard but Talie finding her, and so soon after, had her panicking. She swiped some loose strands of hair back from her face and called her Fae connection to the fore.

"Of course I have," Talie said. "Your hood fell off. I saw you."

"Someone could be glamouring as me."

Talie snorted. "I guess that's possible. Stay away from the warehouse if you know what's good for you."

Molly let her Fae connection tingle into her fingertips.

"Is that a threat?"

"Consider it a warning."

Talie turned on her heel, stalking past the still seated Seymour and into the crowd. Sammy gave her a knowing grin and mumbled goodbye in a spray of crumbs as she hurried after her.

Too busy watching them go, Molly flinched as the kiosk door thudded behind Merry.

"Thanks for the help," she said. "I can manage from here."

"You sure?"

Merry nodded. "More than. Go have some fun. Or some sleep, you look done in."

"Thanks." Molly grabbed her coat. "Let me know if you need me to help out again."

Merry waved her away so she slipped out onto the grass and across the park. She wasn't watching Seymour, and any proximity to him would look extremely suspicious if

Talie was still lurking.

Still she slowed her pace, marking out potential spots to lurk unseen.

"Hey, he's choking!"

A shout tore through the air, followed by several others. Molly's insides rippled with chills as Seymour jack-knifed forwards over the bench, his hands clutching his throat.

White froth bubbled from his lips, his eyes bulging wide as he tried to gasp in a breath and choked instead. Several people clustered around him, but through the chaos of flailing arms trying to both lift and help him, Molly saw the pale green tinge to his cheeks.

She recognised that tinge. It came from ingesting sap of the *goberia* plant, and death was almost instant. The crowd surged back in one widening motion and Molly didn't need to hang around to know he was dead.

Turning on her heel, she slipped into the shadows of the nearest pillar and strode toward the wide lane that led up and down the levels.

First Seymour goes missing like the other artificers.

She let the rhythmic thud of her steps calm her jittering mind.

Then he reappears with no memory of much. Two more artificers went missing overnight. Now he's the first to die, that we know of at least. Question is, did he die because of what I saw?

Goberia was a favourite of several Menagerie assassins, but that didn't mean it was automatically one of them that killed him. Any back alley artificer or healer could get their hands on it for the right price.

Guilt sank in her gut as she hit her level and continued powering along.

Did Talie kill him because of what I saw? Will I be next? Or was he involved in something entirely other that none of us know about?

She broke into a jog. The steady burst of speed stopped the panic from taking over, her fists clenched tight enough for her nails to dig into her palms. Several people on her level often saw her jogging so they wouldn't think it strange.

Act normally. It was the first rule of the Menagerie. *Act normally, then keep your eyes on all that moves, and everything that doesn't.*

Watch, play a role, report back, that was her job with them.

She jogged into her lane and stopped with her hand on her door, slightly out of breath. Lights were on in the building beside hers but thankfully there was no sign of Beryl looming to accost her. She unlocked the door and shut it behind her.

Her first stop should have been the Menagerie to report in, but she needed… she had no idea what she needed. She grabbed a dusty bottle of *Beast* and popped the lid, draining a couple of swigs. No sense getting drunk but the initial buzz would give her the strength to face Marcus.

A loud rap sounded on the door and she almost dropped the bottle. Wiping her mouth with the back of her hand, she took a deep breath and strode forward to open it.

"Have you heard?" Ru charged in without greeting.

She nodded. "I was there."

"You were? What are you doing here then?"

She took another swig and set the bottle down, letting the fierce tingle spread through her muscles before answering.

"Needed a moment. I'm fine."

He grimaced as she straightened her coat and marched toward him.

"You're not, I can tell. I'll come with you. Marcus is away on the higher levels tonight apparently, but you can let Celeste know."

Molly let her shoulders unwind, amazed at her luck. Marcus didn't leave the Menagerie often.

"I was only there for a mo-"

"Don't," Ru shook his head warningly and swept her outside. "Not until we get there. Lock up. At least you look like death, so Celeste will probably let you have tomorrow as a free."

Molly huffed under her breath as she locked the door again and pocketed the key. Ru had every single point correct, but looking like death wasn't complimentary in any light.

She vaulted up onto the nearest beam, Ru moving with innate strength beside her. They clambered up and walked in silence along the girders they arrived at the Menagerie window. Molly slid in first, Ru's feet a soft thud behind her moments later. She lifted her head and scanned the hall, freezing in place as a door opened and Celeste swept out.

"Oh! I wasn't expecting visitors."

Celeste smoothed a hand over her sandy hair despite there not being a strand out of place, giving her linen trousers and immaculate pale gold blouse a quick glance.

"I needed to report something," Molly said, hesitating.

"Alright, come into my office."

Celeste reversed back into the room she'd come out of and Molly followed her in, not entirely surprised that Ru kept pace with her. He was her liaison so probably had as much right if not more to the information than she did.

"Take a seat, dears." Celeste waved a hand at the comfortably padded pink chairs. "Candy? You have too much of a waif about you tonight, Molly."

Molly took the candy if only to have something to do with her hands. Unwrapping it, she sighed.

"I was helping out a friend at the communal park tonight. As I was leaving, the man I've been watching for the past few nights was drinking at a bench. He started choking, frothing at the mouth, then he went green and died."

Celeste frowned. "I need to check your file to see who you were watching, but this is grave news indeed. He was one of the artificers?"

"Yes, Seymour something. He disappeared like the others, then returned for a few days. Then he goes and dies from *goberia* poisoning."

"You're sure it was *goberia*?" Celeste asked sharply.

"Well… I couldn't prove it, but he had the green tint to his skin, the white foam and he was dead in seconds."

Celeste sighed and pushed the candy bowl further across the table to them. Ru obediently took one but Molly still had hers in her hand.

"This is worrying indeed. All these reports of artificers

going missing, and yours was the first to return home seemingly unharmed. Why poison him a day later? If only we'd had eyes on him the whole time, or knew his last movements."

Molly forced herself not to clutch the sweet tighter, gulping as nerves fluttered. She smiled, mindful to keep the movement as relaxed as she could manage.

"If only."

CHAPTER FIVE

"There she is!"

Molly froze at the sound of a lively voice blasting through her open doorway. After a long sleep and enough food to sink an entire level, she was able to spend the afternoon focusing on her shopwork rather than her spying work.

"Found her!"

She grimaced as Sammy appeared in the doorway, decked out in madly furry boots, tights and a black skirt with several ragged layers.

Then she realised who Sammy would no doubt be hollering at and slunk behind her desk, eying the organised chaos. She was waiting for paint to dry, but she needed something else to keep her looking busy.

She grabbed a screwdriver and part of a clock mount she'd been working on, fumbling to find the right kind of screws in her drawer.

"Hi." She hesitated. "No need to shout, it's still early."

Sammy stalked into the room with a wide grin.

"Sorry. Your neighbours are already outside though, so not sure who I'd be waking."

"The pregnant one?" she asked.

Sammy nodded. "Yeah, huge."

"That's not-"

She trailed off as Talie darkened the doorway, her scowl emanating through the air ahead of her.

"What did we say about inside voice, Sam?" Talie asked.

Sammy shrugged and picked up one of the carved keychains from the basket near the door. Molly hovered between hope she might buy one and desire to get them both out before Talie started interrogating her again.

"You said to use it. I forgot. This is cool, can I take one?"

Molly clung to her screwdriver, her mind racing. She had no idea why they were in her shop, but it couldn't be good.

"A pesana each, or five for three."

"Fair." Sammy reached into her pocket. "I'll take this one."

Molly stretched out her hand over the desk and Sammy hurried forward to pay.

"What is all this?" she asked.

Molly shrugged. "Bits and bobs. I fix stuff for people, make gifts. I do odd jobs too in exchange for things."

She lifted her head in time to see Talie's scowl deepen.

"What kind of jobs?"

Molly tensed. "Who wants to know? You're asking a load of questions for someone who doesn't know me."

"That's the point, silly," Sammy added, giving Talie a sharp look over her shoulder. "To get to know you."

"Why?"

Sammy leaned against the edge of the desk and knocked a metal pendulum aside. Molly grimaced and reached out to remove it, setting it safely at the other end.

"Sorry! We want to be friends. Don't you have friends?"

Molly laughed, short and sharp and not in the least bit amused.

"Of course I have friends, but they don't tend to stalk me to my shop."

Technically Ru showed up more often than not, but that was different. The new neighbour Beryl seemed to be happy enough turning up at the door too, but Molly couldn't exactly escape her without moving.

Sammy grinned. "We're special. Talie thinks she's seen you somewhere before, before last night I mean."

"I see." Molly folded her arms. "How did you even find me here?"

Talie tilted her head to the side, eyes narrowing ever further. In the strategically placed lighting that enabled Molly to work in all parts of the room without having to suffer the dim light from the lane outside, Talie's hazel-grey eyes looked almost purple.

"Your boots are worn and your coat has seen better days," Talie announced. "You were serving at a kiosk on the communal level so chances of you being from much lower down were slim."

Molly frowned. "Nice. So you what, asked up and down a few until you found me?"

"Yep." Sammy picked up a weighted blade and almost dropped it. "Oops, sorry. We just asked at the food stands until someone recognised you. He said you were the best fixer of all the levels and that we'd find you down here."

Molly sighed. No doubt that was Sai, always singing her praises so she'd give him another discount on fixing the glasses his son kept breaking.

"Well, here I am."

"Here you are," Talie echoed. "Here a lot, are you?"

"Yeah, keeps me busy. Why, are you looking for a job? I'm probably not the best person to work for. I'm very specific."

Talie eyed the workshop, one eyebrow popping up.

"Clearly. I don't need a job."

Molly forced her shoulders down from her ears. Being hostile wasn't going to get Talie and Sammy off the scent or out of her shop.

"And what do you do then?" She glanced at Sammy. "Both of you?"

Sammy held up her keychain, the wood carved and inlaid with special glass that caught the light and made rainbows dance through the air.

"I'm in school three levels up. Talie is… complicated."

Of course she is. She's working for some unknown faction that's taking artificers like Seymour into random warehouses for Faerie knows what reason.

Molly couldn't match Talie's raised eyebrow for derision so she smiled instead.

"Clearly."

Sammy glanced back and forth between them, her wide grin never fading.

"Well, this is fun. Are you here every day then?"

Molly nodded slowly, tearing her attention away from the hostile stiffness of Talie's shoulders. They both knew she was word-tangling her way out of admitting who she was, but for some reason Talie was playing along rather than charging in.

"Rain or shine, yeah."

Sammy's mouth quirked ruefully. "I'd love to feel the rain. I know they sometimes simulate the feel of it to keep a sense of the seasons but it's not the same."

"Rain is cold," Talie snapped.

"Have you ever felt it? Ever been outside the citadel? No, you haven't, so shush. Have you ever been outside, Molly?"

Molly smoothed down a clutch of paper being terrorised by Sammy's wandering hands. If they stayed much longer everything she owned would be in a haphazard pile on one side of the room.

"I've barely even left this level," she admitted.

Easy to say because the Menagerie never asked her to go much further than three levels up or down, and each citadel tower had several.

"Hmm." Talie took a step back. "We should be going, Sammy."

Sammy pulled a face. "Fine. Can I come back? You can show me how everything works."

Molly couldn't help smiling, helpless at the thought of Sammy being let loose on some of her work.

"That would take a long time," she said. "I can't stop you coming back. If you do, next time I'll give you a price list in case you ever need anything fixed."

Sammy nodded. "Great! I'll leave old grumpy-orbs at home next time. Bye Molly!"

Talie rolled her eyes as Sammy danced past her, giving Molly one last arctic look. They might have even made it out unscathed, but Ru almost dashed into them on his way in.

A look passed between him and Talie, a widening of both sets of eyes, a subtle veering apart. Ru stalked into the room, glancing over his shoulder once more before dumping a tub of *offke* onto the desk.

"Who's that?" he asked.

Molly waited a few seconds before hurrying to the door and peering out. Talie and Sammy were nowhere to be seen but she closed the door anyway, deliberating whether to tell Ru the full truth. He might insist she go and tell the Menagerie everything, and they wouldn't be impressed.

"The bouncy one? I met her yesterday while helping Merry out at the kiosk."

Ru frowned. "And the other?"

"Her sister. What brings you rushing in here like *oricadae* are at your feet?"

He stared for several excruciating moments. She kept her muscles relaxed, her head slightly tilted, expression curious, but her pulse raced as she sought for a way to distract him. Then she noticed his clothing, the fitted black trousers much finer than any of the jeans she'd seen him wear before, and a smart blue shirt with the long sleeves rolled up to the elbows.

"I came to give you some news from Celeste," he announced. "Apparently, two other artificers have returned with no memory of going missing."

Molly stopped ogling him. "The most recent two?"

He nodded. "Celeste says they're short-handed at the moment, something to do with Marcus taking several to the lower levels, so we're it."

"We're what?"

"It. The surveillance, the trackers, the investigators, everything." He ran a hand over his black hair with a weary huff. "You've been promoted, kid."

CHAPTER SIX

Molly was still staring in astonishment, lost for words as Ru held out a large sturdy paper bag.

"What's this?" she asked.

"Clothes. We're going down and we need to blend in."

Molly grabbed the bag and peered inside.

"Wow. How far down?"

She pulled out a soft pair of linen trousers in muted dark blue and a pale grey cotton shirt. At the bottom were a pair of brown ankle boots, so shiny they had to be new.

"As far as we need to. We have to blend into the crowds as much as we need to use the rooftops, so pack a small bag to take."

"What about the shop?" she asked.

Ru rolled his eyes, glancing around at her sanctuary.

"It'll still be here. Think of it like a short holiday if you have to."

Molly thought of all the things she had still to fix, but they'd have to come back to sleep at some point, and sleep was a luxury she sometimes went without.

I can work through the night or through the day.

"Okay, outside then while I get changed."

"Might want to brush your hair as well," Ru smirked. "I think Celeste mentioned make-up at the bottom."

He nodded to the bag and shut the door behind him, leaving her in silence.

The clothes were new but if Celeste had chosen them then they would be fine ones, not so fancy they'd rip easily if she had to run or hide, but expensive enough to blend in on some lower levels.

Molly changed into soft trousers of thick, forgiving black fabric and a stretchy blood red blouse. She also spared a moment to add a second pair of socks to her feet so the stiff leather of the boots wouldn't tear them to shreds. As she ran a brush through her hair, she fixed a couple of final bits on various projects, then faced the cluster of make-up at the bottom of the bag.

Her guardians had insisted she attend the basic schooling until fifteen, or Lily had at least, but after that she chose to focus on her fledgling business and apprentice with Basil instead. Then they both passed in the freak carriage accident two levels below, and she'd inherited the workshop while their cottage had reverted back to the citadel's ownership.

None of her education, schooling or otherwise, had involved make-up. She could hold a basic glamour for a few minutes, ward against attacks for longer and the charm gift was useful, but she had zero make-up experience.

Tucking it into the bottom of her rucksack, she piled clean jeans, underwear, extra socks and a couple of sweatshirts on top.

Ru knocked on the door to hurry her along, but she took

the time to scrub her hands clean and wash her face before opening it and grabbing her coat.

He eyed her over with a frown.

"What?"

"You look… different."

She pulled a face. "Isn't that the point?"

He didn't answer as she shut and locked the door, only led the way to the main lane and started down toward the next level. She hurried after him, drawing alongside as the sun emerged from behind the clouds beyond the glass. The urge to find a way out of the citadel swelled, to feel that sun directly on her face along with the real wind, not the simulated effects the fans and vents hidden among the levels produced.

"What's the plan?" she asked, keeping her voice low. "Do you have addresses?"

He nodded. "I do, a brother and a sister who live side by side."

"How convenient."

"My thoughts exactly."

They dodged around a group chatting and wound downward. As they passed the communal park, Molly risked a glance toward the bench where Seymour had met his gruesome end.

"Do we have time to stop?" she asked.

Ru frowned. "I suppose we can get lunch. I bet you've barely eaten. Roll or pocket?"

"Meat pocket please."

She reached for the pocket of her trousers before remembering it didn't have one, then started to wriggle out of her rucksack to find her change pouch.

"On me." Ru waved a hand and sauntered off toward the food kiosk. "Wait here."

With him occupied, Molly neared the bench and cast a careful look around.

The bench was free of any stain but the park clean-up crew would have disinfected it already and picked up any debris. She ran her fingertips over the soft grass, peering at the decidedly grubby underside of the picnic bench to keep an eye on Ru's progress. The legs, seats and tabletop had been polished like new, but clearly the crew didn't bother cleaning the bits that wouldn't be seen.

A subtle glint caught the light. Molly ducked lower, her heart pounding when at what she saw stuck to the underside of the table. Reaching out, she tugged at the small disk attached to the wood until it came free.

A metal coin was tethered to what looked like a friendship bracelet in black and brown threads. The metal had been painted with the basic outline of an eye inside a star with five curling points.

Molly slipped the bracelet into her pocket as she straightened up and slid onto the seat. Moments later, Ru turned away from the kiosk with two food parcels wrapped in brown paper. She grabbed hers from him and tore into it, hunger growling the moment the smell hit her. The bracelet might be nothing relevant and it could wait until she'd finished her meal.

"Is there anything specific we're looking for?" she asked, wiping her mouth. "Strange behaviour, certain subjects, or weird symbols…?"

Ru folded their wrappers up and shook his head.

"We watch, we report back. If they move, we follow them. If we find anything, we go straight to Celeste."

Molly stood up with a groan.

"The usual then."

Ru grinned. "Exactly, isn't it exciting? This is everything you've always begged me for. More exciting assignments, more responsibility. Okay, it doesn't come with any more pittance pay, but still. "

"Not how I envisioned it." Molly started toward the walkway. "I know the Menagerie protects the citadel, and everyone says it's an honour to be a part of it, but things aren't exactly getting better on the upper levels."

Ru stuck his hands in his pockets as they strode out of the park side by side, the sun sending prisms through the glass to dance across the lane.

"Progress takes time, and so many levels are a lot to manage," Ru said. "You should take my arm."

"Er… what?"

"Put your hand on my arm like we're out for a leisurely stroll."

Molly glanced around. A few more levels and she would be further down than she'd ever been before. The buildings built from brick and stone looked much the same as those on her level, perhaps a bit bigger, with the lanes reaching inward to the central core of the citadel tower itself, but then she spied one with a tiny front garden. It was barely big enough for three people to stand in together, with only a low border of ragged brick to define its boundaries, but it had plants growing inside it.

She wanted a garden. Orbs, she wanted the whole realm outside, from the wild woods that held all manner of horrors if the rumours were to be believed, to the dazzling silvery glint on the horizon that was apparently the sea.

Fae went out there of course, often rich types that could afford guards, but most born in the confines of the citadel never stepped beyond the vast walls of glass.

She wanted to see the whole of Faerie, to find out all the secrets nobody else seemed able, or willing, to explain to her. Like how the Fae lights worked. They came on when needed, but nobody could explain to her what made the light itself, or how. Even her teacher at school had been depressingly vague about it, and she had a feeling that there were so many Fae in the citadel with no idea how half of the lives they lived worked, and no care to find out.

"Mol?"

Ru's voice jolted her from her thoughts and she pressed her hand to his upper arm, frowning at him when he chuckled.

"Like this." He grabbed her hand and threaded it under his elbow. "I forget you don't get out much."

She shrugged. "Too busy being busy. How many levels down are we going?"

"Twelve."

"Twelve?!" she gasped. "That's middle territory. Is it true they have jewels in the walls of their houses?"

"Not a clue. That far down is as new for me as it is for you, but I doubt they'd have actual jewels. We'll find out."

She nodded. They would find out and a fleeting thrill of excitement buzzed inside her chest. She slid her free hand into her pocket and let her fingertips pass over the bracelet.

"Say… Ru?"

He groaned. "That's trouble."

"What is?"

"When you use that voice all drawn out and hesitant. It means you're going to ask me to do something."

She grinned. Exactly the mood she wanted him in, dreading that she was going to ask something huge so she could wheedle something less huge past his inevitable relief.

"I'm not saying now, or even today, but if we are going downward, could we see the library?"

He wouldn't refuse her, she was almost certain of that. He sometimes brought her library books to borrow because he was able to go down a few levels more than she did without sticking out too much, and the library was seven levels below hers.

"You don't have an access card," he reminded her.

"I know, but I just want to see it. Didn't you say you had some stuff you wanted to look up? We can come at night when-" she lowered her voice to a whisper. "-when everyone is asleep."

He sighed, rubbing a hand over his face.

"You're going to get me in trouble one day," he grumbled.

She grinned. "Is that a yes?"

"*If* we can get away from duties, and *if* we have time, then maybe. I know someone who works the evening shift sometimes, so we may be able to get you inside without argument."

Molly let her smile do the talking as they moved down another level, this one with many more tiny gardens than the first.

If she was clever about it, she would be able to find out if the emblem on the bracelet was anything to worry about.

CHAPTER SEVEN

"It's… amazing!"

Molly twirled in a circle, her face turned upward and her mouth open. She managed three rotations of awe before Ru clamped a hand on her shoulder and held her still.

"Don't draw attraction to us," he whispered.

She nodded, shrinking herself small and following him across the vast flagstones of the library's entrance hall. Behind glass walls on either side, towering far higher than she could ever hope to see, were countless shelves of books. She'd imagined a room or two but this was bigger than her mind could even comprehend, the nighttime darkness obscured by several lights glowing ahead of them.

"Don't mention I lent you any books," Ru muttered. "You have to wait here as well, no coming inside with me."

Molly nodded, her mind twisting back to her plan. Neither the brother nor the sister artificer, whose names Ru wouldn't tell her, had left their houses during the day. Only once they went to bed and showed no signs of sneaking out did Ru agree to leave their post and go back up to the library.

A tall man behind the library's front desk lifted his head, his face morphing from recognition to wariness when he spotted them.

"Hi, Vic." Ru smiled and leaned his forearm on the counter. "I need to check some facts in a couple of books, no need to take them out."

Vic eyed Molly as she gave him her best 'I'm going to be absolutely no trouble' smile.

"Okay, Ru. You know where and what you need?"

Ru nodded. "Yep, won't be long. Molly's going to wait right here for me."

Vic sank behind the counter as Ru strode into the gloom and out of sight behind the rows of bookshelves. Molly assessed the space. Smooth stone pillars flanked the length of the room along with towering panes of glass which separated the hall from the actual books, so not much chance of getting up high without using staircases. Lots of dark corners but no guarantees there were many doors or exits beyond, whether open to her or otherwise.

She spied a sign for the toilets and sidled up to the counter.

"Could I use the ladies please?" she asked.

Vic hesitated.

"We're going to rush off again after," she added, calling her connection forward and spilling charm into her words. "Then I'll be gone."

He nodded. "Of course, no problem. Over there and to the left, at the end of the corridor."

"Thank you."

She kept her pace steady as she walked toward the toilets, but the moment she was out of sight she broke into a run. Two doors later and she found a shortcut into the enormous vault of books behind the glass wall.

Keeping an eye on Vic through the glass, she crept through the shelves. Ru had explained the layout before and given her some indication of where he tended to sit when he looked for various things. She'd memorised the layout, one of her more idle pursuits that she used to entertain herself while working, and headed straight up a staircase to the citadel history section.

If there were any records about the mysterious eye symbol, she would find them.

"*Symbols and signifiers*, nope," she murmured to herself. "*Histories of the Fae*, enormous. *The Omens of Fate, Conspiracies and Conspirators*, probably not."

Each time she flicked through and discarded a book, she checked the desk and the surrounding area for signs of Ru. He might only need a short while or he might be ages, but she couldn't risk missing him and being 'in the toilet' for too long.

Knowing him, he'd come in to find me.

A soft thud echoed nearby, a door shutting, and footsteps tapped on the wooden floor by the stairs.

Molly flinched behind the nearest bookcase and peered through the shelves, her pulse pounding as she recognised the person striding down the stairs.

Despite the gloom, the lights were bright enough for reading by. As Talie reached out for the banister, something small fluttered out of her sleeve. She disappeared down the stairs and Molly waited a couple of seconds before hurrying across the floor to find out what she dropped.

A scrap of paper lay crumpled on the wood.

Molly ducked down to snatch it up, watching through the glass as Talie said something to Vic before pulling her hood up and speeding out of the library entrance.

Molly uncrumpled the paper, eyes wide as she read the few short lines.

'Twelve parts yew to one part nightshade, twice swill with oia residue, distil once and steep for three days.'

Nothing immediately telling, if anything it sounded like some kind of poison, but Molly's gaze stuck on the tiny image inked beside the words, the crude outline of the eye slightly wonky inside the star with curling points.

She pocketed the paper alongside the bracelet she'd taken from the park table and jogged down the stairs, hovering at the edge of the toilet corridor until she saw Ru emerge.

He looked around and she walked into sight, watching as his gaze flickered to the sign above her head before he grimaced at Vic and swept her out of the library.

"Find what you were looking for?" she asked.

Suspicion flashed across his face. "Yes. Why are you being…"

"Squirrely?" she offered.

"Yeah, that."

"What do you mean?"

He sighed, coming to a stop and turning to face her.

"Something's going on that you're not telling me. You

didn't once beg me to sneak you into the library itself, which means you probably already found a way to do it. Vic didn't even seem to notice you when we left, and he's eagle-eyed on a bad day, which means you had reason enough to try charm on him."

She shrugged, walking on and waiting until he was forced to follow. She could tell him what she'd found, the bracelet and the piece of paper Talie dropped. It wasn't like she was hiding them from him exactly, just delaying the actual telling.

Talie seems to get everywhere. The park where Seymour died, the warehouse he went to, my shop where-

She frowned at Ru. "How do you know her?"

"Huh?"

"The girl at my shop. You asked me how I knew her, but how do you know her? You both looked at each other very… squirrely-ly."

"That's not a word."

She clenched her fist around the items in her pocket.

"Nice try. How do you know her?"

He chuckled. "Jealous? When would I have time for anyone but you, Mol?"

He could keep his secrets if he wanted to, but she wasn't willing to let him. Winding her compulsion gift around her, ignoring the subtle stab of guilt that came with it, she willed him to want to tell her.

She had learned young that the trick with compulsions wasn't to make the person do something, because they'd immediately wonder why if the action was out of character for them, and Fae were naturally suspicious souls.

He wants to tell me everything he knows, she willed.

Ru's gaze fixed on her and her insides twisted.

"Ah, Mol, I'm sorry. I'm being unfair. Look, you can't tell anyone this, okay?"

She nodded. "You can trust me to be discreet."

Discreet was not the same as promising to never tell a soul and normally he'd have noticed her sneakiness, but the compulsion wound tight around his instincts.

"Marcus gave me some details about an underground movement," he explained. "Very scant mentions but he thinks they're the ones taking the artificers. They don't know why yet though, so it's our job to try and find out what we can."

"Thank you for telling me."

She forced a smile past the growing guilt as he slung an arm around her waist and guided them back onto the path leading down to lower levels.

"Marcus insisted we need to find their identifier. Once we know that, we'll be on the lookout."

Molly inched her hand into her pocket and drew out the paper and the bracelet.

"Something like this?" she asked.

He frowned. "What are those?"

She explained, glossing over the indignant look on his face, and held both items out to him. He swiped them from her and eyed the paper.

"Does that make sense to you?" he asked. "Have you seen this sign before?"

She shook her head. "No and no. You know more than I do already about this resistance or whatever they are."

"They're the enemy. Those artificers have been returned with their memories gone, and some Fae that aren't artificers haven't returned at all don't forget."

The thought of Seymour flitted through her mind and she shuddered.

"Don't remind me. Do we need to go and report in?"

Ru's arm slid away from her waist as he pocketed both the bracelet and the scrap of paper.

"You go get some rest, you look exhausted. I'll report in for the both of us."

Molly nodded. "Okay. I was going to tell you."

Eventually.

He started walking away toward the nearest available surface to vault up onto the girders but turned back to face her, a stern look marring his handsome face.

"Make sure you do, Mol. How can I keep you safe if you start keeping secrets?"

CHAPTER EIGHT

Going up three levels from the workshop barely even registered the afternoon after her illicit library visit, but Molly wore the fancy red shirt Celeste had given her over her smartest pair of jeans and made sure to brush her hair.

She stood in front of her old school, wondering if she was doing the right thing despite knowing she probably wasn't.

It was on the glass side of the lane, a long building with the playground at the front. Molly eyed the fading rays of sunlight playing over the grass. She remembered sitting there in baking hot summers, pulling blades of grass apart to make whistles and making idle chatter with friends who she slowly drifted apart from the moment she chose the workshop over further schooling.

The doors clanged open and a cascade of people tumbled out of the doors. She watched the crowd, looking for a familiar face.

"Molly!"

Sammy's head bobbed up over the crowd then disappeared, reappearing over and over like a doll on a springboard as she got closer. Molly noted Sammy's black trousers and t-shirt, an understated choice of outfit compared to the few times they'd seen each other before.

"What are you doing here?" Sammy asked.

Molly ignored the question, because she couldn't exactly say 'I'm here to get all the dirt on your sister from you'.

"I used to go to school here."

Sammy frowned. "Oh, you're not here to see me then. Are you meeting someone?"

"No, not unless I want to explain what I've achieved in my short life to teachers. I was passing by."

Nice and vague, the past tense of passing by giving no indication of when so it wasn't a lie.

Sammy's expression cleared as she dodged a huge group of boys charging past.

"What does no longer in school even look like?" she asked. "I'm daydreaming of it nearly every day, but mostly it's about staying in bed until the afternoon."

Molly laughed. "No such luck. I get up early to fix things, I'm in the shop most of the day then I eat and sleep a bit. Sometimes I go to the shop, sometimes I go to the park. Life goes on."

"Well that's… nice, if you enjoy it. I want to go down the levels and sing in the finest song halls one day."

"That'll take some doing."

Sammy sighed, bouncing up onto her tiptoes to see over the still milling crowd.

"I know. I want to perform already on our levels but Talie insists I wait until I'm sixteen. Only fifty-two more days."

Molly shuffled sideways so she could lean against the

nearest length of wooden fence surrounding the grassy park in front of the school. She had no idea how to bring the conversation around to Talie's mysteriousness, but she managed a smile as Sammy looked her way.

"I'm sure you'll do great when the time comes," she insisted. "It's nice that you have someone to look out for you. She takes her job as your sister very seriously by the sound of it."

Sammy rolled her eyes, shoving her hands in the pockets of her trousers.

"I know. It's sweet but she's madly over-protective. Even when she disappears at night I have to… I shouldn't have mentioned that."

Molly kept her expression neutral as her pulse picked up.

"Secret tryst?"

Sammy pulled a face. "I have no idea. She tells me I'm not allowed to leave the house until she comes back. She walks me to school every morning as well."

"And picks her up at the end."

Molly froze as Talie's unimpressed voice echoed beside them. She sucked in a deep breath and turned her head to find Talie a few feet away with folded arms, the remnants of the crowd leaving a wide gap as they dipped around her.

"Molly thinks I'm going to be great as a singer," Sammy sang.

Molly tensed as Talie's glower deepened and fixed on her.

"Does she? How nice. What brings her all the way to a school I wonder?"

"Stuff," Molly retorted. "And I am here you know, no need to talk about me in third person."

"This was her old school," Sammy added.

Silence fell between them and Molly eyed the situation over Talie's shoulder. The crowd was thinning fast so she would have a clear jog back to the shop, assuming Talie didn't try to physically stop her.

I could maybe take her in a fight, not that I'll need to.

"Well, nice as this is, I have things to be doing," she said.

Sammy nudged her elbow with a wry grin.

"Will you come and see me perform? It's only the end of school celebration, but it would be so fun to have you there."

Molly nodded. "If I can, I will. Drop a flyer or something by the shop."

Conscious of the time with the sun fading fast above the glass ceiling of the level, she had to get back before Ru appeared for another night of surveillance. If he found her absent he'd ask all sorts of prying questions and she wanted to avoid that wherever possible.

"Okay, well, see you," she said.

Sammy's goodbyes echoed behind her as she broke into a jog and headed toward the lane leading downward. Sammy's words about Talie being out every night filled her mind and set her curiosity tingling.

She definitely doesn't seem the social type, so maybe she's at that warehouse every night. Maybe even as part of this resistance group against the Menagerie Ru mentioned.

She didn't dare look back once and puffed into the shop

with no sign of Ru, shrugging off her fancy cardigan and pulling a more ragged one on.

The moment she slid into her seat and picked up a hammer, the dim lane-light from outside darkened.

"Did you leave?"

Ru strode into the room and shut the door behind him, his voice breathless.

"I jogged, why?"

He frowned. "That's it?"

"I did some jogging up a couple of levels and back down again, is something wrong?"

She dropped the hammer back onto the desk and stood up, rounding the edge to stand in front of him.

"Ru? What's going on?"

He sighed. "I've been watching the gruesome twosome all day. No sign of movement but I did catch a glimpse of that symbol you found on a similar bracelet in the woman's house."

"Similar how?"

"Same design on the metal coin but the threads of the band were gold and blue."

Molly rubbed her top lip, her mind racing through the information. Someone stuck the first bracelet on the underside of the table where Seymour died. It could have even been him. Talie dropped a piece of paper with the same symbol on it and some cryptic wording that made no sense after being seen interrogating Seymour in the warehouse. Now two of the artificers who were kidnapped and returned had a similar bracelet with the same symbol.

"Why are they being taken?" she muttered. "Artificers

have arcane skills, and some are able to weave Fae magic with certain gifts. No doubt that's why they're being taken, but Seymour had absolutely no clue about what had happened, yet he knew where to go."

Silence swelled as she thought about the warehouse, and she lifted her head in time to see Ru's eyes darken.

"What do you mean?" he asked.

Her insides twisted, realisation dawning.

"What?"

"You said he knew where to go. Where did he go?"

Molly took a step back as Ru folded his arms. He was between her and the door but it wasn't like she could run from her entire life just to avoid him. Compulsion was an option, but manipulation was a dangerous tool to become reliant on, and she'd used it on him once already despite promising herself long ago that she wouldn't.

"I told you I followed him, right? Well, I might have followed him a tiny bit further than I initially told you."

"Molly," Ru groaned, pinching the bridge of his nose. "Right, tell me everything, I mean it, and we'll work through it together. I have no intention of getting you kicked out of the Menagerie, but I can't keep you safe if you're not honest with me."

Molly sidled back to her desk and sat down, grabbing a pair of glasses she was fixing and using her fingernail to wind the tiny screw in.

"I followed him to a warehouse. He went in through the door and I found one of the service hatches higher up. I watched as someone interrogated him, something about him waking up after a party but having questions. I didn't stay long enough to find out what they were talking about."

Ru huffed a sharp breath through his nose and stalked to the desk, pressing his hands on top as he leaned over her, his broad forearms bunching.

"Did you recognise who he was talking to?"

Molly grimaced. She couldn't lie. She'd also been thinking they should be tailing Talie after all her involvement so far, and what easier way to do that than with Ru's permission?

"You know you asked me yesterday about the girl that was here? The one you looked at weirdly?"

"You're kidding."

She shook her head. "She was definitely interrogating him, not the other way around. Then she's at the park when he died. Then she's sneaking through the library and drops that piece of paper-"

"The paper wasn't under the table with the bracelet?"

Oops.

Molly aimed for a guilty smile despite knowing it didn't work on him.

"Not exactly, by which I mean not at all. I found the bracelet under the table and figured I'd have the quickest look through the library."

He straightened up, grabbing handfuls of his hair as he paced away and back again.

"How did you get that past Vic?"

Molly shrugged. "Asked to go to the toilet. Worked well enough in school."

Ru's face contorted, a struggle of emotions passing through his eyes.

"This is what's going to happen," he announced. "You are going to continue making friends with her, while I-"

"I'm not exactly friends with her. She's suspicious of me more like."

"Rightly so," he muttered.

"Maybe, but it's more her sister that I'm friendly with. Besides, she started it."

"Probably because they want information. You can't trust them, not even if you want to."

Molly nodded. "I know that. I wasn't sure if you'd turn me into the Menagerie for disobeying orders, so I figured I would find some stuff out first in case it led to nothing."

Ru sighed, rounding the desk and grabbing her hands to pull her to her feet. She tensed when he didn't drop the contact, heat racing across her cheeks and flutters bursting in her gut as he gazed down at her.

"My first priority is to keep you safe," he murmured. "I can't do that unless you tell me everything as it happens. I definitely don't want the Menagerie to get rid of you, but we have to trust each other, okay?"

She nodded, mesmerised by the closeness of his steely blue eyes.

"Okay." She hesitated. "I think we should be following her instead of the artificers. Sammy said she goes out at night, which would fit with what I saw in the warehouse."

Ru's gaze roved over her face, no doubt searching for more secrets. A tumble of disappointment flipped in her gut as he let her hands go and stepped away, but immediately his expression was all business.

"You may have a point. Celeste told me we had full

reign to do what we need to do to get this uncovered, so let's do it."

"I don't know where they live though," Molly said.

Ru shrugged. "We're bound to bump into them again if you have already. I get the feeling she'll be finding ways to seek you out as well, even if it is through her sister. Make friends with whichever one you can."

Yay. Molly pulled a face. *Talie's going to love that.*

CHAPTER NINE

"Don't go in without me."

Ru's words danced in Molly's head three days later. Three whole days of watching the two returned artificers with only the occasional break to go back to the workshop, or to lurk around the upper level shops in case Talie magically appeared to guide them somewhere unsavoury.

Molly grabbed her miniature toolkit each morning, more suited to jewellery making than wood or metal work, and took a small project with her to work on. She debated whether to tell Ru about the school and Sammy, but short of lurking outside the school gates where there was little room to hide themselves, she also didn't want to get Sammy involved. Her instincts told her Sammy was innocent of whatever skulduggery Talie was involved in. So every time Ru grumbled about needing to find out where they lived or hung out, she murmured vague agreements and doubled down on whatever project was in her hands at the time.

She glanced up at sundown on the third day from their perch high above the artificers' houses, almost toppling over in excitement. She tugged Ru's sleeve and pointed toward the main lane.

Talie had a long coat on, the collar pulled up to obscure her face. Molly eased to her feet and balanced with her arms out as she moved across the girder, Ru's footsteps tapping behind her.

"What is she doing this far down I wonder?" she whispered as Talie powered up the lane.

"Not a word," Ru muttered. "See where she goes first. If it's somewhere normal, then you can drop down and talk to her."

Molly shuddered as his breath gusted against her neck and pulled a face. Talie wouldn't be keen to talk to her, and without Sammy as a buffer there wouldn't be any reason to either.

They kept to the beams above as they tracked Talie out of middle territory, past the library and toward Molly's level.

"She might just be going home," she suggested.

Ru shrugged. "So then at least we'll know where she lives."

They passed the workshop and continued on up, but Molly had a feeling she knew where Talie was heading. Her pulse pounded, her cheeks flushed from climbing sixteen levels, but with Ru at her back she kept going.

Down below, Talie glanced left and right, back and forth, then slipped into the lane leading to the warehouse Seymour had gone to.

Molly beckoned over her shoulder, hoisting herself up the beams until she reached the service hatch. Ru followed her lead, but the moment she squeezed inside and made room for him on the beam, he pressed a finger to his lips with a fierce look, a warning.

As if I'm a child.

A loud hum of conversation filled the air, but nothing distinctive enough to pick out. Molly eyed the wood underfoot for any lingering spiders and dropped to a crouch, balanced in place as she recalled the unfortunate bird incident that had happened last time.

A door slammed down below and the muttering ceased.

"We'll make this short." A terse, masculine voice filled the silence. "The Menagerie are getting too close for comfort. We've had a couple of run-ins on lower levels, and the whole situation with the artificers is getting more convoluted by the day."

The man talking paced back and forth, his silvery blonde hair cascading down his back as he shovelled his hands through it.

"Run-ins," Molly whispered. "Marcus?"

Ru shrugged, his gaze fixed on the small group below. Of the seven gathered, Molly noticed Talie was the only younger one. The rest were a mixture of fully grown adults, none of whom Molly recognised.

"What do we do then, Phoenix?" one woman demanded.

"We could fall back a while," suggested another. "Or we could mount an attack."

Molly gripped the edge of the beam, her knuckles turning white.

"We're not strong enough yet, Calendula," the first man, Phoenix, insisted.

"Then what?"

Phoenix sighed. "We send someone in. Not sure who, or how yet. We need to keep to our posts until then. Don't come here unless you have business to or you've been summoned."

The apparently bloodthirsty Calendula folded her arms.

"We're not as weak as you imagine," she grumbled. "We could fight. Draw them out on our own terms."

Phoenix rolled his eyes and pointed to the door.

"Out. Do as you're told for once, and we'll get through this unscathed. We have a lot to achieve and nothing, not even the Menagerie, will stop us."

Molly glanced at Ru as his head turned toward her.

"I'm going to report in," he murmured. "Leave it a minute then go straight to the shop. Stay there until I come back."

Before she could argue, although she had no real reason to other than weary petulance, Ru twisted gracefully on the beam and darted out of the service hatch.

Molly dropped her gaze back down to find three people still clustered together, Phoenix, Talie and one other woman.

"Calendula's going to be a liability," the woman insisted.

Phoenix tilted his head back with a groan and Molly inched back into the shadows.

"She's more an asset at the moment, Nia, and one we can't afford to go without. I can manage Calendula though, don't worry."

"What are we going to do then?" Talie asked, glancing between them. "It's one thing to harvest artificers for their gifts if the replications still aren't taking, but-

"Rumour has it the cheap imitations don't last, it's true," Phoenix insisted.

The woman nodded. "We'll figure it all out, don't worry. The most important thing is to get eyes on the ball."

Silence drifted and Molly prepared to stand up.

"Why are you both looking at me?" Talie's indignant voice echoed through the warehouse. "I'm not going to any ball!"

"Let's walk and talk," Phoenix suggested.

Molly bit her lip as they started toward the other end of the warehouse. She hadn't heard of any ball, not that she would usually, but with or without Ru gone it sounded like something they should know.

He didn't say not to follow the lead.

She conveniently ignored the clear instruction he'd given her to return to the shop and eyed the crossing beams in front of her. She would just follow them through the partition wall into the next room, then turn back.

Creeping along, their voices floated up to her.

"You've got to be kidding," Talie insisted.

The woman laughed. "We'll neaten you up nice, do your hair, find you a dress. All you have to do is observe."

"What if someone talks to me?"

"Talk back. Say you've been invited by a wealthy patron but you're not entirely sure what his intentions are, then excuse yourself."

"Ew."

Before she could complain any further, a young man hurried up behind them.

"Calendula said she saw someone flitting across the beams by the roof," he said.

Ru. Molly's heart squished. *Surely he's not getting careless.*

Phoenix wiped a hand over his mouth and sighed as he stopped beside a door. Molly balanced on the beam above them, her pulse pounding. Any attempt to turn now would likely either kick dust on their heads and draw their attention up, or make noise to the same effect. Keeping her breathing light, she held her position.

"We all need to be wary," Phoenix insisted. "I'll leave you to discuss the specifics. It's only twenty three levels down, so not like you'll need too many gems and jewels. Maybe a nice feather in your hair."

"Shove off," Talie muttered to much laughter.

"The ball is the day after tomorrow," the woman said, ignoring the previous protests. "Come back tomorrow evening and I'll kit you out."

Talie folded her arms but the woman swept after Phoenix, leaving Talie standing alone at the edge of the warehouse.

Molly took a deep breath and started to inch around to go back to the hatch, until the voice stopped her dead.

"Creeping around again, Molly?"

CHAPTER TEN

Molly dropped her chin to her chest, peering past her outstretched arm.

Talie turned and tilted her head up, looking her directly in the eyes.

Molly took a step back. She'd disobeyed Ru's order, which was bad enough. She'd been seen, which was probably worse.

"They'll have posted watchers in the alley now," Talie added. "You won't get out through the hatch unseen. I'm guessing that's how you've been getting in, although I'm not sure why."

Molly darted back across the beams with less care than she could risk, slamming her hand into one of the upright ones hard enough to shake dust over her. She peered out of the hatch, hoping with everything she had in her that Talie was wrong.

Fae couldn't lie, but they learned to misdirect easily enough.

Three men were lounging by the end of the lane, a crate between them with a jug of something drinkable inside on top. They each held a handful of cards, but given the way their gazes were darting around, the cards were mostly for show.

"Crud." She grimaced and sank back against the pillar.

"Sammy thinks you're her friend," Talie called up. "For that reason alone, I'll get you a way out of here unseen."

Molly hesitated as Talie crossed the warehouse floor and stood glowering up at her.

Oh orbs, what if she thinks I'm sneaking in because I have a crush on her? Better that than me spying for the Menagerie, but still, embarrassing.

Knowing Talie couldn't lie but could definitely change her mind about helping at any point, Molly navigated across the beams and dropped onto a tower of boxes, sliding down to land on a bunch of sacks.

"Come on, you can't be found here," Talie muttered.

Molly clambered to her feet and flinched out of the way as Talie reached out to grab her arm.

"What, in this magical room full of boxes?"

Talie pulled a face. "No, the warehouse. I don't know what your involvement in any of this is or why you keep sneaking about, but you're in way over your head."

Molly choked down the urge to snap back anything that might suggest she was part of an enemy organisation. She couldn't tell Talie a single thing about herself, but she could try and dredge as much from the situation as she could. It was either that or admit to Ru she'd gotten caught again and still gained them nothing.

Even though he was the one who was seen.

"Why?" she asked.

Talie grunted something under her breath, heading at a striding pace toward the door Phoenix and the other woman had gone through.

"Didn't catch that," Molly said.

"You weren't meant to. Come on. If you get caught here, it'll be trouble for both of us."

Molly hurried to her side.

"You didn't tell them about before?"

Talie shook her head, easing open the door and peering around it.

"No. I should have done. Would make this so much easier, but Sammy would never forgive me."

"Right. So, what is this place?" Molly tried.

"None of your business."

Talie herded her through the door into a long hallway. The strangest urge to smile rumbled up but Molly forced it away.

"Fair. Just being friendly."

Talie opened another door and slipped through, holding it open behind her. Molly inched inside and stared at a flight of wooden steps leading down into gloomy darkness.

"Where are we going exactly?" she asked.

"Out the long way. It's not the nicest route but you'll get yourself caught otherwise."

Molly craned her neck to look further down the steps but couldn't see past the end.

"I can move around easily enough without getting caught," she muttered.

Talie scoffed. "I've seen you twice lurking around now. How many times have you actually been in here?"

Molly considered that as Talie started down the stairs and she had no choice but to follow.

"None of your business."

Talie huffed something that might have been a disbelieving laugh.

"What is this place anyway?" Molly asked.

"Service stairs down to a refuse tunnel that's no longer used. Maybe I should have blindfolded you."

Molly smiled, sudden amusement at Talie's irritable prickliness giving her the urge to see how wicked she could get away with being.

"That would have made our grand escape much slower though, you'd have to keep steering me."

"Or I could let you bash into everything."

"I'm loud when I walk into things."

"Maybe I should have covered your mouth as well."

Molly jogged a few steps to keep up with Talie's powering stride.

"Aren't you afraid once I know the way out I'll be able to get back in?"

Talie shrugged. "Next time I'll let them find you. Way less hassle for me. Besides, nobody and nothing comes in the way we're going. Only way is out."

The ominous suggestion filled the air between them. Molly couldn't imagine Talie using the water pipes, industrial or otherwise, but maybe there was a service tunnel.

As they passed under a light, she looked down at Talie's wrist. She couldn't see any bracelet, but with the long sleeves that didn't mean it wasn't there.

"We're going to have to work together to get out of here by the way," Talie added. "You can take direction when you have to, right? You're not completely hopeless?"

Molly frowned. "How do I know you're not going to stab me in the back?"

"Why would I do that after getting you down here?" Talie groaned. "Why would I bother?"

"Well, I don't know what you're into."

"Don't flatter yourself."

Molly ducked her head to hide her grin as the stopped in front of a large weighted pulley system on ropes as thick as her arm.

"One has to hold the door shut, one has to hold the balance rope steady," Talie announced.

"And I'm…"

"Holding the door shut."

Talie pointed to a few planks of wood nailed to make a rickety gate, some of the nails halfway hanging out.

"Where does it go?" Molly asked.

Talie grinned, the effect almost frightening in the gloom.

"Down."

Common sense and the voice in Molly's head arguing 'is it safe' warred with her absolute determination not to let Talie see an ounce of doubt or fear.

"What do I do?" she asked.

Talie opened the gate and waved her arm until Molly stepped inside, testing the bare wooden board with a few taps of her foot first. The idea of using compulsion to test if Talie was somehow deceiving her bubbled up, but Talie strode into the cart with no hesitation at all, pulling the gate shut with one hand and pointing at it with the other.

"One hand on the cart, one on the door to pin it. If you let it fly open it'll knock against the shaft and unbalance us, and these ropes have been here a long time. Very ropey."

Molly shoved her hand onto the cart with a death grip and clutched the door shut with the other. Twisting to look over her shoulder, she watched as Talie untied a rope tethered to a hook on the shaft wall, wound it a couple of times around her hand and her elbow in a large loop, then tapped her hand on a big blue button.

Molly strangled the scream in her throat as the cart shot downwards. Flickers of wall shot past in the dim glow from the cart's lamp, a frightening blur of murky brown. She clung to the door with all her might, wishing she could close her eyes but not trusting herself to keep the door exactly in the rickety frame it kept trying to bounce out of.

The cart jolted and Molly squeaked. She couldn't look behind her, frozen in place, but the cart was stationary.

"You can let go now," Talie said drily.

Molly forced her fingers open and straightened up, wrinkling her nose as the stench of decay hit her. Talie brushed her aside with a firm shoulder and opened the gate, stepping out and leaving it to bang back in place.

"You won't be coming out in the nicest of areas," she added. "But if you're quick-footed you can get back up to your level safely enough."

Molly pushed the gate open and followed Talie down a bare brick corridor lit with stark, flickering bulbs. She inched a hand up to her nose, breathing through her mouth instead.

Talie led them to a large metal door and Molly waited, ready to bolt the moment it was open.

"Orbs alive, today of all days," Talie muttered.

Molly tensed. "What? What's wrong?"

"They've locked it. Usually it's open but they must have had the bat problem again. They keep getting in to go up the chutes."

Molly clenched her fists and shoved them in her pockets, her arms rigid at her sides.

"We have to go back up then."

Talie shook her head. "It's a refuse cart. It's not built to take loads up, only down. Unless you're feeling strong enough to pull the whole thing back up by hand?"

Molly took a step back. Ru would probably be on his way to the workshop by now, unless Celeste or Marcus got him talking. He'd wonder where she was.

Will he come back for me?

She had to hope he did, although she didn't want to be the reason he strayed into enemy hands.

I don't need to rely on him, I'm smart. Think.

She eyed the door. The lock was metal and not likely the kind that would be pickable without a specific tool, not one she had in her miniature kit.

"There's no other way out?" she asked.

Talie grimaced. "If there was, would we still be standing here? I think we've both run out of luck, Princess."

Molly snorted. In the bog of panic clouding her mind, the nickname said with such a withering tongue, pulled at her attention.

"Princess? Really?"

Talie shrugged. "You fell from the beams last time all dainty-like with a huge white banner flapping like a train. It fits."

Molly decided not to dig too deeply into that, if only to avoid having to discuss how often she was making mistakes lately. Instead she eyed Talie, tense shoulders and alert eyes, but with every ease of movement, like a predator waiting for prey.

Or a predator who had once been prey and learned fast. Like the large songbirds rumoured to escape from cages on the noble levels. They sometimes flew up the levels looking for a way out with their claws scraping on roof tiles, sunshine flashing over their pale wings as they fluttered over the beams.

She shuddered.

"Okay, Sunshine."

Talie was quiet for a moment as they walked on.

"I'm no sunshine, more like a girl's worst nightmare."

"If you can have a ridiculous nickname that doesn't fit for me, I can have one for you. Now, when's the next refuse pick-up?"

Talie cocked her head and Molly folded her arms across her chest. In the whole time they'd been moving along together, she hadn't even thought to use a protection warding.

"Probably tomorrow," Talie said. "But we can't be caught in here either way. Just stop yammering for a moment and let me think."

Molly wanted to yammer purely out of pettiness but it

wouldn't help either of them. Talie stalked back toward the cart muttering something about Molly staying put, but Molly edged closer to the door.

With a frown, she pulled out her mini toolkit and rifled through. Extracting a screwdriver, she approached the door's hinges. The lock wouldn't budge, set into the metal so it would need to be open to be removed, but the hinges were reachable.

"What are you doing?!" Talie hissed.

"Performing arts, what does it look like I'm doing?"

The screwdriver slipped in the screw, the head almost too small to have an effect, but Molly had learned long ago when to push and when to take care.

"So, what exactly is this place?" she asked, keeping her tone purely conversational.

"Are you serious? You know I can't tell you that. How about you tell me what you're doing here?"

Molly grinned. "You know I can't tell you that. Much like whatever mysterious nonsense you're doing here."

"You're not going to keep asking?"

Molly shook her head. "Nope. I should really concentrate on this, so if you're done yammering…"

She let the taunt land, grinning at the door as Talie huffed behind her.

"Typical. The one time we're somewhere quiet and you aren't talking."

"Tell me then."

"No."

Molly shrugged. "Okay."

She dropped the first hinge at her feet with a satisfying

clang, crouching down to start on the second.

"You missed one," Talie announced, tapping the middle hinge with far too much satisfaction.

"If I do that one second, the door will try to tilt or twist. Makes it harder to do the last one. Balance is important."

She waited a few seconds, but apparently she'd finally beaten Talie on comebacks.

"Why are you even bothering to help me anyway?" she asked after the bottom hinge was undone.

Talie sighed. "I have my reasons."

"Like what?"

"Nothing I'm going to tell you. I meant it when I said you're in way over your head. Go back to your shop and forget all of this."

Molly ignored the warning and shunted her shoulder against the door as the final hinge came free. Talie pressed her hands against it too and together they lowered it to the floor.

"What will you say about the door?" Molly asked.

Talie shrugged. "Nothing. Go right at the end of the lane, then left and you'll hit the main spiral. You're five levels below your shop, so I'd move quickly if you want to avoid being stopped."

"Stopped by who?"

"People who won't bother to ask a young woman questions before taking a leap. Don't want the boots asking why a young woman is sniffing around the refuse level. I'd jog actually, if I were you."

Molly stepped outside, eying the towering brick walls either side of her followed by the pungent smell of rubbish nearby. She could easily vault up to the girders and climb, but she didn't want Talie seeing how easily she could do it and wondering why. She also had her Menagerie tattoo if the boots did find her, but explaining to them would mean explaining to Ru and likely to Marcus as well.

Maybe I'll keep this a secret for now.

"I guess I'll see you around then," she said.

Talie rolled her eyes. "Try not to."

Molly took a couple of backward steps so she could keep Talie in sight.

"I'm sure Sammy will come to say hi if I don't," she said.

Talie's face shadowed and she heaved the metal door up from the floor with astonishing strength.

"Don't bring Sammy into this. She's got nothing to do with any of it."

The door slammed into place between them, and Molly would have put pesanas on Talie holding it shut until she was sure Molly was gone.

A loud crash echoed nearby, jolting Molly out of her astonished staring contest with the metal door. She would need to go back up to the workshop and find either some excuse for Ru, or more likely a suitably meek explanation for what happened.

Oh orbs. He's going to kill me this time.

CHAPTER ELEVEN

"What took you so long?"

Ru looked up the moment she jogged red-faced through the door of the shop. She'd avoided going the way Talie suggested, using the door as safety enough to vault up to the beams, and up and up until she was on her level again.

"They weren't finished talking when you did your mad dash," she explained, pressing one hand against the desk to regain her breath.

He groaned. "I'm going to regret asking, but tell me."

"They were talking about the missing artificers and mentioned something about gift replication, and how they've only got cheap imitations so far. I didn't even know that was possible. Then they said Talie had to go to the ball twenty three levels down to keep an eye out. She wasn't happy about it."

Ru rubbed a hand over his mouth. "That… is wild. Gift replication is a myth, or at least everyone thinks it is."

"Clearly not everyone."

"And they're going to have a presence at the ball? We should go too then."

Molly shook her head, using the ebbing of his panic as a sign to sneak around the desk and collapse in her chair.

She pulled her toolkit free and set it on the desk, deciding she wouldn't tell him about her trial by refuse chute unless she had to.

"It's so many levels down, I'm pretty sure they said twenty three. I've never been down anywhere near that many levels before, and how are we even going to get an invite?"

Ru frowned. "Leave that to me. I'll take this back to Marcus now, but promise me, I want an actual promise, that you won't go on any tasks or errands for us without me. Take tonight to rest up, okay?"

"Okay." She nodded. "I could do with catching up on some work anyway tonight. I don't try to get into trouble you know."

He chuckled. "Could have fooled me. I'll go now and bring some food on my way back."

"You're coming back after?"

"Of course." He grinned over his shoulder as he walked toward the door. "If we have an evening off, where else am I going to spend it?"

He left her mulling that over and strode out of the shop without a goodbye.

He doesn't mean it like that. She was almost sure. *We're friends and he's my liaison.*

Amusing herself with the dusty remnants of a teenage crush she'd once had on him, she let her mind wander and set to fixing things. She'd almost wandered so far into daydreams that her mind was half asleep when a loud knocking made her jump.

"Only me."

Beryl bustled in without waiting for an invitation, leaning at a very pregnant angle to peer at some of Molly's carved keyrings in the basket by the door.

So relieved that Ru hadn't interrogated her closer and that she'd escaped the mysterious enemy den unscathed, Molly smiled.

"Hi. Want a keyring?"

Beryl looked up. "Might do. I wanted to ask if you can fix a chair."

"Sure. What's wrong with it? Missing a leg?"

Beryl ambled to the desk before Molly noticed the sack in her hand. She lifted the sack and upended the whole thing onto the table. Smithereens of wood tumbled out, shards and lumps of all sizes and shapes clattering across her already messy desk.

"I- wow." Molly stared at the chaos. "Did someone throw a fireball at it?"

"No, the baby's father decided he wanted to fix the wobbly leg."

"By falling on it?" Molly struggled to keep a straight face.

Beryl grinned. "He slipped on a patch of soap on the floor first, dropped the hammer on it, tried to catch the hammer and ended up smashing himself and the chair into the wall."

Molly grabbed a few of the larger pieces and laid them out, reaching about to line everything up.

"It won't look exactly like new, but I can put some wood filler and varnish here and there, and it'll be sittable on. Probably worth keeping soap off the floor though, or him at least away from the soap."

Beryl laughed, then groaned with a hand on her stomach.

"He's lucky I let him in the house at all. How much do you want for it?"

Molly mentally calculated the time it would take her and how much material she would need. Given that she might have to try and buy some fabric to make a ballgown, because she couldn't expect Celeste to dress her for every Menagerie occasion and Marcus was firmly against freebies, she risked pricing upwards.

"Fifteen pesanas."

Beryl frowned. "That's all?"

"Well, unless you have a fancy ballgown laying around with a matching mask."

The words leapt out before she could check them, her cheeks burning instantly.

"I might be able to dig one out if that works better. Be worth more than fifteen pesanas but I doubt anyone's going to wear it again." She tapped her stomach. "When do you need it by?"

Enough fabric and thread to account for inevitable mistakes would probably set her back about eight pesanas, plus a mask, but this way she could save herself time, which was well worth the extra few she would have saved from earning fifteen.

"Day after tomorrow," she said, raising her hand to hide a large yawn.

Beryl nodded. "Gown and matching mask, consider it done. Where's the party?"

Molly froze, her weary mind racing through potential ways she could word-tangle a suitable answer. Knowing Beryl, even as little as she did, she wouldn't put it past the woman to want to come along, baby and all.

"The school does a dance for previous students," she said.

No lie because they did after the oldest class graduated. She'd gone to hers, secretly delighted when Ru agreed to escort her on a friends date. She'd technically promised to attend another one as well to hear Sammy sing so it wasn't even word-tangling, if she thought about it really generously.

"And you're going?" Beryl asked.

Her attention was on the shop now, but Molly couldn't answer without lying, unless she asked a question which usually sounded sarcastic or saying something suspiciously vague.

So she shrugged.

"Not my thing usually," she said. "I should be able to get the chair done in maybe three days' time."

Beryl nodded. "Great, thanks. We've got the family coming to visit, and Faerie knows that took so much faffing to organise, so we're going to need all the strength of furniture we can get."

With that ominous statement lingering, she shuffled out of the shop with an airy promise to bring the dress by the next evening. Molly had no idea what level Beryl had lived on before, but she would have put money on it being further down if Beryl had access to dresses.

Exhausted, Molly found her comfiest sweatshirt and

wriggled into it, toeing off her boots and pulling on fluffy socks. Even if Ru did come back, she wasn't going out again for anyone.

By the time she'd pulled the screen aside that hid her bed during shop hours, she was only willing to let him come in because he was bringing food. The scant remnants in her tiny kitchenette at the back of the room weren't enough to cobble a proper meal together.

Footsteps thudded in the doorway at the same time her stomach growled.

"I'm starving," she called out, still searching the counter for her favourite mug.

"Never mind that!"

She twisted around in alarm. Sammy's frantic voice was overshadowed only by the look of pure panic on her face.

"Sammy? What's wrong?"

"Talie's not come home."

"I- Wh- why would you think she'd be here?" Molly asked.

Sammy wrapped her arms around her middle.

"I didn't, but I don't have anyone else to go to."

Molly stared, her jaw dropping. She balanced one hand on the counter as her mind raced down the levels back to the metal door.

I can't admit to Sammy I was with her earlier either, or she'll ask why.

Pulling off her fluffy socks, she shoved her feet into her softer shoes she used for nights of proper climbing.

"Do you know where she might have gone? Doesn't she usually spend nights doing her own thing?"

She couldn't remember what anyone had told her and what she knew through spying, panic pushing her into action before thought.

Sammy shook her head. "She goes out at nights sometimes, says she's working or meeting people. I've been told over and over not to ask how the bills get paid, and she gets really cross if I pester her about it."

"So what makes you think she's done different tonight?"

Molly paused in pulling on her coat. She couldn't rule out Sammy's arrival as some kind of enemy tactic either, whether by Talie or whoever she was working for.

"She always comes home for dinner," Sammy insisted. "Always. There's never an excuse and she's never late. She gets panic attacks sometimes, and I shouldn't have told you that but I'm worried. I thought maybe she was late but it's getting later and now it's too late and-"

"Okay, take a breath." Molly rubbed her forehead. "Why don't you go and check out the kinds of places she usually hangs out?"

Sammy hesitated. "What are you going to do?"

"Ask some friends. Trust me."

It was a big ask, but Sammy nodded immediately.

"Okay. There are only a couple of places. I'll meet you back here?"

Molly nodded. "Yeah."

She wanted to reassure Sammy that everything would be okay, but if someone had found Talie coming out of the refuse door, or perhaps holding it like a miscreant trying to steal through it.

Who would steal from the rubbish? She grabbed her keys. *More likely she's lost track of time or having to wait for a safe time to leave. Or she's been delayed. Or this is some kind of trap.*

She hurried to the door with Sammy beside her, only to run straight into a broad, solid chest.

"*Oof.*" She stumbled back. "Ah, Ru. Um…"

He eyed Sammy warily.

"Sammy's worried her sister has gone missing. I said I'd help look."

Ru grimaced. "I'm sure she's fine."

Sammy eyed him up and down, her hip tilting to the side and her arms folding.

"You can't know that. She *always* comes home for dinner before going out."

Ru held up the bag of food and Molly's stomach backflipped obediently for it, but she couldn't risk leaving Talie in the rubbish tunnel if she somehow hadn't made it out unscathed. Sammy was technically underage still, a dangerous situation to be in if Talie didn't return and the boots got involved.

"Keep it warm for me, please?" she asked.

Ru rolled his eyes. "For Faerie's sake, she's a sixteen-year-old girl. They're always out with someone and losing track of time."

Molly's mind slowed at the same time as Sammy's irate face crinkled.

"How do you know she's sixteen?" she demanded.

"She looks it, or roughly Molly's age anyway."

Sammy seemed one step away from stamping her foot,

fists clenched and her eyes flashing.

"She never misses dinner. She promised she wouldn't."

Molly pressed a soft hand to her shoulder, flinching away when Sammy jumped.

"Sorry. You go check like we discussed, and I'll go do my thing."

Sammy nodded and shoved past Ru with such speed she almost sent him through the doorframe, even though she was only two-thirds his size.

"Molly..."

She held up a hand. "Nope. I won't live with myself if something happened."

"You can't go poking around! You can't be seen there."

"I won't be seen. If I find Talie, I'll tell her that Sammy's worried about her."

"And if you don't?"

"Then I'm no worse off than I was before, but Sammy will be. In or out?"

She jangled the keys at him. After a few seconds of silent stand-off, Ru put the food bag on her desk and strode to the door, turning until his unimpressed glare was framed in the lamplight outside.

"Come on. The quicker we find her, the quicker we can eat."

Molly brushed past him and pulled the door shut behind her to lock it.

"You'll feel good after doing a heroic deed," she suggested. "We'll start at the warehouse."

She hadn't told him about the cart and the refuse hall several levels lower down, but if it came to it she would admit the whole thing.

"It'd be so much easier if you'd made friends with her like I suggested," he muttered as they hurried along. "How easy would it be to orb her and say 'hey, your sister's panicking about you, give her a call'."

Molly slowed the pace as he turned to her, realisation dawning on his face as it did on hers.

"Why hasn't her sister tried orbing her?" he asked.

"Maybe she has. Maybe she can't answer. Maybe something's actually happened. Or maybe they don't have an orb each, or even one between them."

Worry speared through her and she broke into a jog, spinning around when Ru didn't appear beside her.

"Ru, come on!"

He pointed behind her, then folded his arms across his chest as she turned again.

Molly stared, uneasiness fluttering in her chest at the amount of sheer relief that flared as Talie came to a stop in front of her, eyebrows raised and arms folded.

"I can't seem to get rid of you lately."

CHAPTER TWELVE

Molly waded through the relief pounding inside her and fell back on disagreeable goading instead.

"Well stop worrying your sister then," she snapped. "I've had her racing into the shop panicking because you've missed dinner and she has nobody else to go to."

Ru appeared right behind her but she ignored him, focused solely on Talie's face. The subtle dip of anxiety was brief, a fleeting flash of emotion, then she clamped it down tight.

"I'll have a word with her. I got caught up in something and left my orb at home."

Ru's folded arms knocked Molly's side as he jostled forward.

"Need to be more careful."

Surprised he wasn't doing his usual routine of trying to charm everyone around him, Molly stared between him and Talie, both sending out acidic vibes as they locked eyes.

"It won't be happening again, believe me," Talie muttered.

Molly waited a few moments but they were still staring each other out without a word.

"Okay, not sure what this is but knock it off, both of you," she said. "We need to find Sammy."

Talie broke the glaring contest first.

"Did she say where she was going?" she asked.

"No, just that she'd check the few places you might hang out. We agreed to meet back at the shop."

Talie pulled a face. "After you then. Knowing Sammy, she'll get through the couple of places we go to in a few seconds. She's a fast runner."

"We'll send her home, don't worry," Ru suggested.

Molly hesitated. Ru had said she should try making friends with Talie and Sammy, and he was the kind of person to buy way too much food.

"Not something I'm trusting a stranger with," Talie said. "I'll wait outside if I have to."

Molly sighed, wiping a hand over her face.

"No need. Assuming we can all get there without killing each other first, there should be enough food for four."

Ru stared at her like she'd grown two heads, and she tried her best in her responding glower to remind him that they were meant to be finding out more from Talie, not alienating her. He gazed at her for a couple of seconds, then shrugged, letting his arms drop to his sides.

"Enough for three. I'll check by tomorrow morning, Molly. Get some rest, and don't stay up all night working on commissions either."

Before she could stop him, he turned on his heel and strode toward one of the side alleys. Guilt curled around her chest, squeezing tight, but she could apologise tomorrow and remind him of their overall mission.

It's not like he was expecting this to be a date or anything. Was he?

She started back toward the shop with Talie a pace behind her. The thoughts jangled around in her head, chaotic enough that they reached the shop without saying a single word to each other.

Molly unlocked the door and led the way inside, the instant scent of food hitting her right in the hunger-zone. She fussed around fetching three plates, some cutlery and trying to clear space on her desk without disturbing anything fragile.

Talie picked up one of her carving knives and flicked it artfully between her fingers, like it belonged there, like she was used to handling the weight of blades as the metal clinked softly against her collection of silver and black rings.

"So… this is enough to pay for whatever it is you do all day?" she asked, waving a hand at the shop.

Molly shrugged. "It pays the bills. If I need more, I work more. People are generous when they think they might need a very niche favour at some point in the future as well. A broken pair of glasses fixed quick. A handy gift for a forgotten birthday, that sort of thing."

She almost mentioned Beryl and the dress out of a strange swell of unexpected nerves, but then Talie would demand to know what she needed a dress for. She would probably guess the truth too.

Talie nodded but didn't reply, her gaze flicking to the food as Molly pulled it out of the bag.

"I won't bother asking what you do," Molly added. "I

know you'll only brush me off. I don't have Sammy in my orb but if you can connect to her, you can use it."

Sammy had mentioned Talie had left her orb at home, but Molly didn't bother asking why Talie had one, even though they weren't cheap to get.

I saw her inside the library as well, and those member cards aren't easy to come by without a referral.

She lifted her head to find Talie staring at her, not in a considered way but as if her mind was stuck, her eyes fixed and glassy.

"Are you okay?" she asked.

Talie blinked hard. With a tiny shake of her head, she leaned forward to peer at the food instead.

"I'm fine. She'll be here in a minute anyway."

"Not many places to check?" Molly asked, still unnerved by the sudden staring.

Talie shrugged. "Something like that. We go to the park. I take her to school. She walks herself home sometimes. We go to the shop. She insists on going to the live song shows sometimes. I've been saving up to get tickets if *Siren-Sing-Along* ever performs here but it'd probably be far too many levels below for us to afford any."

Amazed that Talie was speaking so much, let alone giving her actual information, Molly pushed one of the food cartons across the desk.

"Sit down and eat. It's not a meat pocket but the food is good from Mirabella's. Cheap and cheerful but tasty. I sound like an advert."

She bit her lip, moving cartons around needlessly as she

opened them and Talie perched on the edge of her spare chair.

"We like Mirabella's," Talie offered. "Every birthday dinner Sammy has needs to be from there."

"Ru says the same."

"That's the gargoyle who was flanking you earlier I take it?"

Molly tried to look disapproving but failed, her smile twitching.

"That's not nice. He's been kind to me. Not sure why, or how much we're trading in terms of conversation here, but he's protective and you're not exactly being upfront with who you are. No point asking who I am either probably, so we'll probably need to sit in silence until Sammy reappears."

Talie shrugged but conceded with a tiny quirked smile of her own.

"Relax, Princess, I won't ask. You've been nice enough to share a meal with us so we'll pretend we're not whoever we are for tonight."

Charmed by that idea, Molly dug her fork in the carton of spiced rice.

"Fair enough. Tell me about who you aren't tonight then."

Talie sighed. "Not much to tell. We live a few levels up. Sammy goes to school. I train in the gym up two levels a lot, do odd jobs for those that need them. You're pretty lucky to have this place though."

"I am. The workshop is my safe haven. Ru always tells me I need to have a good clear out but my clutter is organised down to the last bolt and nail, and I know where everything should be by looking."

Talie nodded, inhaling a mouthful of food before speaking.

"I imagine it's nice to have a skill, something others need that you can trade on. I'd never be able to sit still for long enough."

Molly risked a smile. "I can believe that. I like it though. Hearing the occasional tap of footsteps outside the door as people pass, and when I charge things from the generator, the whirring is friendly so I don't feel alone, even though I am more often than not. Occasionally the neighbours have a shouting match, or someone drops something huge a few levels below that shakes and rumbles the foundations, but mostly it's peaceful."

Talie reached over for one of the food tubs, and Molly eyed the narrow set of her wrists, her collarbones, wondering if she often went without to make sure Sammy ate enough.

"If it weren't for the synthetic floral scent they keep pumping out of the vents, this place wouldn't be so bad."

Molly laughed. "True, but you can't have everything. I just cover it with the smell of oil and sawdust. Sometimes I pretend I'm out somewhere in the wilds of the realm, or even another realm of Faerie entirely."

"Nice idea." Talie sighed. "We're stuck in the citadel for life though, but you keep on dreaming. You never know."

"TALIE!"

Molly almost lobbed the rice at the door in alarm.

Clutching the carton in her hand, she huffed a startled breath as Talie swung around on her seat.

"There you are. Hungry?" she asked.

Sammy strode into the room, hands on hips. Delighted that she wasn't in the firing line, Molly grabbed cartons and started dealing herself a hearty bowlful to hide her grin behind.

"Hungry?! You didn't come home for dinner! You left your orb on the table! I've had no idea where you are or if you're lying in a gutter somewhere!"

Talie sat still in the face of Sammy's anger, but Sammy clearly wasn't going to let her off the hook without a killing blow.

"If you wanted to come here and have a date, you could have just run home and let me know!"

Molly froze with a forkful of food halfway to her lips and half a mouthful still not finished.

"Snotadate," she mumbled.

Sammy folded her arms. "Oh. Why not?"

"Sammy." Talie's tone was full of warning now.

"She thought you were interested in me at first," Sammy added. "But she's really glad you aren't. So am I, no offense."

"*SAMMY.*"

Molly risked a glance at Talie's rigid shoulders and slightly pink cheeks.

"I'm sure that's not true," she soothed, terrified to even consider it. "This isn't a date either, so sit down and have some with us. Please?"

She couldn't do anything about the obvious pleading in

her tone, but Sammy eyed them both for one final moment before sinking into the last available chair and grabbing the nearest carton.

"As it is, I heard something really weird when I was at the shop just now."

Talie shifted in her seat. "What's that?"

"Still not talking to you." She looked pointedly at Molly instead.

Amused, Molly repeated the question while Talie rolled her eyes and grabbed the paper bag of hot rolls.

"One of the missing people was raving about having his memories coming back," Sammy announced. "He was harping on to anyone who'd listen that the Fae in hoods had copied his gift and given it to someone else."

"Oh, wow." Molly snuck a look at Talie, noting the pinch around her eyes and the absolute absence of any other noticeable emotion. "Which one? One of the artificers?"

Sammy leaned forward. "No, that's what's so weird. The artificers returned, but the others, the servants, one of the boots and the cobbler, didn't. But it was the man from the boots who was in the shop."

Talie tapped her roll on her plate, staring at it.

"How do you know?" she asked.

Sammy eyed her, then Molly, until Molly wearily repeated the question.

"Butch who runs the shop said so. Someone calmed the man down but Butch was talking to whoever was in front of me and they recognised him."

Molly's heart sank. "What happened to him?"

"The boots arrived and were closing in on him when I left. It's probably some kind of psychosis from whatever happened to him though. Everyone knows gifts can't be stolen, not unless you're like a queen or king or something, and we don't have any of them here."

"Everyone knows," Molly echoed, unable to word-tangle anything more eloquent.

She flinched as Sammy leaned forward, eyes narrowed as she glanced between them.

"Are you sure this wasn't a date? You're both being weird."

On firmer ground there, Molly set her fork down.

"Definitely not a date, and you don't know me well enough to tell when I'm being weird or not," she teased.

Sammy grinned. "We'll fix that. I like your shop and I like you too. What gifts do you have?"

"Enough, Sam," Talie grumbled. "It's rude to ask."

Molly shrugged. "I have a charm gift, comes in handy sometimes. What about you?"

She reached out to grab the bag of rolls at the same time as Talie. Her fingertips slid over Talie's knuckles by accident. She flinched, the reaction only marginally less reactive than Talie's.

"I don't have one yet." Sammy didn't seem to have noticed their awkward fumble. "I'm lying in wait for some unsuspecting noble to walk by in need of saving somehow. Rumour has it a lot of the other realms have courts where you can go and work off a debt in exchange for a gift, but we don't have anything like that here. Have you ever left the citadel?"

Molly shook her head. "Nope, where would I go? I got lucky with my charm gift because my guardians got it for me, but I have to make my own luck since they died."

"Well if this gift replication rumour turns out to be true, maybe I can share someone else's."

Talie frowned. "It's never as golden as the opportunity sounds. You pay less at the start and end up paying forever after."

Molly grabbed a roll and split it in two. The only two ways to get a gift was to be born with it by grace of Faerie, which was rare, or to be gifted it by court Fae. She knew her charm gift was bartered for by her guardian from a passing low ranking noble when she was ten, she remembered it well enough, but her compulsion must have been a birth-gift.

Not knowing who her parents were had its drawbacks and advantages, but the only thing Lily and Basil would tell her was that her mother had been too cloaked to be recognisable when she handed Molly over as a baby, and they'd cared for her ever since.

"Thank you for the meal," Talie said. "We'll leave you to it."

Molly stood with them, relieved even though she was finally beginning to relax around them. It was easy in those moments of chatter to forget she was still working for the Menagerie and Talie was still part of an unknown faction who were talking about gift replication and missing people. Thoughts of Seymour filled her head as she followed them to the door.

"Thanks for feeding us," Sammy said, hovering at the

desk in no rush to leave. "We could invite you to ours next. It's not much, not a great workshop or anything, but we'd cook something nice. Talie can when she chooses to."

Talie clamped a hand on Sammy's shoulder. "She's being polite, Sam. Time to go."

Molly opened her mouth to argue, even though she could feel exhaustion tugging at her eyelids. She tensed as Sammy leaned forward and gave her a tight hug.

"I'll just say bye," Talie muttered.

Molly nodded. "Probably best. It was kind of okay not being who we are for a bit."

That earned her a smile, and she shut her door with a tiny flicker of warmth blooming in her chest.

CHAPTER THIRTEEN

Ru didn't check in the next day. She half expected him to skulk in at some point, moody until she managed to make him smile and forgive her, but he didn't. When Beryl popped by to apologise and say she would most definitely have the dress ready before the next evening, Molly was almost done with the chair. So focused on her work, she decided if she wasn't able to go to the ball it was no big shame after all.

The thought kept her calm enough to eat and sleep herself back to some sense of normality, until Beryl bustled on the evening of the ball with a large bag hanging over one arm and a smaller bag clutched in her free hand. Molly eyed Harvey trailing behind her with a wide box, his hair a mess.

"One dress with effects as promised," Beryl huffed, heaping the whole lot down on the nearest chair.

Harvey grinned. "I offered to bring the lot over myself but she's still mad about the chair. She gets independent when she's mad."

Beryl pulled a face at him and unzipped the larger bag.

"Now, I thought this would be more your colour. Fit for the finest ballrooms in all of Faerie."

She pulled out a pile of pale gold, tiny purple sequins catching the dim light from the lamp Molly kept meaning to replace. The bodice was fitted but the skirts flowed when Beryl gave it a weary flourish. Edging closer, Molly traced a reverent fingertip over the tiny slithers of purple woven through the fabric.

"The sleeves take a bit of attaching," Beryl added. "Harv, put the shoes down before you drop them."

"I didn't even think about shoes," Molly admitted.

Beryl sank onto another chair, her cheeks pink.

"Go on then, pop it on. It's corseted at the back so it should fit you."

Molly picked up the dress with careful hands, taking a slow walk to the screen around her bed as she inspected the handiwork. Whoever had made the dress was unbelievably skilled, and as she peered closer the sequins became tiny chips of purple gemstone.

"The slightest hint of amethyst," Beryl said.

Molly undid the ties and slithered into the dress, doing her best to tie the corset over her chest before wriggling the dress around the right way. She glanced in the small mirror beside her bed and watched the way the skirts swished and swayed around her legs, hiding all but her feet from view.

"It's beautiful."

She shuffled out, blushing when Harvey whistled and Beryl threw a small pair of pliers at him.

"Can you cope with stilettos?" she asked.

Molly froze. "Um… I don't know. I've never worn heels before. Never had to."

Beryl held her arms out until Harvey ferried the box from his hands to hers. Shoes flew through the air seconds later, and Molly struggled to stay in place when one nearly took out a clock hanging on the wall.

"Aha. Wear these." Beryl chucked a pair of pale gold slippers at Molly's feet. "Then we'll put your hair up and fix your mask."

Molly allowed Beryl to fuss around attaching some floaty sleeves to the dress that bared her shoulders and slit up the insides to show part of her arms, aware of Harvey inspecting various parts of the workshop with undisguised curiosity.

"What does this do?" he asked.

Molly held still, wincing as Beryl scraped her hair back firmly enough to remove her scalp from her skull.

"It's a weighted bottle scale, for weighing potions and tinctures."

"Wow, cool! What about this?"

Molly blinked. "That's a screwdriver."

"For driving screws, got it. You about done, love of my life?"

Beryl huffed. "Don't rush me. Alright, all done. Put your mask on and let me see the full effect."

Molly took the mask, a golden, spindly thing that glittered and curled around her eyes. She'd expected a full face mask, but this wouldn't do much more than cover the bridge of her nose and her eyebrows.

"Is that real gold?" Harvey asked.

"Of course not," Molly answered without thinking. "Real gold would have more weight to it. My money's on pulped card covered with lacquer."

"It's pretty, that's all that matters," Beryl insisted.

Harvey nodded. "It is. If you need a chaperone, Molly, we can recommend a suitable one."

"You don't know any suitable ones," Beryl retorted. "None that would be suitable for Molly anyway."

"You don't know that. I *could* know suitable ones."

"But you don't."

"But I could."

Beryl scowled. "You don't though."

Harvey grinned. "I could though."

"You're more likely to know absolute miscreants."

"True, but you and your sisters would be the most miscreant-y of the lot."

"Oi!" Beryl folded her arms over her stomach. "You make us sound awful."

"Only the best kind of awful."

Molly sought for a way to kick them out without actually kicking them out, but their bickering seemed to be sweeping them toward the door anyway.

"Thank you for the loan," she said, loud enough to draw their attention. "The chair is ready if you want to take it."

Beryl frowned. "Oh, right. I'd forgotten the chair."

Harvey moved forward as she looked expectantly at him. Molly pointed out the chair, grimacing as he picked it up in hand by one leg.

"Enjoy yourself!" He called out over his shoulder, using the chair to jostle Beryl gently outside. He even shut the door behind him as Molly pressed her hands to her desk, slouching over with social exhaustion.

How did she even get a dress this fancy in the first place? She smoothed her hands over the skirts, twisting gently to watch them flare and flutter. *I wonder if Talie's finding this whole dressing up thing as weird as I am.*

She smiled at the thought of Talie scowling and being stuffed into a ballgown against her will. Searching inside the smaller bag Beryl had left behind, she found a small fabric purse of identical gold to the dress with a drawstring opening, neat enough for a ball but big enough to fit her orb and some pesanas in.

Unless Ru doesn't bother coming to pick me up. She bit her lip.

He'd never forgotten or rejected her before, even after they had arguments, but he hadn't checked in or popped by like he usually did. She wasn't even sure what exactly upset him so much about her inviting Talie and Sammy round for food. There would have been enough for the four of them, and she was almost certain he wouldn't have expected the evening to be a date.

A firm knock at the door had her heart leaping, but she took a second to settle herself and finish picking up the shoes Beryl had scattered around before calling out.

"Sorry, it took me a while to get-"

Ru stopped dead in the doorway, staring at her dress.

"It's a loan from the neighbour in exchange for fixing a chair," she explained. "Will it do?"

He held up a bag, his gaze still fixed on the dress.

"I brought these from Celeste," he murmured. "But yeah, that's… yeah."

She bit down a smile as he cleared his throat and walked

inside, kicking the door shut behind him. He dropped his bag beside the ones Beryl had left behind and Molly took in his suit, navy blue like midnight ink, from the jacket and trousers to the waistcoat and tie. With a pale blue shirt on underneath and his black hair slicked back, he wouldn't need a charm gift to have all the well-bred lower level ladies fluttering.

"What instructions have we got then?" she asked, a trill of nerves flaring in her chest. "Oh, I almost forgot. Sammy said when she was looking for Talie in the shop, one of the missing Fae was in there talking about how his memories were coming back and how they stole his gift."

"Gift replication?"

"I'm not sure, but it was the man from the boots, not one of the artificers, so it looks like he's been returned as well. I didn't want to seem too interested with Talie around, but she looked uneasy about it."

Ru sighed. "I don't get a good feeling about her. You need to be careful, especially as she's involved with the enemy."

"We don't know who they are yet," Molly countered.

Ru hesitated. After a tense moment, he chuckled and held his elbow out to her.

"Come on. You're right, there's still a lot we don't know, which is what tonight is about. You look great, by the way."

She grinned. "Thanks, should hope so too. You look fine enough to charm all the nobles, or however high up the social chain we end up having to go."

He bowed low as she slipped her hand into the crook of

his arm. She wished then that she had some of those fancy elbow-length gloves she'd seen in old story books and some of the orb-casts on *The Faerie Net*'s socialite channels.

"We won't have access to the lifts from here, but I have organised a cart instead."

Molly followed him outside, stopping only to lock the door, and stared in amazement at the open-topped cart at the end of the alley. She'd seen several carts running up and down, often pulled by a single Arumpus, sometimes a pair of Arumpii, but she never imagined she would actually end up getting a ride in one.

The wooden cart was polished to a high shine, from the spokes and the four wheels to the double wooden seat behind the driver's bench.

"How?" Molly asked, her jaw dropping.

Ru laughed. "Got to arrive in style. Mind your dress on the edges."

Molly took the hand he held out for her as they approached the cart, and the silver Arumpus between the spokes tossing its spined neck in a showy display. The driver tapped his fingertips to his peaked hat as she climbed up to the seat behind him, and Molly glanced back at the alley to find Beryl and Harvey watching from their doorway.

She gave them a wave and shivered as Ru slid an arm around the back of the cart, perilously close to her bare shoulders.

CHAPTER FOURTEEN

Molly hung over the side of the cart as they descended the levels, her eyes wide as clustered buildings with several front doors gave way to more smart brick and individual gardens, nicer paving of the lanes and eventually even bigger buildings.

"How did we even get invites?" she asked.

He pulled two smart rectangles of ivory card trimmed with gold from his jacket pocket.

"Celeste has contacts apparently," he murmured, slipping them back in.

"I wonder why she's slumming it on the upper level offices of the Menagerie then."

He chuckled. "She probably doesn't live there. You know Marcus likes the Menagerie to fly under the radar, and a lot of what happens on the upper levels is brushed over and hushed up."

"True, she dresses nicely and has access to ballgowns and changes of clothing for me that wouldn't fit her, so she's clearly got some serious coin."

Ru lifted a hand instead of answering, but Molly didn't need help noticing the vast building looming in front of them like a ghostly white castle.

"It's like something out of a storybook," she whispered.

Ru nodded, his eyes wide. "You can say that again. Remember the plan. Socialise but give nothing away. Don't let anyone take too much of an interest in you either. If they do, be clingy, it's a surefire way to send them running."

"Is that how you manage to chase off all the girls?" she asked, nerves dancing under the humour.

The cart rolled to a halt in front of enormous double doors, wood lined with curving metal, and Molly waited for Ru to jump down before taking the hand he held out to her. She flinched as he drew her close, his breath brushing her ear.

"As long as I've got the important one by my side, yes, the rest can chase themselves away."

He placed a midnight blue mask over his face so that only his mouth was visible amid the dark sequins, then straightened up and tucked her hand through the crook of his arm without asking.

He's being silly, she reassured herself. *No point getting all fluttery for nothing.*

Molly held her skirts with her free hand as they ascended the stone steps and approached the open doors. Ru held out their invitations to a man on the door, who was dressed so finely that Molly bet his uniform cost more than her yearly workshop costs.

She eyed the opulence of the entrance hall as Ru led her toward the clamour and clang of the ballroom at the end, her slippers scuffing over red and gold carpet. The only other place she'd seen such fancy carpet was the

Menagerie, but this was far above and beyond anything even Marcus could probably afford.

"We'll take a walk around the edge of the room first," Ru said.

Molly nodded, barely hearing a word. Fae whirled in front of her in a coordinated dance of flowing skirts and bright colours, the firelight picking up the glinting sparkles of countless gemstones and jewellery.

"Can we go by the food table while we're walking?" she asked.

Ru squeezed her fingers with his arm but didn't answer, steering her past the cluster of chairs and tables and onto a circuit of the ballroom's edge.

Molly risked a glance at him as they passed the food table, which was piled high with ornately arranged pastry towers and mixed fruit sculptures, but he was too busy eying the crowd to notice her quick fingers.

She swiped a tiny spherical pastry, popped it in her mouth and stifled a groan of delight.

"We should separate."

Ru twisted to face her and she almost choked on the pastry. Gulping it down, she dabbed the corners of her mouth with her fingertips.

"If you think that's best," she said, her insides bubbling with anticipation.

"I'll try to be seen by some well-known faces in case I can slip into one of their conversations," Ru murmured under the pretence of drawing her close to whisper secrets in her ear. "You should do the same and see if you can get someone to talk to you. I'll come back for a dance."

Before she could find some way of teasing him about his dancing to settle her nerves, Ru stalked off into the whirl of the crowd. She watched him go, then glanced back and forth for some sign of someone she might recognise.

Even Talie would do right now.

A dignified bell broke the crowd noise, all heads turning toward the entrance and one of the many uniformed men standing on a small raised platform.

"Lady Carrington," he announced.

Murmurs filled the air, and Molly bounced onto her tiptoes to get a better look at the woman sweeping into the room with all the air of a royal.

Burnished brown hair curled artfully around a circlet of roses, revealing a pert nose, ruby lips and the kind of stare that would cut battle-hardened warriors in half. As the regal gaze swept the assembled crowd, Molly had the urge to shrink away in case she was seen, but someone like Lady Carrington wouldn't spare a glance for someone like her, masked and gowned or not.

Molly followed her example and assessed the crowd around them. Several people were dancing again and across the floor Ru was already charming a cluster of women, laughing as they fluttered their fans and their eyelashes at him. Molly stifled a giggle as one of them leaned forward to pat his arm and almost fell half out of her dress.

All that wealth and she still can't keep her chest in properly.

"Who are you?"

The voice echoed beside her, not loud enough to draw

attention but sharp enough to insist on being obeyed. Molly turned her head and gasped.

"Well?" Lady Carrington snapped.

Molly curled her toes inside her slippers instead of clenching her fists, nerves slowing her tongue as she sought for something to say. This was a noble right in front of her, someone who could gift or possibly even curse, depending on how pleased or disappointed she was.

"My name is Molly," she answered.

Lady Carrington eyed her up and down, the frown beneath her dusky blue mask deepening.

"Who are you affiliated with?"

Molly channelled her inner Beryl with a touch of rising hysteria, forcing a wide grin.

"My companion is around somewhere, charming everyone in a dress no doubt. I'm only here for the food."

Lady Carrington huffed a noise that could have been either a snort of derision or an incredulous laugh. Molly shuffled a step back. No doubt Lady Carrington also had all sorts of perilous gifts at her disposal.

Pulling her Fae connection around her, Molly summoned up her charm gift, the sensation of it tingling up to her cheeks and out through her lips.

"Your dress is exquisite," she said. "If I can be bold, the colour suits you."

Lady Carrington nodded. "It does. Whereas you clearly have a statement in mind over a choice of fashion."

"I don't know what you mean."

"Clearly 'bold' is a theme for you, especially to wear the colours of royalty if you're not part of the royal family."

WHAT?!

Molly glanced down at the gold dress woven with purple crystals. Beryl hadn't said anything about royalty.

Maybe she doesn't know. As if any of us are going to be in situations where anyone knows the rules of royalty.

"The dress belongs to a friend of mine," she admitted. "I'm borrowing it for the evening. Had I known, I'd have chosen something a bit more on my level."

Lady Carrington's lips thinned. "And what is your level?"

Molly bowed her head, indignation at the dismissive tone firing inside her chest.

"Actually somewhat useful to society. Excuse me."

Each step she took toward the food table was a struggle, the fear that her attitude would get her killed for insolence or used as some kind of spectacle tearing at her nerves. It took all her effort not to plaster her hands to the table when she reached it and slide under it to hide.

A quick glance proved Lady Carrington had moved on to more important social conquests already, but Molly stayed alert and only helped herself to four more tiny pastries while doing so.

Ru had moved on from his new fan club, deep in conversation with a couple of men, and Molly risked leaving her safety zone to amble past a cluster of people gesticulating wildly.

"-rumour that some madman was causing trouble in some far up level, going on and on about gifts being stolen. I tell you, if we don't start taking these levels in hand, we're going to have absolute anarchy soon."

Molly tilted her head to hear better, her gaze fixed on a nearby statue with dedicated intensity.

"Theoretically, it could be possible to steal gifts," a woman said. "But that would require a conduit and such things are a gruesome business."

"True, we're about the finer things in life, not the macabre."

"Indeed. The decorations tonight are extremely satisfactory, like that Arvasquez there. Are you a fan of Arvasquez, dear?"

Molly froze. It was possible the woman was talking to someone else entirely, but the softened tone that came with the question was what the motherly always used for the young. The fact that she was also in fact a huge fan of the famed Fae sculptor's work and able to recognise the statue, mainly because Arvasquez had started in practical masonry before moving over to art and Basil had found her a book on it from a passing merchant, confirmed it.

She turned as elegantly as she could, fixing a smile on her face.

"I am indeed," she agreed, modifying her tone and inflections to match theirs. "Her early work especially, although her artwork is superb."

She wondered what Ru would say if he could hear her now playing at being some finely bred young lady.

Probably laugh himself into next week.

"Ah, her early work is interesting," the woman said, waving away her companions.

Molly glanced over her shoulder to keep track of Ru,

but her attention snagged on a flash of dark hair, all shiny and sleek, before she could find him. Talie lifted her head sharply as if she'd sensed Molly's attention on her, and Molly turned quickly back to her conversation, her heart picking up an erratically panicked beat.

"I couldn't help overhearing you mention all this artificer news," she tried. "Not a very nice business. Is it true that gifts could be stolen?"

The woman chuckled. "Stolen implies they could be used elsewhere. It is possible to remove Fae from their gifts though, not just by royalty of course, but by process."

"You said it would be gruesome, something about a conduit?"

"Now, what's a lovely young woman like yourself taking an interest in such things for?"

Molly heard the subtle note of warning beneath the airy tone and hastened to laugh, the sound ever so slightly strangled.

"I don't attend these things as much as others do," she tried, pushing her charm to the fore. "I've been told before that knowledge of current events is expected conversation. We can return to Arvasquez if you prefer. I could talk about her all night."

She checked out the woman's bare arms but found no sign of a certain bracelet. Her charm seemed to have worked though as the woman relaxed and waved a dismissive hand.

"These balls are overrated, but we must do our duty and turn out. All this worry about the artificers going missing and returning with no memory will be nothing more than an anecdotal morsel by time the next one rolls around."

Molly doubted it, but before she could find a way of turning the conversation to something useful, Ru appeared beside her. He bowed his head to her conversation partner before holding out a hand to her.

"I promised you a dance," he announced.

"You did." Molly nodded, smiling over her shoulder. "Excuse me."

She took Ru's hand and got halfway to the dancefloor before realisation set in.

"I don't know how to dance," she hissed.

Ru grinned. "Neither do I. Copy the others and we'll muddle through."

Molly bit her lip, eying the couples around them. Several women were dancing with one hand on their partner's shoulder and the other hand in hand, so she did that. Ru's free hand landed warm and firm on her waist and she shuffled back and forth, trying to let him guide her even though she could see how he was doing it wrong.

"That's enough of that," she muttered. "Did you get anything useful?"

He shrugged. "Nothing we could trade on. We'll do another round of conversations separately, then together?"

"Okay. You're better at it than I am though."

"What, dealing with people?"

She nodded. "Yeah. I've already backchatted Lady Carrington and spent too much time talking about Arvasquez with the other one."

Ru rolled his eyes as he guided her to the edge of the dancefloor and hurried off for another attempt at charming whoever he could get close to. Wishing she had a fan, Molly wiped a hand over her clammy brow.

There were doors to a terrace right behind her.

Doors to a terrace that would have some kind of shadowed corner.

A shadowed corner that would probably have some service steps to the girders between the level and the one below it.

Molly checked nobody was watching her, nobody who might see a reason to follow her at least, and slipped outside. Alone on the terrace, she trotted past bountiful bushes full of bright pink blooms throwing out a hazy sweet fragrance and toward a dark patch near the wall.

A soft breeze brushed her face and she tilted her head up, her jaw dropping when she noticed how. Unlike her level, or any she'd visited before, this one had small partitions of the glass boundary removed. The air on her cheeks wasn't the artificial stuff pumped out like she was used to, but fresh and real from the realm beyond the citadel.

The closest I've ever been to outside of the citadel is a breeze in the night.

She pressed a hand to the glass to steady herself, closing her eyes to soak it in. Such a simple thing, and yet she'd seen some of the old orb-wave broadcasts from elsewhere in Faerie explaining about Fae who could realm-skip to whole other realms, or simply walk through their own as far and as often as they liked without restriction.

Nobles probably came in and out of the citadel every day on lower levels, but for people like her the outside realm was a mere escapist fantasy, let alone other realms entirely.

By time someone worked their way down far enough, they'd probably be in so much debt they can't leave, or too old to remember it.

Unwilling to get caught on her own, she found the wooden service steps leading underneath the level and hurried down. The world of metal girders and wooden posts was the one she knew, and she breathed a sigh of relief at being out of sight.

I'm not built for balls and glamour. She grinned in the semi-darkness. *At least Talie looked like she was as grouchy about it as I am.*

She would go up in a minute, rejoin the charade and let Ru do the talking until it was time to leave. Maybe after one last kiss from the real outside air first.

Footsteps tapped quietly on the stairs before she could bring herself to move, the sounds too soft for someone not to be sneaking up on her.

She tensed, ready to whirl around and catch them off guard, to run past or push them if she absolutely had to.

"Are you following me, Princess?"

CHAPTER FIFTEEN

Molly stared at Talie, her face half-lit by the lamps from the level above. Her fitted black gown of velvet with sequins that glimmered in the dim glow was at odds with the stiff posture, but it was definitely Talie's eyes glowering behind the slip of black mask. Molly didn't want to say yes to the question, even though Talie was the reason she was there, at least inadvertently, but the evening had already put her at odds with her own sense of peaceful equilibrium so attitude came easily.

"Down here? It looks more like you're following me."

Talie cocked her head. "Not what I meant and you know it. We always seem to be on different sides."

"What side are you on then?"

Talie smirked, glancing around at the wide ledge they stood on.

"The side that keeps Sammy in school and both of us in food, shelter and occasional heating. How about you?"

Molly faked a smile. "The side that keeps my workshop open and the occasional guest fed."

"Yeah, Sammy's still determined to have you over. She's been trying to bake."

Molly opened her mouth to answer with sarcasm but

hesitated.

"That's really nice of her. She's sweet."

"Unlike me?"

Molly shrugged, her cheeks flushing. "I don't know you. Every question gets a vague answer."

"That's like the orb reader calling the book informational. Do you want to dance?"

Molly blinked. Somewhere in her awareness of the situation, she knew Talie had asked her to dance. She also had Ru probably looking for her upstairs, assuming he'd put his growing fan club down for long enough to notice she was missing.

It's just another type of dance. She wants information from me and I want information from her. It's a fair game.

"Alright."

She stepped forward, relishing the surprise flaring in Talie's eyes. Awkwardness curled in her gut but she held her hand out, palm up. Talie could take it or back down, but Molly wouldn't let her win this one.

Talie's hand slid into hers a second later, warm and firm. Molly's stomach tangled into immediate knots as Talie took her other hand and placed it on her shoulder.

"You know how to dance?" Molly asked.

"Sammy wanted to learn, and I wanted to make sure nobody took advantage of her while she did."

Molly tried hard not to smile at the thought of Sammy dancing with people and Talie following behind them with some kind of weapon to beat at their legs with.

"There at least you're ahead of me then," she admitted. "I've never found a reason to learn to dance."

Talie didn't answer as her hand slid tight over Molly's hip. She took a step to guide them sideways and Molly settled into the soft swaying steps back and forth.

"You know Lady Carrington well?" Talie asked.

Ah, and it begins.

"Nope."

"She approached you."

Molly grinned. "She did."

"Why?"

Determined not to make it in any way easy, she frowned, pretending to think.

"Why do you care?"

"It'd be a big help to me if you told me," Talie admitted through a rigid jaw.

"What's it worth?"

"My unerring gratitude."

Molly snorted, laughter spilling out. "You couldn't even try to make that sound genuine. Fine, it's no big secret or anything. She wanted to know why I was wearing gold. I can't remember exactly what I said but I doubt she'll be inviting me round for tea and finger pastry anytime soon."

Silence fell between them and Molly's attention fixed on Talie's hand soft against her hip. She wasn't heavy-handed like Ru, or dragging her about either. It was a gentle give and take of movement, both of them mimicking the tentative dance of the questioning.

"And Ursula Fen-Brigad? What did you speak to her about?"

Molly frowned. "The woman with the big hair? We talked about Arvasquez. She's a sculptor, mostly art but some of her earlier work was more like mine, fixing or building functional things. Although her experimental period apparently caused a lot of things to explode, so not much is known about that part. Do you want to know what Ru and I talked about as well?"

"What you and your boyfriend talk about is nothing to do with me." Talie sniffed.

Molly pulled a face. "He's not my boyfriend. He's been kind to me and he's my closest friend."

She conveniently left out any mention of her teenage crush on him and silence dropped around them again.

They were on opposing sides of a much bigger mystery, at least until proven otherwise. They couldn't even go two seconds without squabbling, but as Talie took a baby step closer so that her hand rested on Molly's back, Molly couldn't meet her gaze, afraid in the face of some truth she'd barely even scratched surface of yet. Because this back and forth, the suspicion and their strange habit of being drawn to each other, it was something deeper and more naturally savage, beautiful in some kind of desperate darkness.

"You're still my enemy," she murmured.

Talie nodded. "Yeah, but we don't have to be for tonight. Temporary truce because those out there, up there, don't matter. Tonight is a gap in time where I'm just me and you're just you."

"No spies or secrets."

"Exactly. Now, dance with me properly."

So, Molly did. She stepped closer, her hand splayed over Talie's sequinned waist, her gaze finally settling on those startling hazel-grey eyes ringed with hints of sunshine.

Talie smiled, and in that moment it was every realisation Molly had never fully known.

"What if someone comes down and sees us?" she asked a while later.

Talie shrugged. "We're wearing masks. We do what we have to for survival if something happens."

"By dancing away from everyone else?"

"We're having our gap in time, but if you want we can play three questions."

Molly smiled. "Is that the way you get Sammy to stop talking then?"

"Sometimes. You ask me three, and we both have to answer, unless we can't."

"Let me guess, you can't answer most of the ones I should be asking."

"Who knows? Give it a go."

Molly considered what she might ask, torn between duty of asking about Seymour and the warehouse, or asking more about Talie herself.

"Okay. What goes on at that warehouse?"

Talie tensed, her shoulders stiff under Molly's fingers.

"I'll get in trouble if I tell you. Besides, it's meant to be both of us answering all questions."

"I could tell you what I think is going on," she suggested. "But don't answer if you'd rather not. I'll find out somehow."

Talie groaned. "You're better off letting it go. What I can tell you is that there's a side that wants to control the citadel and others who want to set people free."

Molly knew enough about sides, and she guessed Talie knew she was part of the Menagerie now as she clearly wasn't anything noble or aligned to a guild.

"In that case, what I can tell you is that I know there are two sides, potentially several if you include guilds and nobles and all sorts. Second question, is the gym training your job? How do you pay the bills?"

Talie laughed. "That is a very invasive question, but yes I earn money from the gym."

"And I earn money from the workshop. Okay, final question. If you could do anything, go anywhere, what would you do?"

"I…" Talie sagged. "I try not to think that far ahead. You?"

Molly let her brush the question aside. Talie wasn't going to tell her anything she could use, but getting to know her on a personal level settled something restless inside. Making friends with Talie was also technically sort of exactly what Ru had told her to do, even though the mere thought of that duplicity made her insides sink.

"I'd want to go out beyond the glass and see the realm maybe, travel a bit," she admitted. "I can work anywhere given the right tools, although the workshop is home. There are so many questions I want answers to, like how things in Faerie function."

Talie nodded, her chin dipping onto Molly's shoulder, the soft wisp of her hair brushing Molly's cheek.

"It's good to have dreams sometimes."

A loud clamour of noise drifted down from the level

above, muted by the structure.

"He'll be wondering where you are," Talie said.

Molly grimaced. "Yeah, he's going to be furious. So, how do we do this, truce until we're out of sight, or do we count to three and start fighting?"

Talie chuckled. "We walk away. We go back up to the ball. We keep running into each other and avoid fighting unless we have to."

"Say hi in the street and all that?" Molly joked, humour safer than the unexpected swell of melancholy.

"I don't know if we can go that far." Talie hesitated. "It's not like this is a *Carrie's Castle* book and we're going to be running away together. We both have consequences. I don't know what yours are, but I imagine you must have them."

Molly nodded, even though she wasn't so sure anymore. The Menagerie was more like an employer than a family, although their motto, *Forever Entwined by Bonds of Blood and Loyalty*, forced everyone to pretend otherwise. Ru was her liaison and her friend, but she had an inkling deep down that if he had to choose a loyalty, he would go to the ends of the earth for the Menagerie whatever its faults.

"I never found any *Carrie's Castle* books," she said. "It's meant to be good though."

Talie frowned. "No library card?"

"Nope. Where would I get the referral from?"

When Talie pulled away and stepped back, Molly did the same, turning the space between them from respectable to wary.

"Go home, Molly," Talie said softly. "Don't look back

either."

"Why not? Going to stab me in the back?"

Talie laughed. "No, not if I can help it. Go."

Molly turned and strode toward the archway. She'd have to explain away her absence, to Ru at least if not to the menagerie, but she could do that easily enough.

Don't look back. Don't look back.

Talie's words circled in her head. She waited until she was through the archway and walking up the stairs before turning her head and glancing back.

She wasn't entirely surprised to see that Talie was already gone.

CHAPTER SIXTEEN

Molly inched into the ballroom to find the crowd in chaos. Several people were rushing past her, others clustered in tight groups, the buzz and mutter of panic flitting around the room. She tensed as Ru stormed toward her, reaching out to grab her wrist.

"Where have you been?" he hissed.

She hesitated. "Asking questions. What's happened?"

"Another artificer's gone down." He glanced over his shoulder. "Right here."

Molly peered around him, trying to catch a gap in the crowd to see what had happened. A fleeting flash of a lump covered by a tablecloth, but little else through the gaggle of arms, legs and puffy skirts.

"Let's go," Ru muttered.

Molly nodded, almost yelping out loud as he pulled her by the wrist toward a side door. Molly didn't want to work out how he knew exactly where to go, but the side door led them down a corridor and out through glass doors into the night. Several carts and carriages waited but Ru hurried past all of them and toward the lane leading up.

Only another twenty two levels. Molly grimaced, relieved beyond belief that Beryl had been sensible about the shoes. *I doubt Ru would stop for anything, let alone fancy footwear right now.*

"Not a word until we get back," he insisted.

Molly settled for jogging along behind him, her free hand holding her skirts up. She wanted to ask questions but his attitude would need settling first, something she really wasn't in the mood to pander to.

Her cheeks burned as they ascended the levels at a dizzying pace, the cold air chilling her bare shoulders. By the time they reached her workshop, her vision was beginning to blur. She went straight to her desk after unlocking the door and eased her feet out of the slippers with a groan.

"What's with the mass panic?" she asked. "You almost sent me tumbling a bunch of times we were moving so fast."

Ru settled against the door, dropping his head back to regain his breath.

"There'll be mayhem as soon as the boots arrive and we weren't there as ourselves, but I doubt anyone will think to come looking for guests this far up."

Molly dragged herself behind her bed screen and pulled on jeans, shimmying out of the dress and wrapping herself in her most comfortable sweatshirt. With fluffy socks on and a mug of cold *offke* in hand, she settled herself at her desk.

"Did you get anything useful before everything kicked off?" he asked.

She grimaced. "Not exactly. I was trying to find out more from Talie without giving anything away. Then we split and I came straight to you."

Ru pushed away from the door and came to take a seat opposite her, resting his forearms on the table.

"It's a complete mess." He sighed. "Marcus is convinced there's some kind of anti-Menagerie faction massing on the upper levels, which would fit with what we saw your friend doing in that warehouse."

"But why would they? What do they have against the Menagerie?"

She ignored the acidic way he called Talie her friend, her mind a jumble of things she didn't have the energy to even consider, let alone figure out.

"There are whispers that Fae don't like the control the citadel holds, especially the higher-ups," he explained. "The Menagerie isn't known to most but with the boots reacting to independence so firmly, we need to step in on occasion. Some say it's one of our own gone rogue, but Marcus thinks it's more likely someone spilling secrets out of weakness."

She wiped a hand over her face. "Maybe, but what does that have to do with artificers disappearing and losing their memories though? Why take them in the first place?"

"Who knows?" Ru leaned back in his chair. "Perhaps they're being used to build something that'll bring us down. Whatever it is, we need to find out."

"Do we know anything about the one that died tonight?"

"We do and it's getting more dangerous. To risk taking down a high nobility figure like Lady Carrington-"

Molly gasped. "I spoke to her, she asked about my dress."

"I noticed. Even more reason to get you out of there immediately. She's- *was* a big champion of the citadel freedom movement, and now she's dead."

"Was it *goberia* again?" she asked, thinking of the fancy food.

"No, much more overt than that apparently. Word is she got stabbed between the ribs with a long needle."

Molly twisted her hands into fists. *Such violence.*

"But, she's not an artificer," she reminded him. "How do we know it even has any relevance to the others? How do we know any of them have any relevance except for the missing memories?"

Ru pulled out his orb and rubbed his thumb over the pearlescent gold-brown surface. It beamed a vision onto the desk between them, Ru swiping his thumb until the image became a video of an old *Faerie Net* report.

"Lady Boena-May Carrington, experienced wielder of both elemental and persuasion abilities, has raised her voice to support the citadel freedom campaign."

Ru tapped the orb to still the image and poked at the frozen Lady Carrington.

"Look there, can you see on her wrist?"

Molly leaned closer until her head was almost beside his. It was hard to make out on the image, but she recognised the two-colour band woven around Lady Carrington's wrist as she waved for the cameras.

"It's the eye, the same one I found where Seymour died." Molly sat back, stunned. "And she was experienced at artificer gifts like elements."

"It could be nothing or it could be everything, but if the

enemy are attacking the nobility-"

"But if she's one of them, why would they attack her?" she insisted. "Why go to the trouble and risk of killing her when she's championing their cause?"

Ru shrugged. "Maybe she changed her mind or stepped out of line. Even nobles can outrun their uses eventually."

"They're still people. Two people are dead, whether there's something going on or not. Nobody deserves to die for any of this."

Ru sighed, a softness falling over his face as he smiled.

"I forget how moral you are sometimes."

"Is it so hard to not want people to die?" She stuck her tongue out at him. "I may not be some high-bred noble but even I know that if we start saying one person deserves to have their life obliterated, then we can say it about anyone given the right angle."

Ru eyed the dress she'd draped over the screen with a sigh.

"Maybe you're right," he said. "That dress really is beautiful. It's a shame we didn't have a chance to dance more, and you barely had any time to try the food."

Molly snorted. "It's probably best I didn't, not until we know what killed her. Do we have any idea who it might have been?"

Ru rolled his eyes and pushed out of the chair, moving around the desk to sit on it in front of her.

"I'm trying to compliment you."

She frowned. "Why?"

Ru leaned down, the subtle scent of sweat and him wrapping around her as he pressed a warm, fleeting kiss to her cheek. She stared in addle-minded amazement as he straightened up and cleared his throat.

"I'll report in to Marcus now."

Molly lifted her hand to her cheek as he strode toward the door, shoulders stiff.

"He's back?" she asked, more for something to say than actual interest.

He nodded with his hand on the door.

"Back to normal."

As he pulled the door open and slipped outside, shutting it quietly behind him, Molly sagged over the desk.

Nothing is normal now.

CHAPTER SEVENTEEN

Molly hugged the dress tight the next morning, bags hanging from her fingers as she walked the short few steps to Beryl's front door. She knocked with her forehead in the absence of any free hands.

Orbs, what if she's sleeping and I just woke her up?

She took a step back as the sound of footsteps echoed out of the open window and the door swung open.

"Oh, hiya." Harvey eyed the dress. "Have a good night?"

She nodded. "The dress was great. Can you thank Beryl for me?"

"Thank her yourself." The weary grumble echoed from behind Harvey's shoulder. "Glad it was useful. Someone should get some fun out of it."

Harvey dutifully took the dress and bags and disappeared into the gloom beyond. Molly risked a quick glance, but all she could see was another doorway which meant their home was one of the larger ones with two entire rooms.

"Did you hear?" Beryl added. "Some posh lady several levels down bit the dust."

Molly hesitated until her mind caught up, realising

Beryl meant the death of Lady Carrington.

Murder. Someone stabbed her with a needle.

"Yeah, I heard. I can't imagine how painful it must be to get stabbed," she said.

Beryl frowned. "Who got stabbed?"

"Lady Carrington, isn't that who you mean?"

"It is yeah, but she wasn't stabbed. It was poison by several accounts, *goberia*. Weird brew, hard to make as well so I've been told."

Molly's skin chilled, the ripples clawing through her muscles.

"Perhaps there's some secret society offing people for their gifts," Harvey suggested.

He'd ridded himself of the dress and accessories, but Molly couldn't stop herself from staring at him, wondering how someone who seemed so silly all the time could get to the truth without even realising.

"Molly?"

Ru appeared beside her before she could recover from the shock, or ask how Beryl knew it was *goberia* poisoning and not stabbing. She twisted around to give him a quick grimace before fixing a smile on her face.

"Just dropping the dress back, I'll be inside in a minute."

Ru ignored her suggestion and stood right beside her with his hand held out.

"Hi, you must be Molly's new neighbours." He shook Harvey's hand. "I'm Ru."

"You're around a lot." Beryl's tone was entirely accusing.

Ru hesitated before turning on his most charming smile. "Someone's got to keep Molly out of trouble."

"Hmm." Beryl eyed him up and down, her nostrils flaring. "We'll see. She's been a model neighbour so far, so I don't want to hear of any young men leading her astray, and there are far too many of those in the world."

With a dark glower in Harvey's direction, she disappeared inside. Harvey pressed a hand to his forehead and risked a sheepish smile.

"It's the hormones," he stage-whispered. "The baby is due soon."

Molly nodded. "No problem. Let me know if you need anything, or... I'm not good with kids, or babies, or anything like that, but if you need something fixed."

Harvey waved them away and Molly led Ru back to the shop, baffled by Beryl's sudden hostility.

"What's the plan then?" she asked.

Ru sank into a chair by her desk and she took her usual seat, picking up some sandpaper and a figurine she was smoothing out.

"Well, if you haven't had anything from your new friend, we go back to tailing her. Until we can find out where to find her, considering you didn't think to ask, we'll take a few shifts watching the artificers who are still alive this evening."

Molly rolled her eyes at his flippancy.

"Fine. I need to go to the shop at some point before then, but I really want to finish this first." She hesitated. "Beryl said she'd heard from multiple sources that Lady Carrington had been poisoned. She even mentioned *goberia*."

She left the suggestion hanging as Ru sighed.

"It's possible, either that or the rumours are fixed to align the death with the other man's."

Seymour. Molly thought disagreeably. *His name was Seymour.*

She had no great affection, or even feeling, for the dead artificer she'd followed, but he was still Fae, still had feelings and a life. Even a wife. Molly's chest panged with a twist of sympathy.

She opened her mouth to reply but the door swung open and smashed into the wall before she could. Leaping to her feet, Molly stared from the basket of keychains now scattered over the floor to Sammy's wide eyes and frantic breathing.

"Sammy, what-"

"They've taken her!"

"Who?"

Sammy doubled over, panting.

"Talie, who else? The boots came to take her because they said she's been implicated in killing some random lady from lower down, something about that bracelet she always wears and a potion she had in her shoe."

"Wait, she had a potion in her shoe?" Ru demanded. "What potion?"

Sammy lifted her head and glowered at him.

"I don't know, but she kept it for emergencies she said, in one of her old shoes at home. She refused to say anything so they carted her off."

Molly gasped, her mind racing.

I can't say I was there last night in front of Sammy, but Ru and I both know Talie is innocent.

"Mol." Ru's tone was laced with warning. "There's nothing you can do."

He knew her well enough to think she'd go haring off to confirm Talie's innocence, but the boots likely wouldn't even believe she'd been there herself, and if they did they'd take her as Talie's accomplice without asking the right questions.

"I need to speak to my tutor at school and see if they can help," Sammy insisted.

Molly flinched as Sammy stumbled in front of her, gripping her hands tight.

"Please, I know you know things. You must do if Talie's been looking for you. If you can do anything, please help us."

Molly had no words as Sammy's desperate gaze flicked over her face. Without waiting for promises or reassurances, Sammy dashed out of the workshop as quickly as she'd entered.

"Don't do anything rash," Ru said, moving to stand in the doorway. "Even if Talie didn't kill anyone herself, she's probably part of the group that did."

Molly frowned. "What makes you so sure?"

"Because if she wasn't, she'd be a part of the Menagerie by now. She's not one of us, so she's got to be the enemy."

"But you know and I know she was with me when Lady Carrington was killed."

Ru rubbed a hand over his hair and glanced over his shoulder.

"You can't let anyone know that though. Don't break the rules, not even for good reasons. Keep your head down, say nothing."

Why not? We were there on Menagerie orders, and he told me to make friends with Talie for information.

Molly reached behind her and clutched the edge of her desk tight.

"Okay."

Ru's gaze narrowed.

"Promise me."

She nodded. "I promise I won't go to the boots to rescue Talie or anything, orbs alive, I'm not stupid."

His expression softened and she kept her expression the same, tamping down on any possible flicker of deceit showing.

"I know you're not, but you're too honourable for your own good. I've got some things to do, but stay here and get your work done. I'll come get you when it's time for patrol, okay?"

"Okay."

She didn't need to smile to reassure him, tensing as he crossed the room to fold her into a hug. Uneasy, she relaxed each muscle just enough to convince him she was accepting the contact, then tensed again the moment he left the workshop.

She'd promised him she wasn't going to the boots, and she would keep that promise. With her panic driving her on, she grabbed her pesana pouch and pulled her coat with the hood around her shoulders.

He didn't say anything about not going to the

Menagerie though.

Ru might have some questionable morals when it came to right and wrong, no doubt powered by his intention of protecting her and the Menagerie, but Celeste would listen. Even Marcus had to be fair in the face of someone being wrongfully accused, and he had the power to intervene.

Beryl was lurking outside her house still so Molly walked steadily along the main lane, smiling at anyone she passed. The moment she found a suitable vantage point away from any potential onlookers, she lifted her hood and vaulted up the nearest pillar.

Scaling the side of the building until she got her balance on one of the girders, Molly traced the familiar steps down to the Menagerie. The hall window was always open, unreachable by anyone who hadn't learned how to climb to it.

Taking a deep breath and lowering her hood, she made her way to Celeste's office and knocked.

No answer.

She grimaced, glancing at the double doors to Marcus' suite of offices next. Celeste would have been preferable, but Sammy's panicked face swam in her mind and she strode toward the doors with a deep breath.

The Menagerie prided themselves on keeping order. They had to be the ones willing to do the right thing.

The moment she knocked, silence fell. In that absence of sound, she realised there had been voices on the other side before. Footsteps thudded closer and she braced herself to explain.

Marcus gave us permission to attend the ball, or Celeste

did at least. I wasn't anywhere he won't know about, and I don't need to mention everything that happened before that.

The door swung open and her resolve sputtered. Marcus stared at her with narrowed eyes, his cheeks pink with what looked dangerously like irritation.

"Molly? What are you doing here?"

She glanced past him, her eyes widening as she noticed the two men in boots uniforms and the girl standing between them, her arms clamped in their hold and her hands tied behind her back.

Talie had a bruise blossoming on her cheek and Molly's gut twisted.

"I…" She stood straighter. "I didn't realise you had company, sorry. It's about her though, Talie I mean. She was with me last night. Whatever she's being accused of, I don't think she could have done it."

When in doubt, cover the lies with so many truths they don't think to dig any deeper.

Marcus stepped back, beckoning her inside. She tensed even further as the door clicked shut behind her, while Talie stared at her like she'd just announced she was somehow the father of Beryl's baby.

"I don't think you understand what you're saying," Marcus warned.

Molly grimaced. "I do, I really do. I might not know specifics, but-"

"This girl has been found with incriminating evidence in her possession that means she might have murdered one of the citadel's most beloved nobles."

"But she was with me when it was happening."

Marcus took his time returning to his desk and sitting behind it, his hands steepled in front of his face.

"And what do you know about what happened exactly?"

Molly hesitated. "Rumours are saying that Lady Carrington was murdered with *goberia,* like that other man was in the park. *Goberia* only takes a minute or two to take effect, and even less time to kill."

"This is what I was trying to tell you idiots," Talie interrupted. "I wasn't there when it happened. How could I have poisoned anyone? And loads of people have *goberia* lying around. It's hard to make but so easy to get if you know who to ask."

"That's enough out of you," Marcus snapped.

She rolled her eyes. "Did you notice my bottle was still sealed? How could I have used it to poison anyone?"

Marcus leaned back in his chair, one ankle hooking over the other knee to leave his foot tapping thin air, a sure sign he was in a foul mood.

"You said yourself *goberia* easy enough to get if you know where. You could have had two bottles."

Talie snorted. "On what I make in this cesspit? I barely have enough to feed myself."

Molly's insides plummeted.

I should have told her to take the leftovers the other night.

She saw Talie move before the boots did, recognising the duck and leg sweep movement that sent the man holding her stumbling sideways. He clung on until Talie ducked and sank her teeth into the flesh of his hand. With a feral yowl, he let her go. Before anyone could recover, she kicked out at the second man, catching his hip. He flailed but another kick pushed him toward the open window.

Marcus was on his feet, but Talie swiped her hands against the sharp edge of a bronzed statue and sliced through the ropes.

"Don't let her get away!" Marcus shouted.

Molly leapt forward to get between them, thoughts and common sense far away. Marcus stilled, his gaze turning predatory as it flicked between them.

"You need to listen," Molly insisted. "We were both outside when Lady Carrington died, for longer than a few minutes."

Marcus clicked his fingers and Talie squawked in outrage as the cut ropes wriggled through the air to re-bind her wrists.

"Why were you outside when she died then, Molly?" he challenged.

"Because whatever you believe Talie's done, whatever side you think she's on, I'm on our side. I wanted to find out if she knew anything so the Menagerie could do the right thing."

Marcus was silent so she added a desperate plea born of pure frustration.

"That's the whole reason you sent us down there in the first place, right?"

"I knew you weren't some unknowing innocent," Talie muttered.

Molly glared back at her. "Are you serious right now?"

"Enough." Marcus reclaimed his seat. "I get your part in this Molly. Your loyalty isn't in question. But we have to consider she now knows who you are. That puts a mark over your head that doesn't exactly do us any favours."

Molly nodded. "If she vowed not to tell anyone-"

"Oh I'm not vowing anything, Princess."

Molly closed her eyes, frustration leaking out. She decided she would deal with Talie once she was done saving her ungrateful behind.

Marcus eyed them both.

"I need to consider this carefully," he said. "One of our enemy being, shall we say, 'taken care of' isn't going to make much difference. It would however send enough of a sign to the enemy that they need to back down."

Molly tensed. "What do you mean, 'taken care of'?"

The office doors opened before Marcus could reply, although Talie's derisive scoff gave enough of an idea what she thought his words meant.

Celeste swept toward them in a waft of sweetly fragrant perfume, Ru hurrying behind her with flushed cheeks. So surprised that the 'business' he was so quick to rush off for was him coming to tattle to Celeste, Molly couldn't help glowering at him.

"Ru's told me everything," Celeste announced. "I know I'm likely overstepping, Marcus, but you know me. I couldn't resist the drama."

She walked to his desk and sat herself on it, smiling around at everyone. Given the resigned sigh from Marcus, he was used to her holding court in his office.

"Is this girl a friend of yours, Molly?" Celeste asked.

Molly shrugged. "Not exactly. We keep running into each other, and I suppose I'm friends with her sister now. I told Marcus already that Talie was with me when Lady Carrington died, so he can't use her as a poster girl for punishment."

Celeste nodded, rubbing a finger over her bottom lip thoughtfully.

"It is a bit of a pickle. We release her and we run the risk of the enemy being aware of us, but Molly does have a point. It's unbecoming to start using girls as punishment fodder for things they haven't done."

"We did cover her face to bring her here," one of the boots said reproachfully.

Talie huffed. "Orbs, like it's difficult to count each step bump of a new level then feel how many times the tinpot cart you dragged me into turned right or left?"

"So not helping," Molly muttered.

Celeste laughed. "A clever brain is always a benefit to organisations such as ours, but someone must take responsibility for the deaths. Nobody knows what truly happened, but rumours spread fast and we'll have mass hysteria soon."

Molly waited for instructions to be issued, perhaps a manhunt for the killer with increased resources. Even being dismissed from the office, or even the Menagerie, would be worth it to make sure Sammy got Talie back safely.

"What do you say, Molly?" Celeste asked.

"Er... huh?"

"We don't want to draw attention to the forces massing against us and trying to uproot us, so we need to ensure we find a way to keep all sides in line."

"What does any of that have to do with me?"

Celeste stood, glancing at Marcus. He nodded, although he didn't look happy about whatever plan Celeste had cooked up.

"The world outside the citadel is changing. The Holly Queen is growing in her power and the Oak Queen will be grasping for control. It won't be long before she sets her sights on the citadel as a conquest."

"Why would she do that?" Ru asked.

Molly had all but forgotten him and ignored him when he sent her a despairing look. She hadn't betrayed the promise she made him, not technically.

"We keep our secrets close but they know we have many treasures," Celeste explained. "Why wouldn't a queen want to conquer somewhere that has resources and folk fit enough to fight?"

Molly cleared her throat, drawing all eyes to her.

"What does that have to do with me though?" she repeated.

"If you accept a different kind of assignment, we will let your friend go."

Molly frowned. "Why can't you let her go based on the fact she's not done anything wrong?"

"So noble. We could, but this way everyone wins. If you agree, she goes free. There needs to be a balance, and we can't prove she didn't do it. Someone could be compelling her to lie to us."

"Oh sure," Talie muttered. "Eye witness to my whereabouts, local knowledge that *goberia* isn't that hard to get, but I'm still stuck with false charges."

Celeste ignored her. "Wouldn't you be excited to see more of Faerie for a while, Molly?"

Molly opened her mouth to argue, but the words filtered into her head before others burbled out of her mouth.

"Wait… you're saying I would need to leave the citadel?"

Talie scoffed. "I wouldn't. Don't do anything on my behalf."

"Hush." Celeste snapped, her face brightening again as she eyed Molly. "You would be perfectly safe, but we need someone to go to the Oak Queen's court for a while. No different to spying inside the citadel really. Same job, different location."

To leave the citadel, to feel the warmth of real air on her skin instead of the regurgitated gusts from the fans. She might even be able to ask about the many burning questions she had. Someone at a royal court had to understand the intricacies of Faerie well enough to explain it to her.

She wiped a hand over her face.

"I'm not all that great with people," she admitted. "And what about my workshop?"

Celeste slid off the desk with a shrug.

"We'll keep it here for you of course. Nobody will take it over while you're gone. It's a good opportunity, and this way as long as your friend doesn't step out of line again, we'll respect her space in return."

"So either I do what I'm told and save an innocent person, or I refuse and you punish her to spite me?"

Marcus sighed. "Everything is transactional. Everything. There's no getting past that."

"In an ideal world, it wouldn't be necessary," Celeste added. "But this isn't an ideal world. We have the safety of the Menagerie to think of, and you're a part of that, aren't you?"

Molly's heart sank as Marcus drummed his fingers on the desk, a sure sign his tolerance was stretched thin.

"We could let her go, risk her running to the resistance telling them everything, but this would also indirectly endanger you. If we were forced to retaliate, who would we be forced to target next? Her? Her sister?"

Talie's cheeks paled and for once, she was silent.

"Or we can make a deal that secures everyone some measure of leverage," he added. "You are still a part of the Menagerie and on an exciting assignment for us. She and her sister are left alone in return."

Molly bit her lip and thought of Sammy, too uneasy to look at Talie's ashen face hidden beneath a mask of anger.

She had no choice.

"You promise?"

Celeste laughed. "Oh my dear, I'll vow it if you need me to. We'll release her on the basis of no evidence, and she'll be free to go back to whatever life she lives."

"I am right here you know," Talie grumbled.

Molly knew well enough how the real world worked. The Menagerie would release Talie only to use her as a way to track other members of whatever group Talie was a part of. Talie would know that too and not be able to risk endangering anyone by stepping out of line.

And I would be going to an actual royal court.

"How long for?" she asked, glaring at Talie as she groaned quietly. "What? It's not like you're going to miss me or anything, and I'm doing this for… myself."

She choked back Sammy's name as it bubbled on her lips. The less she gave them about Talie's life the safer she and Sammy would be.

"You should choose wisely," Marcus said. "You say this girl isn't exactly your friend, so how much do you really know about her?"

Molly hesitated. "Well, not a lot really, but it's still not right-"

She froze as Marcus lifted a hand, flinching around when Talie made a soft choking sound. Her eyes widened.

"Tell Molly everything you know about her," he demanded.

Molly shook her head. "She doesn't know anything about me."

"Marcus, enough!" Celeste snapped.

Talie clenched her eyes shut tight, but Marcus' command seemed to pull words from her lips.

Almost like a compulsion.

"I know more about you than you think," Talie said. "It was my gift that took your memories of the night your guardians died."

CHAPTER EIGHTEEN

Celeste stalked across the floor toward Molly, but she was rooted to the spot, too busy staring at Talie.

"What do you mean?" she asked.

"Don't be silly, what could she possibly know?" Celeste asked, her hand firm on Molly's shoulder. "Come now, we'll have some tea in my office-"

"You think your guardians died in a carriage crash, right?" Talie said, her tone wooden even though her expression was anything but. "You don't remember them being taken, beaten right in front of you. I did that."

Molly shook her head. "How is that even possible?"

"Enough." Celeste insisted, glaring absolute damnation at Marcus.

Talie shook herself, her face contorting.

"My gift lets me take people's memories. If I hear them speak, I can wipe the memories they tell me."

Thoughts of Seymour, of the artificers returning with missing memories, and the hazy recollection she had of the time after her guardians' deaths filled her head, nausea burning through her chest.

"Why? Who would do that? Basil and Lily weren't a

part of anything like this!"

Before she could protest, Ru had her arms pinned to her sides and Celeste snapped her fingers. The office wavered, disorientation making everything sway in a carousel of blurry colours and a swirl of purple-grey mist. As the air righted itself, Molly recognised Celeste's office.

"I'm sorry you had to hear that," Celeste insisted, giving Molly's shoulder a gentle pat. "We knew about your past when you came to us, but tales can be murky at the best of times. You didn't seem to remember anything so we decided it was best to see if your memories resurfaced naturally."

Molly wrapped her arms around her middle, hunching in on herself.

"My guardians were beaten when they died?" she mumbled.

Ru appeared beside her and this time she didn't tense or fight or glare as he wrapped his arms tight around her. The one constant always putting her safety first, he was the only one she could rely on.

"It doesn't matter now," he said softly. "Whatever happened is done, and you can take some time to work things out."

Molly nodded. First, she had to make sure Talie was returned to Sammy, with or without her supposed involvement in all things past. Through the confusion, one thing she could be sure of was that Talie wasn't doing much by choice.

The citadel has always been my home, but the queen's court could be a way out. If I somehow earn enough money, I could even buy my debt from the Menagerie.

Nobody had managed it, not that she knew of. A debt with the Menagerie was for life, no matter what honeyed words were said at the time of agreement. The indifference over using an innocent girl for a war against the Menagerie's enemy unnerved her as well, but being involved in such a war, even at a distance, worried her even more.

Space. She needed space. *The queen's court will give me that.*

She lifted her head from Ru's chest, wriggling free of him.

"I'll go to the queen's court, but only if it's not for too long. I don't want to spend years or anything there."

Ru nodded. "And I'm going with you."

"Marcus won't like that," Celeste said, her lips twitching with amusement. "I'll have a word with him about it, don't worry. Perhaps sending two of you in would be best anyway."

"How are we even going to get anywhere near the court though?" Ru asked.

Celeste grabbed her sweet bowl and held it out. Ru grabbed a handful and gave one to Molly. She took it and ate it for something to do, her insides still churning.

"Let me worry about that," Celeste promised. "We can probably get you in soon, so finish any work or affairs you need to sort in the next day or so."

Molly folded her arms, forcing herself to catch Celeste's eye.

"I'll be making sure Talie makes it home as well."

Celeste waved a hand, smiling with amusement.

"We have no intention of not honouring our bargain, my dear. The boots will be taking her home as we speak."

Molly nodded. "Good. We're still meant to be the good side, and I'm starting to have serious doubts the way people have been behaving lately."

Ru cleared his throat but she ignored him and fixed Celeste with a sharp look. Irritability fuelled by worry kept her strong where she normally would have conceded, remembered her place and piped down.

"There is one thing I would have you do when you get to the queen's court," Celeste said. "An errand that I would undertake myself if I could."

Molly stilled. "Go on."

"It's nothing awful, don't worry. We know very little about what the enemy here do, and these artificers going missing… Well, there's definitely an element of giftery being involved. We have many great texts at the citadel library, but the queen's library will have countless more."

"You want us to steal a book?"

"I want you to take and memorise some information from a book, yes. Don't steal it under any circumstances, it can't be done."

Molly couldn't help wondering how many times Celeste had tried, or had someone try on her behalf, to know that with such certainty.

"Which book?"

"It's called *Potions Most Foul and Fae*. There is a chapter inside on gift extraction."

Molly froze, Seymour's words to Talie about his

missing gift and the mention of gifts being removed she'd heard people talking about at the ball ringing in her head.

"Gift extraction?"

Celeste nodded. "We need to know what the enemy are planning, and to know that, we need to know what signs to look for. Bring me everything you can from that chapter, can you do that?"

Molly bit her lip, her mind raging.

"How would I even get into the library? I bet it's restricted. Unless I got myself onto a cleaning crew of some kind."

"Excellent idea. Do what you must, but nobody can catch you with that book, understand?"

"How do we even know where it is?"

"I have the layout of the palace, or the parts of it that are core parts of the realm, in my head," Ru said. "We thought this might happen someday."

Another thing he hasn't shared with me. How much else has he been hiding?

Going to the queen's court to lurk for information was one thing, but sneaking into a royal library to steal it was entirely different.

"You can't have some kind of actual librarian or historian ask to go in on some diplomatic information sharing mission?" she asked.

"There aren't any, none we can spare."

"But…" She struggled desperately for some kind of excuse. "Wouldn't a more experienced Menagerie member might want the chance to do this?"

Celeste rolled her eyes. "What sort of Fae would want

to spend their days sifting through dusty old books? Knowledge has its place, heritage absolutely, but by choice? No, I think not."

"Right. Well, I'll do what I can, but until then I've left the workshop unattended. Excuse me."

She headed for the door, Ru right behind her like an overprotective sentinel. He might not be happy about going to the queen's court, but he'd offered readily enough and she didn't ask him to either.

"Wait, both of you." Celeste approached them. "Arms out."

Molly lifted hers and tensed as Celeste grasped her hand, turning it palm down so that her Menagerie tattoo was visible. With a pass of her hand over Molly's wrist, Celeste mumbled something under her breath and the tattoo vanished.

"Slight glamour," she explained as she did the same to Ru. "I'll be able to remove it when the time comes for you to return. Now, the queen's court is said to be quite a wonder when the regent is in a good mood. Have some fun while you're there, but get the information from that book without being found above all else."

She waved a hand as they stepped out into the hall, and a second later the door thudded shut in their faces.

Molly approached the window with weary limbs, determined to go straight to Sammy's school and find a way to check Talie had made it home okay.

Then I have some serious questions for her.

The progress across the girders and down into the first unoccupied alleyway was slow. Ru didn't say a word as he followed her, only whipping out a hand to steady her when her grip slipped once. She didn't challenge him on following her back to the workshop either, because she needed to make sure she locked the door before going to find Sammy and Talie.

The moment they were inside the workshop, Ru pressed both hands to his face.

"I'm going to pretend you took temporary leave of your sanity," he muttered.

Molly folded her arms. "Well I'm going to pretend you weren't completely unfussed about letting Talie take the hit for something she didn't do."

He lifted his head, irritation flashing in his eyes.

"It's nothing to do with that. I went to Celeste to ask her to help!"

"Help with what exactly? You clearly know more than you've ever told me."

He hesitated. Molly wanted to storm past him but he was blocking the door, and he deserved to be heard out before she demonised him completely.

"I told her everything that happened, and asked her to help, what else could I do? I figured she'd put a word in for Talie, which is exactly what she did. Now you've got us signed up for some mad errand to a completely different part of Faerie."

Molly nodded. "Yeah, that was unexpected, but you didn't have to volunteer."

He stalked toward her and grabbed her hand, staring at it as he toyed with her fingers.

"As if you're going without me." He smiled, his

irritable mood dissipating like magic. "The queen won't have a court left if I let you go alone."

She skipped over the mention of him letting her, too perturbed by the weird sensation of his hand moving over hers.

"Well, hold that thought," she said, gently tugging her fingers free. "I'm going to go and see Sammy's okay."

Ru rolled his eyes. "Of course you are. If Talie's there, don't get involved in anything. Quick hi, bye and thanks for all the trauma."

Molly ignored that suggestion, dodging around him and heading for the door.

"I'll be back in a bit."

She didn't hear what he grumbled as she shut the door behind her. He might have things to do but she had an inkling that he would be there waiting to make sure she returned, so she didn't lock him in.

We're unlikely to go snooping tonight now so maybe I can get all my commissions finished before we leave.

She didn't need to go to the school in the end to charm Sammy's address out of them. Lifting her head, she saw the whirlwind coming right to her.

"Thank you thank you thank you!" Sammy gushed.

Molly froze, rooting her feet as Sammy bashed into her, arming winding around her neck.

"I- what did Tal-"

"Oh she didn't tell me a thing, growled at me not to say a word, but I know you had something to do with it. Overheard her muttering some profanity about owing you now, so thank you! Will you come back home with me?"

Molly hesitated. "I don't-"

"We don't have much but Talie said she'd get us some fancy food to celebrate her not being offed by the establishment." Sammy rolled her eyes, still holding onto Molly's shoulders in a death grip. "Probably not fancy by your standards as it's not either of our birthdays, but still. We owe you."

"You don't owe me anything," Molly sighed. "But sure. I can't stay long, and I can't stay for food as I've got loads of stuff to get back to, but I'll pop by for a bit."

It was exactly what she shouldn't be doing, especially now Sammy had reassured her Talie was home safe.

Sammy grinned and finally let go of her shoulders, only to grab her hand and start towing her along instead.

Why is everyone so obsessed with handholding?

Molly let herself be led, bewildered. She had questions for Talie, who probably wouldn't answer them unless she used compulsion, but somehow she was as nervous to see her again as she was eager.

Sammy led her up five levels, then down a short alley on the core side. There were a couple of doors set in the brick walls either side, all shut, and a dead end with dull graffiti scrawled on it ahead of them.

"You have to say hello to Mister Boots," Sammy insisted, pointing out a disgruntled looking ginger cat. "It's bad luck otherwise."

Molly pulled a face. "Um, hi."

Mister Boots hissed at her in reply as Sammy opened one of the doors nearest the dead end and left it wide open behind her for Molly to follow. Molly inched inside and shut the door, glancing around. The single room had no windows but wasn't much smaller than her workshop, with a small corner kitchenette on the left and a sectioned off partition that no doubt led to the bathroom. She tried not to smile as she spied a definite discord between two sides on the right.

The corner nearest the door was a burst of colour, from flashes of amateur art on the bare walls to bright throws on the simple floor-bed. Across the room there were no flashes of colour, just a second identical bed with even more threadbare sheets, two books and a decrepit pair of shoes on the floor.

No need to guess which side is whose.

The gloom near the kitchenette shifted and Talie walked toward her, no sign of smile or welcome on her face. Her eyes were ringed with shadows and her lips were pressed thin, enough that Molly regretted not refusing Sammy's begging in the lane and going back to the workshop after all.

"Sam, go get the dinner in," Talie said. "Pick whatever you want."

Sammy took the pouch Talie handed her and grinned at Molly.

"You two clearly have stuff to talk about, but can I come by the workshop soon?" she asked.

Molly shook her head. "I'll be away for a while, so it'll be locked up. Not sure when I'll be back."

Sammy's smile dimmed, but she pushed another hug on Molly, holding tight for several seconds before letting go.

"Well, you'll be back someday. This isn't goodbye. Oh,

I need your orb details!"

Talie rolled her eyes as Molly dutifully handed them over and waded through Sammy's insistence that they stay in regular touch, especially when the next season of *Siren-Sing-Along* started.

She couldn't tell Sammy that she wasn't going somewhere inside the citadel, so the orb messages wouldn't reach her.

Sammy hugged her one last time.

"I have a friend at school who knows everything about orb-waves," she murmured. "Meet me on the Kayla Crane fan forum and I'll reach you wherever you are."

Molly sucked in a breath, too astonished to formulate words as Sammy hurried off in a flurry of promises that she would be back with food.

Does Talie know about this? Was it somehow her idea?

"I guess I'm supposed to say thank you," Talie muttered the moment the door was slammed.

Still stuck on the idea that Sammy knew someone who could communicate outside the citadel, unless it was someone word-tangling mistruths to sound impressive, Molly blinked in Talie's direction.

"Huh?"

Talie scowled. "I said I'm supposed to thank you."

"I'd probably die of shock if you did."

She filed away the mysterious outer-citadel orb situation for future consideration and eyed Talie warily.

"Why did you do it?" Talie demanded. "Why even bother sticking up for me?"

A tiny smirk crept over Molly's face, the sight of Talie

all but openly squirming about being in her debt an utterly delightful thing to behold.

"You know I can't tell you that," she teased. "But you need to be careful and watch your back better. If you do step out of line, they won't hesitate."

"Yeah, I heard. Well, I owe you one I guess."

Molly nodded. "Then tell me who made you wipe my memory."

Talie grimaced, turning away and heading toward her bed.

"I can't say, literally physically can't. You had a lucky escape though, believe me when I say that."

"There's nothing at all you can tell me that might jog my memory?"

Talie shook her head. "It's not your memory anymore. That's how my gift works, you tell me a story and I siphon that information right out of your head."

Molly stared in horror, only able to believe it because Talie was as Fae as she was and couldn't lie.

"Exactly. Not so much a gift as a curse, and one several would be happy to use me for."

Molly winced at the bitterness in her tone, but the astonishment seemed to have welded her tongue to the roof of her mouth.

"I… well…"

Talie laughed. "It's okay. I don't expect a fond farewell or anything."

"The artificers, and Seymour, the one I saw at the warehouse. You wiped their memories too, didn't you?"

Talie said nothing for a long moment, her gaze fixed on

Molly's face and betraying nothing. Foreboding crept in and Molly dredged up a protection warding. Just in case.

"You don't learn, do you," Talie said softly. It wasn't a question. "Leave this place, the citadel, the bad things going on. Leave it all behind. You deserve to be free of all of this. Good luck at the queen's court."

It was possibly the kindest thing she'd heard Talie say, but Molly couldn't be in any way happy about it.

She walked to the door as Talie knelt beside her bed, reaching for something in her shoes. Even though that was exactly where Sammy had said the boots found the *goberia* bottle, Molly couldn't dredge up even the pretence of fear the same might happen to her. Talie wouldn't harm her, not unless she absolutely had to.

Molly let her warding drop.

"I hope life gives you everything you deserve," she said softly, opening the door.

It wasn't her place to decide what Talie deserved, but she couldn't bring herself to use a compulsion to get more information. Ru would without a second thought, and Marcus. Celeste might think it was a shame but she wouldn't hesitate if she had to.

In that moment, Molly reaffirmed her previous rule.

Absolutely no compulsions unless it's an emergency.

"This won't be the last time we see each other, Princess." Talie's voice drew her attention back to the room. "You can count on that."

"You mean Sammy? I will do my best to stay in touch if it makes her happy."

Talie shook her head and approached with something

held on her outstretched palm.

"Leave her out of this," she murmured.

As she leaned close, Molly smelled the hint of berries from her hair. Her brain glitched and she took a step back, her insides somersaulting as tingles fizzled over her skin.

"I- what- you-"

She looked down as Talie took her hand and wrapped her fingers around something small. The moment she had a grasp on it, Talie grabbed her shoulder and guided her firmly out to the alley.

Molly had no words as the door shut in her face and stared at the wood in a daze. Only the thought that Sammy would come back soon and find her still frozen there brought her out of it. She glanced down and uncurled her fingers.

A stalk of common moor grass and an acorn lay in her palm, ordinary enough items that had no meaning whatsoever, other than her last name being Acorn.

She had no idea how Talie had come across such random things, or what she meant by giving them, but she slipped them both into her pesana pouch all the same.

She would dry the grass overnight and cast it in resin to keep it, just in case it was somehow something to be taken seriously.

As she walked down the lane with a grudging goodbye to Mister Boots, who hissed at her again, Molly's heart sank.

Maybe that's literally all she could give me to say thank you.

CHAPTER NINETEEN

Talie's gift played on Molly's mind for two whole days, along with the disappointing realisation she was probably overthinking the whole thing. Talie had cosied up to her on the night of the ball to get information, and was forced into her way by Sammy mostly. The gifts were nothing more than a tiny nod of appreciation that settled any debt between them. Job done.

While she tried and failed to keep her mind off Talie, Ru rushed in and out preparing for their journey, so chaotic that Molly had to stop herself from locking the workshop door and pretending to be out.

Celeste had somehow managed to get them into the Oak Queen's court as servants, which still didn't feel real, and Molly spent a night cleaning and sewing up a bunch of old clothes Ru had unearthed so she would have more things to change into.

On the third morning after the ordeal in Marcus' office, Ru appeared with a smart new coat on, his eyes alive with excitement.

"Time to go," he said.

Molly pulled on her coat and grabbed her bag, throwing the strap over her shoulder.

"I'm glad I had time to finish up all my commissions for people," she said, nerves biting at her insides. "The workshop will be okay, won't it?"

Ru nodded. "Of course, you have Celeste's word on it. I don't know how long we'll be away but this is a chance to see more of Faerie before coming home to settle. That's what you've always dreamed of. You can ask your countless questions."

"I don't know about more of Faerie." Molly grinned. "We'll be looking at both ends of a scrubbing brush more like."

Ru chuckled. "Maybe, or perhaps we'll have some exotic chores to do instead. Who knows? It's an adventure. At least we're doing it together. Come on."

She followed him out of the door and locked it, checking it twice and stopping to make sure she had everything in her bag for the umpteenth time. She had clothes, both her small and her mini toolkits, her pesana pouch and Talie's confusing gifts. She'd dried the moor grass and set it in clear resin the moment she returned from Talie and Sammy's, or at least straight after Ru had flapped off on some errand.

She'd then pierced a hole in the resin so that she could wear it on a strong chain around her neck alongside her workshop key, the acorn too.

They fell into step with each other, walking downward. Molly watched the gardens appear, then grow, the stones of the lane cracking less until they were whole, then split only by fountains.

"How far down are we going?" she whispered.

Ru grinned. "The nearest skip-way is a fair way down, but we're almost there now."

"Wow, we're going through a skip-way?"

She smartened her pace, Ru matching it with a laugh.

"How else did you think we'd get to a whole other realm? Besides, you skipped before."

She frowned. "I did?"

"Yeah, didn't you wonder how we got from Marcus' office to Celeste's the other day?"

Molly gaped at him. "Ohhh, that's what that was? Wow, okay."

"There it is." Ru pointed ahead, then grabbed her hand and pulled her to a halt.

She was too busy ogling the queue lined up outside what looked like a gap beneath the parted fronds of a large willow tree, until he turned her to face him.

"I have to ask," he hesitated. "We've been friends a long time, and we're close. I need to know…"

She smiled. "I'm not going to suddenly abandon the Menagerie for the queen if that's what you're worried about."

Not unless all this murder and mayhem has something to do with them anyway.

"It wasn't. Isn't. Molly, I need to know if we'll be arriving at the queen's court as a couple."

Her jaw dropped.

"As in… is that the cover Celeste gave us?"

Her mind started to race, panic warming her skin. She'd spent many a teenage night dreaming of exactly this moment, but Ru had insisted he was her friend and she'd quashed any ailing crush on him long ago.

She became uncomfortably aware of her hand heavy in his warm one as he struggled to reply, charm itself reduced to hesitant awkwardness.

"I'm hoping we might see it as less of a cover and more like something real growing between us."

He's been my rock all this time.

She blinked up at him, not seeing his obvious good looks but all the times he'd supported her in some way or another. Her mind hitched, the memory of dancing in darkness and soft hands on her waist, of several awkward encounters and a gift of nature pressed into her palm.

That is absolutely ridiculous and never going to happen. I probably won't even see her again.

She inhaled sharply, smiling at Ru easily enough. He knew her. He wouldn't push her if she needed time to get used to the idea.

"Let's just arrive as the people we need to pretend to be," she suggested. "We can see what develops. I don't want to rush into anything with anyone right now, and we don't know what to expect as it is."

Ru's breath tumbled out. "That's not a no. I'll take it."

It wasn't a yes either, but as they walked toward the skip-way queue, Molly said nothing about him hanging onto her hand. She would need him and his innate charm where they were going, and she couldn't imagine a life without him either.

They said nothing as the queue thinned, until it was time to step up to the skip-way. The willow fronds were drawn back and she saw the flicker of purple-grey nether.

With a deep breath, she prepared herself to be whoever she had to be.

"To Faerie and beyond."

She stepped forward and nudged her toe into the skip-way, squeaking as Ru moved beside her and pulled her in with him.

The nether folded around them, obscuring her vision as Ru clung tight to her hand. She sensed him drawing her closer, but immediately the haze was dissipating. As the nether faded away, the hive of the citadel realm-skip spot and the chatter was replaced by an ominously imposing silence, and a hall with high ceilings.

Immaculate purple runners lined with pale gold covered flagstone floors, the walls adorned with murals of oak trees, acorns and all sorts of summertime images like Molly had only seen in story books. A grand wooden staircase wider than her entire workshop swept up one of the walls, and even Ru was frozen in amazement, his lips softly parted.

"Wow," she whispered.

"Wow indeed." A brisk voice made them both jump. "You'll be Molly and Ru, yes?"

A short, delicate woman stood nearby. She swiped a hand over grey hair, the piercing blue eyes no less sharp for the wizened lines around them. Her expression softened as she took in Molly's face.

"Yes, that's us." Ru recovered quickest. "Ready to start work."

The woman nodded. "Good. I'm Marthe, and I run the queen's household. She will see you straight away."

"We're going to meet the actual queen?" Molly squeaked, unable to stop the words tumbling out.

Marthe paused. "Of course. She tends not to see new hires personally, but her wills and whims are often subject to change. Come along."

Molly gave Ru a fearful look but he only squeezed her hand before letting it drop, a mask of utter charm falling over his face. Molly patted her hair down as Marthe led them toward two enormous white doors, but she couldn't risk working up a glamour without potentially making a mistake. Her red shirt looked okay, but her jeans were faded and her shoes needed re-soling.

Marthe strode with remarkable speed through the doors and into a vast hall. Vaulted beams that arched overheard were reflected in the marble floor lined with black squiggles, and the austere portraits and landscape tapestries that covered the walls would likely have paid for an entire level of the citadel. Maybe several levels.

At the far end of the hall, a large wooden throne carved into the shape of a mighty towering Oak tree sat on a raised marble plinth. Molly's insides writhed with nerves at the sight of the queen seated there, her golden blonde hair curled around a spindled oak-leaf crown.

Marthe stopped short of the plinth and Molly ducked into a low bow immediately, Ru doing the same beside her.

"Your new hires, majesty," Marthe announced.

With her gaze fixed on her shoes, Molly couldn't see the queen but the sensation of utter power emanated toward them.

"Welcome to my court. You are Molly, and Ru."

Ru nodded. "Yes, your majesty. It's an honour to be-"

"I'm sure it is. We expect hard work here, and above all we prize loyalty. You will be on a trial period until I see fit to swear you into my service. Marthe will allocate your tasks."

Silence swelled and Molly inched her gaze sideways, making sure Ru was still bowing beside her.

"You have an interesting countenance. Rise."

Molly waited for a moment before risking a glance upward.

The queen of Faerie is staring at me. Why is the queen of Faerie staring at me?

Her senses waded through her panic and she stood, hands clasped in front of her. The queen's gaze, a tumult of blazing sunshine and midsummer fire, fixed on Molly's face. Mad thoughts of Talie's eyes, hazel-grey but with more hints of amber, filled Molly's head.

"What dreams fill that head of yours then?" the queen asked. "What desires beat inside your chest?"

Molly gulped. "Well… I want to see Faerie, or more of it at least. I haven't really ventured far from where I was before. I've always wanted to ask questions about how things work. Like Fae lights, nobody seems to actually know how-"

Ru shifted his weight, a subtle sign to silence her. The queen laughed. Molly had no idea if she was meant to bow again, but the laughter didn't sound like an 'I'm going to pulverise you for speaking' one.

"A royal court is as much the product of its regent as it is a product of Faerie," the queen said. "It bends to my will, but perhaps there will be chances for you in future. Work hard and remain loyal, and we shall see."

Molly nodded. "Of course, your majesty."

The queen flicked a hand at them, her gaze roaming the room. Molly bowed low when Ru did and followed a hastily retreating Marthe out of the throne room. The moment they were back in what looked like the entrance hall, a vast doorway open to the sunny elements outside, Molly wiped her hands over her face.

"There are a few core parts of the court that you can rely on," Marthe announced.

She swept them along through lavish halls, the walls adorned with paintings and tapestries, the ornate wooden sideboards covered in beautifully intricate carvings and their tops strewn with uncountable treasures. Molly eyed a shallow bowl of sparkling pearlescent glass and wondered what it would be like to work with such material, to get it to yield under heat and chisel.

"The main hall, throne room, kitchens and bedrooms will all be exactly what and where they are," Marthe continued. "Other parts, like the land beyond the kitchen gardens, walled walks and the lake, may change according to the queen's will. You may step in, only to step out somewhere entirely other, but always inside the court boundaries, which are vast."

She threw open a door and a waft of something meaty and rich floated out.

"Kitchens. You will eat here. Food is served as and when, and we do not keep staff mealtimes. I will give you schedules after the tour and you start tomorrow. The evenings are your own to do with as you please."

Molly's stomach growled as Marthe hustled them into the kitchen.

"There will be areas you can't access, such as master Taz's conservatory, but you won't be expected to. Oh, and the private section of the royal library, that's off limits too, but of course nobody will send you there. Unless they take a disliking to you. Stick to the main floors though and you'll be fine."

Molly's insides flipped uneasily. The library was what she needed to access, but she had no doubt with her luck the book Celeste wanted information from would be in some kind of restricted access area.

"Alfie, we've two new starters," Marthe announced.

A tall, broad-shouldered man reversed his head of tumbling russet hair out of what looked like a giant oven and approached them, a grin on his face and three large pots balanced in his hands.

"Welcome. I'll be feeding you. Any preferences, allergies, aversions, let me know."

Marthe clicked her fingers and a sheet of paper materialised between them.

"Now, Ru, we have you on garden duty." She eyed him up and down. "You look nice and strong. Molly, cleaning duty. Not the most glamorous, but it'll be your job to work your way through all the rooms and collect the contents of the bins. If you see an obvious mess, don't clean it. You'd be surprised how often court Fae leave things that look like mess only to come back looking for it later."

Her head shot up, tilting as though listening to

something, then she sighed loudly.

"Excuse me. Alfie will feed you, and I'll send one of the girls down in a while to show you to your rooms."

She stormed out of the kitchen like a venerable whirlwind and Molly sagged.

"Could be worse," Ru murmured.

Molly shrugged. "I don't mind cleaning. I've been looking forward to seeing a big library, and there's bound to be bins in there."

She flinched as Alfie appeared in front of them, a huge platter containing all sorts of delicious looking things balanced on one hand.

"The library is great if you love crumbling relics. Give me a campfire and a forest full of foraging any day." He placed the platter on a nearby wooden table. "Sit, eat. The staff can usually be trusted to steer you right, so you'll be safe enough trusting anyone in uniform. Yours will already be in your rooms waiting for you no doubt, but eat, enjoy."

Molly sank into one of the sturdy wooden chairs, eying the amazing spread as Ru dropped into the chair beside her.

"So, manual labour begins," he murmured. "We'll get together every evening to check on each other, okay?"

She nodded, reaching forward to grab some still-warm bread and a slather of herby butter.

Ru would need to tell her where exactly she was meant to be looking, and she'd need all her charm to achieve what Celeste had asked of her.

I might even need to take the risk of using my compulsion gift.

The one thing she hadn't asked was what happened if

she failed. She had to hope Marcus wouldn't see that as an excuse to go after Talie again, not that she intended to fail.

Alfie reappeared before she could dwell too deeply and dropped cups in front of them.

"What'll it be?" he asked.

She smiled. "What have you got?"

"We have everything and anything you could ask for."

Ru's eyes lit up. "I think I'm going to enjoy this place."

CHAPTER TWENTY

Of course the princess of Faerie has birds.

Molly flinched as she entered Princess Mayflower's private chambers, scanning the high ceilings for any flap of wings. In the two weeks since they'd arrived at the queen's court, she'd only had to remove bins from the Princess Mayflower's room twice, and both times one of the orbing creatures had tried to divebomb her head.

So far, the cleaning route given to her each morning hadn't taken her into the library, but she was determined to be patient. Then every evening she and Ru would convene in the kitchen, and he'd insist she wasn't to show any more interest in the library until chance took her there, just in case.

Molly tiptoed into the bedroom and left the door open a crack behind her. The air was still enough but that didn't mean a thing where birds were concerned, so she bit her lip and headed straight for the bin. The opulence of the court still amazed her. She had no clue why a private bedroom suite would need so many ornately upholstered chairs, or why the curtains were made from enough ruched material to shelter an entire citadel park. She didn't even dare think about how many clothes and accessories and jewels were no doubt in the various walk-in wardrobes.

She bent down to empty the wicker bin from beside the armchair, dropping to one knee to reach for an errant sweet wrapper underneath.

Before she could straighten up again, the door clicked open. Footsteps tapped on the marble floor as the door thudded shut.

Molly froze.

"Current?"

It was Princess Mayflower's voice, calling for her favourite bird. Molly took a sharp breath as a soft caw echoed and the whoosh of air echoed nearby.

"Mother's being a right pain," Princess Mayflower grumbled. "Her latest mad idea is to get me betrothed to someone to strengthen us as a court. When I asked who, she said she'd compiled a list. It was full of names, all ancient, cruel, or absolute imbeciles."

Current clicked his beak and Molly forced the wash of fear down into the pit of her gut where it bubbled, ready to spew.

"Excuse me, your highness." She stood with her head bowed. "I was clearing the bins when you came in."

She flicked her gaze up one moment, her jaw dropping the next.

Princess Mayflower, well known throughout Faerie for being the youngest of the royal children, supposedly the purest, the most innocent, and the fairest of all with her curling golden hair, had tattoos. Not discreet ones either. Vines of black and gold climbed over her arms, her shoulders bursting with bright purple flowers.

The princess frowned as Current, a large black bird with an inky sheen to his wings, hopped from her hand to her shoulder. Then she glanced down at her tattoos.

"Oh, right. Needless to say we won't tell my mother about this, yes?" she commanded. "I appear as I'm expected to in public, but she'd have a fit if she saw the real me."

Molly blinked hard to clear her astonishment.

"No, I won't say a word, of course."

She grabbed the bin and bobbed a curtsey, sidling the long way across the floor to avoid the piercing dark gaze Current was giving her. He ruffled his wings in warning and she squeaked.

Princess Mayflower chuckled. "Not a fan?"

"Well, no. They can drop on your head and peck your eyes out."

"They wouldn't do that unless provoked, or perhaps unless they're birds of prey. Current here might if I asked him to, but I'd have to ask really nicely. Do you want to hold him?"

"No!" Molly grimaced. "I mean no thank you, your highness, not unless you insist."

The royal smile widened. "I could… but I won't. You haven't been here long, have you?"

"No, your highness. I'm happy to be here though. It's a great honour to serve the royal family of Faerie."

"Maybe it is now I'm the only one left, more's my bad luck. You'd have had a very different experience if my sisters were still here. You really don't like birds?"

Molly hesitated. "I want to like them, but there's just

something that makes me shudder."

"We could acclimatise you. Immersion therapy is all the rage at the moment. Fear is seen as a weakness."

Molly eyed Current once more, inching her gaze over the dark blue wings, the shining emerald tail feathers, the dark eyes and the sharp, sharp beak.

"That's very kind, your highness, but-"

"Settled then. I'll have to do some muddling though. Mother will wonder why we're together otherwise. Have you ever wanted to be a royal maid?"

"I- have honestly never even considered it, your highness."

Princess Mayflower beamed. "Excellent, which means I can get away with much more around you than I could any other maid. My last was… not a good fit."

Every essence of sense screamed at Molly to ask why they weren't a good fit, and how many other maids had been deemed the same, but she didn't dare.

"I'll speak to mother immediately." Princess Mayflower waved her hand, sending Current fluttering up toward the rafters.

Molly winced, cringing into herself and closing her eyes. By the time she risked opening them again, Current was gone and Princess Mayflower was halfway out the bedroom door.

With the bin in hand, Molly hurriedly emptied the rest and left the room. She avoided people in the halls, some in enough long-skirted finery to be part of the nobility and others in matching uniforms to hers, keeping to one side out of everyone's way.

Now and then in the course of her daily duties, her arm would brush the corner of a side table, or her eyes would glance across a priceless relic or dour-faced portrait. She'd instantly wonder what it might be like to grow up in such a place. Then her work moved her on, more often than not bringing her back to the kitchen which acted like an unofficial staff room.

Molly hurried into the kitchen and across the worn tile floor to dump the contents of her bin collection in the larger bin outside. With little else to do until lunchtime, which promised to be delicious given the mouthwatering scents coming from the enormous cast iron pot over one of the many stoves, Molly pulled out her orb.

She'd had regular messages from Sammy, who she had 'met' on a Kayla Crane orb fan-site. Nobody except Ru would be able to tell she and Sammy had known each other before that.

She grinned as Sammy's latest message scrolled across the surface of her orb, something about Talie accidentally eating the poultice Sammy had been learning to make for school and her face looking like she'd swallowed a dung-beetle.

"You should be more careful."

Molly jumped at the sound of Ru's voice humming right beside her ear. She almost dropped her orb but clung to it as she whirled around.

"What are you doing sneaking around?" She pressed a hand to her chest. "It's rude to read people's orb messages."

He raised his eyebrows. "I didn't realise you had any

secrets to keep, not from me."

With her heart still pounding, Molly slid the orb into her pocket.

"I don't, but Sammy's a friend. We got chatting on the Kayla Crane fan-page, you know that." She gave him a meaningful glare, the meaning being 'keep your mouth shut'.

He frowned. "Just don't tell her anything about where we are."

"Of course not, I'm not stupid." She gave him a smug smile. "So not stupid that Princess Mayflower asked if I want to become her personal maid."

She conveniently left out the part about it being because May wanted to use her as an immersion therapy model for her bird fear. Ru's face lit up immediately.

"Amazing, well done!" He glanced around before lowering his voice. "Make sure you tell me everything."

She grasped the undercurrent of his words, yet another reminder that she was here as a spy for the Menagerie, for the good of the citadel. Marcus and Celeste were convinced that the Oak Queen planned to take over the citadel at some point, but the longer Molly stayed at the queen's court, the easier it was to forget the real reason she was there. She thought about Sammy and Talie often, and she missed the freedom of her workshop, but being under the Menagerie's thumb was similar to being under the queen's, and she didn't mind the work when the food was so good and the bed was beyond sublimely comfortable.

Conversation apparently over, she froze as Ru's face loomed in front of her. Before she could blush and turn for his mouth to hit her cheek, he landed a kiss right on her lips. Flutters exploded inside her gut, but he didn't notice her hesitation, striding off toward the kitchen door without a single look back.

It's still weird. She frowned. *Perhaps that's normal though. This is our first stab at a proper relationship after years of friendship.*

They would find their way through the initial awkwardness, she was sure of it. She had no idea how to behave as a girlfriend, which is what Ru now wanted to see her as. He'd even turned down a date with one of the other maids, loudly stating he was spoken for, which had admittedly soothed her ego no end. She smiled and pulled her orb out to message Sammy back.

"Oh, Molly, good." Marthe bustled up beside her. "Some of the nobles have been using the library and left a cleanable mess. Be a dear and go sort it, would you?"

Molly's pulse picked up immediately and she shoved her orb in her pocket, fighting to keep the excitement away from her face.

"Of course. Bins or an actual tidy?" she asked.

Marthe eyed her for a long moment. "Bins, but if there's anything obvious on the tables that needs to go, a quick tidy wouldn't hurt. You know where you're going?"

Molly nodded. "I haven't been inside the library yet but I'll be fine. Leave it to me, you're obviously really busy."

She tensed as Marthe leaned toward her, raising a hand to her face. Soft fingers patted against her cheek and she blinked in surprise.

"You have a good heart. Now, off you go."

Molly grabbed one of the bins from the pile in the far corner and left the kitchen, forcing her pace to remain steady.

Don't look like you're too eager to get anywhere.

She kept her gaze focused ahead. The moment she showed excitement for anything, someone would notice and wonder why. She wound through the vast halls, navigating her way according to the court map Marthe had shown her, until she found the wide, golden archway to the library.

Stepping inside while clutching the bin to her chest, she glanced up. And up. A faint hue of light glimmered above, but the column of the library and the enormous stacks ventured further than she could see, as if the citadel itself had been hollowed out and filled with all the books in Faerie and beyond.

"Wow."

She twisted around, determination filtering past awe as she stared at the polished wooden columns rising between endless rows of shelves, and the wide aisles that were laid with plush blue carpet.

An echo of noise came from the hall behind her and she started forward. Ru had outlined the library's layout to her and she'd memorised it. She needed to go left down the third row of towering shelves, take a right, cross the circular space full of tables and chairs, then down a short flight of steps and check the first four shelving units for the book. She didn't want to dwell too much on how Celeste had such specific information of the place, but she would do as instructed.

Glancing up again, her heart sank. If all the shelves were that high up, she might never find the book.

Unless I compel the librarian to bring it to me, but then someone might found out and ask why.

She shook the doubts aside and moved toward the long wooden desk that served as the librarian's table, keeping an eye out for any signs of movement. She emptied the bin beneath it and set off toward the left.

Left, third row, go right, past the tables and down steps. She repeated the directions like a mantra as she followed them, not a soul in sight.

It's almost too easy.

The wide expanse of space with tables and chairs lined up neatly in the centre had a starry pattern on the carpet underfoot, and a ceiling of deep purple and pale gold artwork above. Molly wished she could abandon the bin and lie down to learn what wonders the ceiling was meant to be showing, but up ahead was a short flight of steps, partly obscured behind a large golden archway. Molly slowed as she approached the arch, gazing at the detailed depictions of oak leaves and acorns.

She looked around but couldn't see anyone. A tremor of foreboding rippled through her as she stepped beneath the arch. Oaks and acorns were a sign of the royal family, and Marthe had mentioned private areas. She eyed the relatively normal ceiling height above and scanned the shelves ahead.

A faded, browning sheet of paper behind a glass frame had some sort of schematic of the area's layout, but whether *Potions Most Foul and Fae* was under 'histories' or 'heritages' or 'miscellaneous', she had no way of knowing.

With her bin in hand, she trailed along the first unit and hunched over to peer at the lower shelves after scanning the upper ones. Section by section, she shuffled along, flinching at every imagined noise.

The first row yielded nothing, nor did the second or third. Her back started to pang from the constant bowing and standing to see the shelves, such a buzzing, irritating pain that she almost missed familiar words.

Anticipation thrilled in her chest as she eased *Potions Most Foul and Fae* off the shelf. She dropped the bin between her feet and balanced the edge of the book on the shelf to hold it steady. The cover was crinkled at the corners, ancient dark green fabric worn and frayed in places.

Leafing carefully through each page, she found the chapter for gift extraction near the end and frowned at the author's looping scrawl.

'Though this book is about the source and history of poisons, it is academically prudent to make record of the oft ridiculed theory revolving around the melding and severing of gifts with such potions. A gift is an expression of an individual soul, intrinsically linked once given, such is the magic and the penalty of wielding. While extraction has been outlawed since the second age and should remain so, in times of great peril, extraction can be a viable method if used effectively, but the essence of the process is in the brewing of the correct infusion.'

Molly tensed as sounds echoed some distance away.

'To extract a gift, a conduit soul is necessary. While this act of using another Fae as a holding vessel or pin for the gift itself is considered somewhat drastic, the original owner needing to hover between life and death for the extraction to take place, there are some studies that prove the life can then be saved once severing has taken place, although all examples have yielded unsavoury side effects to date. The infusion is to be brewed, twelve parts yew and three parts nightshade, which weakens the anchor of the soul for the gift. It must then be swilled with oia residue, distil once and steeped for three days, then brewed one final time with two parts infusion to one part coalbane. This delays the imminent onslaught of death enough for the gift to be released via fireiron melding and thus redistributed.'

Another noise had Molly shutting the book and pushing it back onto the shelf, her gut churning, her mind spinning.

Talie's paper had those herbs on. She shuddered, ducking to pick up her bin. *What in the name of Faerie is she mixed up in?*

It was identical to the wording on the paper Talie had dropped in the citadel library, which Ru had taken the moment Molly showed it to him.

All except the bit about the two parts to one part coalbane, and something about a fireiron, whatever that is.

She hurried along the row toward the archway, worry biting at her. If she told Ru the whole truth, and he told Celeste, then Celeste would tell Marcus who would likely target Talie first to get to the resistance.

If she's as much a pawn in the resistance as I am in the Menagerie, then I owe her the chance to explain first.

She trotted up the steps and across the circular study space.

"What are you doing in here?" A stern voice echoed behind her.

Molly halted, chills rippling over her skin before it flushed hot. She turned slowly, assessing a towering willow of a man with a severe frown on his face.

"Marthe asked me to come and clear the bins," she said, throwing the whole weight of her charm gift into her words.

His glare turned to a frown. "That was the queen's private gallery. You can't be in there."

"I'm sorry, I didn't know it was *her* private gallery."

Technically not a lie, because while it was pretty obviously private, Molly hadn't known it belonged specifically to the queen herself. Her heart thundered as she clutched the bin tight, hoping for a gruff dismissal.

"You're new?" he asked.

She nodded. "Not even been here a month yet, sorry. I'm still learning."

He gave her a thorough look, before sighing.

"There's a mess made in the front stacks. Come on, I'll show you."

Molly gave him her sweetest, most grateful smile and scurried after him as he strode back toward the entrance.

She would clear what she needed to and use that time to figure out what to do, especially now she wouldn't be able to sneak back in to the library, not a second time without it looking suspicious.

As the librarian waved an irritable hand at an absolute chaos of papers, cups and empty plates on a long table between some shelves, Molly set to the task, letting the repetitive movements soothe her nerves.

She repeated the words she'd read until they were etched firmly in her memory as she swept the debris and food remnants into the bin. Clutching it under one arm, she balanced the tray of cups and plates with the other.

The librarian nodded to her as she left, and she smiled back as naturally as she could manage before taking a steadying walk back to the kitchen.

"Ooh, there's my best mug back." Alfie pounced to take the tray the moment she stepped inside.

"I hope you don't mean me," she joked.

He grinned. "Of course not. This mug is much older. You were gone a while."

"Got lost."

"You got lost?" Ru's voice brought her round to face the back door.

She nodded, her gaze sticking on the veins of sweat slicking his t-shirt to his chest, the tiny scratches over his arms and the flush to his cheeks.

"Had to clear out the library bins, but it's like a maze in there."

His eyebrows lifted. "Fair enough. Do you have time? I'm on lunch."

"Take some lunch," Alfie called over his shoulder. "Marthe will find you if she needs you. She can find anyone in this place with a twitch of her nose."

Molly smiled. "I can believe that. Okay, lunch is good."

Alfie clicked his fingers to summon a clean plate and bustled into the chiller room.

"Talk quick," Ru muttered.

Molly hesitated. "Found it. Something about using someone as a conduit for the gift being extracted while the original owner is between life and death. Not cheery stuff. It was basically what I saw on that paper I found, you know with the bracelet I handed in?"

Ru's gaze fixed on her face, his silence making her nervous.

"Eventually. So, that's it? Just the same wording as that bit of paper?"

She made a show of glancing around, checking they were alone as her mind raced with possibilities.

"Twelve parts yew, three parts nightshade, swilled with oia residue, distilled once and steeped for... three days. Oh, and something about using fireiron to extract it as well, but then I heard someone coming and had to bail."

He sighed. "I don't know what fireiron is, but I'm sure Marcus will. That's great. I'll get the info out of here to where it needs to go."

"The librarian caught me coming out though," Molly added. "I told him I was new and lost, but he won't believe that a second time."

Ru wiped a hand over his mouth as Alfie reappeared, the plate now groaning with food.

"Don't worry about that." He glanced Alfie's way. "I'm sure you're doing a great job, and it's easy to get lost. Come on, let's take our lunch out into the sunshine."

Alfie handed her the plate with a wink, his hefty eyebrows waggling at Ru's retreating back. Molly managed a weak smile as she followed Ru, relief that he'd taken her information at face value ruling over any awkwardness at the gossip that might soon be doing the rounds about her supposed love life.

She hadn't told him about the extra mixing with coalbane either, but as she committed the words to memory, she decided not to.

Not yet.

She focused instead on the food as they sat on a bench by the walled garden, surrounded by flowers and the drowsy hum of nearby bees.

Maybe I should keep a tiny part of the information to myself a little bit longer, just to be safe.

CHAPTER TWENTY ONE

Molly woke in the servant dorms to the familiar sound of people fussing around. She cracked an eye open wearily, bemused to find the room still dark. She shared it with five other maids, and a quick tilt of her head showed body-shaped lumps in all four other beds.

"Shhh."

She sat up in a flurry of bedding to find Princess Mayflower standing beside her bed with her finger to her lips.

"Come with me," the princess insisted. "Bring any stuff you have."

Vaguely aware she couldn't say no, Molly shoved her feet into her shoes, bundled her uniform into the top of her bag and wiped her gritty eyes.

She followed the princess out of the room, holding her tongue until they were in the firelit hallway.

"Is something wrong, your highness?"

Princess Mayflower shook her head. "Nope. Mother finally finished whatever background checks she had to do on you so now she wants to interrogate you herself."

Molly's skin tingled. A queen of Faerie wanted to interrogate her. Fae couldn't lie but word-tangling or trying to deceive a queen? Impossible.

Would she know if I used a compulsion on her? Molly struggled to breathe. *Don't be dim. She's a literal queen, of course she would.*

May swept her down the stairs and toward the double doors leading to the throne room. Molly straightened her top, squeaking as May slammed an arm in front of her.

"I'll glamour you, it's quicker."

May waved an arm in her general direction, and Molly stared down at her sleeping clothes wriggling into the vision of her uniform. Before she could even utter a panicked thank you, May opened one of the doors and gave her a helpful shove on the back.

Molly walked into the throne room with her heart pounding. At the far end of the long hall, centred between the two rows of black marble pillars, the throne towered over all atop its white marble plinth. Each step made the hall seem longer with the queen watching her as she approached. Molly swallowed and straightened her shoulders, keeping her gaze on the plinth as she approached and dipped into a bow.

"Rise."

Molly lifted her shoulders, keeping her chin dipped to her chest.

"Mayflower tells me she's chosen you as her next maid."

Molly nodded. "Yes, your majesty, she has."

"Hmm. Do you know what happened to her previous maids?"

"I've heard rumours, your majesty. It's still an honour

to be chosen."

The queen smiled with wicked amusement. "I see. A promotion in rank is often an honour, despite the perils it may bring. Can we trust you to be faithful in such a high profile role?"

"I definitely have no intentions of harming the princess, or anyone, and I will serve her to the best of my ability, to be loyal and faithful-"

"Then I will approve the appointment." The queen levelled a look at her that pierced right through to her already jangling nerves. "Remember however, you are in my employ, not hers. Your loyalty is to the court and the crown. To me. I may find some benefit to this yet and you would do wise to remember it."

Molly nodded, bowing low. "Yes, your majesty."

"I'm sure you have things to be doing."

Molly bowed again for safety's sake and took a few awkward steps backwards before turning and scurrying for the door.

She'll use me to spy on May. No doubt that was what happened with the other maids who all ended up leaving. Oh orbs, did they leave by choice? Or worse?

She walked through the door, mindful to close it behind her, and sagged against the frame.

May grinned. "Nicely done, meek and agreeable is her favourite."

"I don't know about that," Molly muttered.

"So, you officially work for me now. There's a chamber beside mine where you'll sleep, and you can pick one of my bathrooms."

Molly's brain hitched, stumbling over the idea of someone having multiple bathrooms. She'd cleared the bin in Mayflower's bathroom before, but only the one adjoining the bedroom.

"Right, ground rules." The princess swept down the hall toward her rooms. "When we're alone, you're to call me May. I want us to feel on the same level even if we aren't. In front of anyone else, even other servants, I suppose 'Princess' will have to do."

Molly bit her lip. She couldn't exactly say no.

"I will spend one hour a day getting you acclimatised to the birds as promised," May continued. "In return, you will have to fetch my meals, and anything else I ask for, but I draw the line at letting you dress me."

"Well that sounds fair." The early-morning flippancy slipped out.

She flinched as May looked back, but the grin on the royal face wasn't one of cruelty.

"It's absolutely not fair, but this is the Faerie we live in. Take it or leave it."

"Take it." Molly risked a smile. "If I'm not needing to dress you, prin- *May*, what do you need me to do first?"

She hurried forward, intent on at least opening the door for her new mistress, but May reached it before she could and powered inside.

"First, we find you something suitable to wear. Then you can bring the breakfast."

Molly glanced down at her ragged t-shirt and old shorts she slept in as May's glamour faded away, then at the uniform poking out of her bag.

May wrinkled her nose. "You can't wear a uniform if you're to actually be seen with me."

"So, a dress?"

Molly did her best not to pull a face, unlike May, who grimaced.

"Not unless we have to. Go fetch the breakfast and I'll have Marthe find you some trousers and some suitable tops. There will have to be dresses too for social occasions, but today's outing definitely isn't a dress kind of day."

"Okay, your- May. I'll fetch breakfast then. Is there anything you want, or do they usually choose what to serve you?"

May shrugged. "I'll take whatever's coming. They know my tastes."

With that as her guide, Molly hurried out of the room. Halfway down the stairs, she saw the double doors to the throne room open and realised she had faced the literal queen of Faerie without even brushing her hair. Cursing her bad luck, she dashed through the deserted halls until she skidded into the kitchen. Alfie lifted his eyebrows at her entrance.

"The princess wants her breakfast," she announced.

He grinned. "I heard you got promoted. Her maids don't last long, so good luck. If I can keep her in a good mood for you with food, I will."

As he started whipping something in a bowl at startling speed, several people around him whizzed into action on other jobs.

"Did they…" Molly hesitated. "Did they choose to leave? Her other maids?"

Wild thoughts of May disposing of former servants filled her head until Alfie laughed.

"Yeah, with curses ringing behind them. The first hated birds and was found whispering in the queen's ear that birds weren't a noble pet for a princess. After seven days of being constantly pooped on, she quit."

Molly snorted a laugh. "I won't be whispering anything in the queen's ear at least, not unless she tells me to."

"There was one who insisted on eight hours of lessons, until she was mysteriously cursed to repeat the same sonnet over and over at all hours of the day."

Alfie started setting out a sturdy wooden tray, lining it with a tablecloth and plating up a delicious array of pancakes, berries and yoghurt.

"I definitely won't be insisting on any lessons," Molly said, relieved.

Alfie set the tray in front of her on the big island in the middle of the kitchen, then whisked a small plate next to it.

"My favourite though was when Master Taz was still here. He actually faked his own death to get out of a royal engagement, but then he always preferred the dramatic approach in his younger years. Eat before you rush upstairs again. Hers will keep a moment."

Molly grinned, inhaling the smaller plate of pancakes and using the last one to scoop up the berries.

"She'll ask if you want any of hers, but always tell her you already ate," Alfie murmured. "From now on, eat before taking her meals up and say I insist on it. If she asks you to fetch something and you're not sure, ask her to explain. She likes to know things, so she'll want to feel like she's teaching you stuff not the other way around. When you're sure she likes you, then it'll be safe to share food."

Molly nodded. "I get it. Thank you, Alfie."

He patted her shoulder, bustling back to the counter with her empty plate.

"Get that up to her now and mind you don't run into anyone on the stairs."

Molly did as she was told, amazed how many staff members seemed to suddenly be standing exactly where she would have stepped if she hadn't slowed her pace.

Almost like it's happening on purpose.

Unsure if it was the princess' way of testing her, or perhaps even the queen's, or if the other maids were jealous of her new appointment, she dodged and excused herself all the way up to May's room and paused to knock before entering.

"Oh, there you are." May looked up with a frown. "Are you hungry?"

Molly shook her head as she took the tray to the table by the open window.

"I already ate, Alfie insisted," she explained.

May grunted something, but Molly was too busy closing her eyes and soaking up the gentle morning sunshine radiating through the open window, the air fresher and more fragrant than she'd ever known.

"Right, let's get a look at you."

Molly twisted around in alarm to hear Marthe's voice. Rumour among servants was that Marthe was ancient, possibly even serving the royal family before the queen took the throne. As the court's Head Housekeeper, she was also the one in charge of everything.

Molly hastened to stand in front of her, half a head taller and feeling twice as gangly.

"Hmm." Marthe eyed her up and down as May looked on. "Give me five minutes, Princess, and I'll have her sorted."

May nodded. "Thank you, Marthe. That gives me time to enjoy breakfast before we go."

The moment Marthe disappeared, vanishing on the spot to a different part of the castle, May slid into a seat and started eating.

Molly hovered until May tapped the table with an irritable hand.

"Sit down."

Molly sat, holding her hands in her lap and glancing out of the window as May continued eating. The gardens of the palace rolled on to the horizon and she'd had a few hours here and there to walk in them. She wished she could send Sammy a picture, or at least tell her about it, but Ru would kill her if she did.

The moment May finished her breakfast, Molly stood to clear the plates, flinching as Marthe reappeared with a towering bundle of various fabrics in her arms.

"These should fit you."

She shoved them at Molly, who almost dropped them, then vanished the tray with a click of her fingers.

"Wow." Molly's jaw dropped.

Marthe's lips twitched. "Quite. Now, go pick something smart. When you're in this palace you represent the staff, but outside you represent the family itself."

May leaned back in her chair with a grin. She whistled and Molly crunched in on herself as Current flapped down to land on the table.

"No need for formalities where we're going, you know that Marthe."

Molly hesitated. "May I ask where we're going so I can dress appropriately?"

"Wouldn't worry about it," May insisted. "We're going to the one place I can find some common sense."

Molly wanted to repeat the question but she got the feeling May was both not used to having to repeat herself to maids and also pausing for dramatic effect. When Molly didn't say anything, May grinned.

"We're going to visit my brother."

CHAPTER TWENTY TWO

Molly had heard scant tales of the royals in her life. The citadel boasted access to several orb-cast streams including news channels, and of course reports of the recent battles had trickled through, but then she reached the palace. There were hundreds of channels, not a handful. More than she could possibly sift through without spending all her time on it.

She knew that the Oak Queen's son, May's brother, was king consort to the Holly Queen, but not much more than that.

So when May introduced Molly to her troll realm-skipper, Lavender, and they boarded an ornate little carriage with long wooden handles at the front, Molly had no idea what to expect on arriving at the Holly Queen's court.

Absolute chaos was not it.

"Why is there an eight foot statue of me in the atrium?!"

The voice blasted through the air, full of incandescent female rage. Molly eyed the clusters of people standing in the enormous hall, then gazed in amazement at the place itself. Dark red beams arced up overhead, light emanating from even further above than that, a ceiling so far up it was basically invisible. The walls on all sides were covered with ivy and holly, butterflies a riot of colour against the green. Molly spied several golden gates amid the foliage too, but didn't get a chance to look any further.

"I didn't order this!" The shouter insisted. "Nobody in their right mind would order this! I look constipated!"

May grabbed Molly's elbow and steered her toward a semi-circular wooden counter with an unimpressed elderly man behind it. When they got close enough, Molly could see his tie had tiny pencils on.

Then she noticed the pink-cheeked young woman standing on the other side of the counter with her fists clenched.

Molly's insides flipped at the sight of the Holly Queen, no less fearsome in jeans and a *Demolition Ducks* hoodie. Without waiting to be told, Molly bowed low.

"It says 'item deliverable to Taz Elverhill'," the man with the tie announced.

The queen froze. "Oh he is *so* dead."

She turned before Molly could snap her gaze to the floor, so Molly got the full effect of the royal frown beaming down upon her.

"Who is this and why is she down there?" the queen asked.

May sighed. "She's new. We don't bow here, Molly. Nobody bothers."

Molly waited a second then straightened up, bowing her head instead.

"My brother really has surpassed himself," May said, delight singing in her tone. "Oh, there he is."

Molly risked a look up in time to see the king consort of Faerie strolling out from one of the golden metal gates.

He saw the situation, and the unfortunate statue, and turned on his heel with a wicked grin.

The queen charged after him, chaotic black hair flying behind her.

"Come back here you absolute-"

"I regret nothing!"

Molly wiped a hand over her face.

"That's… something."

May laughed. "They're not normal but it's fun. Come on, I know where we're all meant to be meeting."

Molly followed her through a similar golden gate to the one the queen chased the king consort into, eying the bare brick walls behind the grills warily.

"Elbows in," May announced cheerfully as she banged the gate shut. "I can be myself here, but probably best you still call me Princess for now. There are always ears at Mother's court, always listening, but here there's not much I want to hide."

Molly tensed as the lift shot upward, the sudden gust of wind ruffling her hair as her stomach swooped and plummeted.

"Are we just here for a family visit?" she asked.

"Not exactly. I'm probably the closest to my brother out of all my sisters. I never tormented him like they did, but Mother is being extremely tight-lipped about the goings-on in Faerie, so I'm here to make sure they don't end up fighting each other if there's a wider enemy out there."

"A wider enemy?"

May nodded as the lift slowed to a halt, the light of a hallway settling on the other side of the grill.

"There have been rumours that the Faerie citadel is in a state and both queens are worried about it."

Molly froze. "The… citadel?"

"Yes, it's been around for a long while but gossip says it's flourished in the past thirty years or so. It also functions outside the law of Faerie legally, a no man's land uncontrolled by either queen or by any court."

Molly forced her face into what she hoped was mild curiosity, but May opened the grill and strode out without looking her way.

The Menagerie is basically a glorified court, Molly thought, rushing after her. *It's entirely self-sustaining though, with no need for much trade or input from outsiders.*

The hallway led past paintings, and one random hole in the wall that had been ceremonially roped off with ribbons of red and green velvet, to large double doors at the end. Memories of having to face the Oak Queen through a similar set of double doors that morning surfaced. Molly took a deep breath and forced herself to walk straight past them and into a large office.

The entire high-ceilinged room was decked in rich purple drapes, with grey-framed mirrors and an enormous dark-wood desk that had macabre carvings and spiky edges.

The woman behind the imposing desk caught sight of them, nodding rather than bowing her head to May. Molly tensed as the woman eyed her next, the look prolonged and scrutinising from beneath the curtain of dark hair. A relative of the Holly Queen's, Molly decided, tensing as the woman's bright purple lips thinned in her direction.

"Hiya, don't mind me."

The voice was so familiar that Molly flinched.

In the corner of the room stood a woman, only older than Molly by a handful of years, and almost identical to Beryl.

The nose was a little more ridged, the hair bright green instead of bright purple, but she could have easily mistaken this woman for Beryl's sister.

Even if she was, I can't admit I know who Beryl is, and what are the chances they're in any way linked?

She sidled after May, who boldly took one of the chairs. Molly stationed herself behind it and wished she could have a chair too. The woman behind the desk was still glancing her way with those narrowed eyes as the queen and king consort swept in.

"Sorry, domestic matter," the queen muttered.

Molly bowed her head even though nobody was paying any attention to her. She breathed a tiny sigh of relief when the queen chose to remain standing, as did the king consort.

"As the delegation from the Oak Queen's court, I can confirm we have nothing to report," May announced, looking idly at her nails.

"Hold on." The woman behind the desk held up a hand. "Are we all accounted for?"

She nodded at Molly, who froze as all eyes turned to her.

"This is my new maid, Molly," May said.

The queen frowned. "Are you sworn to the oak court?"

"No, your majesty." Molly lowered her chin and gaze before shaking her head. "But I am serving to the best of my ability. This position is new."

May sighed. "Mother has already interrogated her. I doubt she's likely to stab me in my sleep, or any of us in a meeting."

Molly looked up, alarmed.

"I honestly wouldn't."

The queen's lips twitched. "I'll take that. Well, I'm Demi, this is Taz, and that's Queenie."

"I think we all know who we are," Queenie said drily from behind her desk.

The queen rolled her eyes. "Fine, just being remotely decent. We don't have much news either sadly."

Molly was still struggling with their utter informality, having to remind herself that these were the most powerful Fae in all of Faerie, even more powerful than Celeste or Marcus.

"The citadel is an all but impenetrable fortress," the king consort admitted. "We can't get any kind of service going in because they seem to do everything in-house. Even performances are limited. We can ask for access but we'd be followed from entrance to exit which gives us no chance to investigate."

Molly couldn't avoid the tiniest stab of pride as she thought of the citadel. She both missed it and didn't. She liked the people she'd grown up around, her workshop, the park, even if the air was filtered rather than fresh. She definitely could do without the subterfuge and having to deal with the Menagerie's resistance drama.

She snuck a hand into her pocket, her orb warming with notification of a message, no doubt from Sammy about Kayla Crane's concert. The idea slammed into her, and she opened her mouth before she could check herself.

"I-" She froze.

The words dried on her tongue. May eyed her up and down.

"Is this a suggestion thing or a 'you need the toilet' thing?" she asked not so helpfully.

Molly bit her lip, uneasy under the queen's piercing gaze.

"You can share whatever's on your mind," she said gently. "It won't go against you."

Molly gulped. "Um… I'm part of the Kayla Crane fansite. One of her other fans I'm kind of friends with said she's holding a concert at the citadel."

"Really?" The queen's eyebrows raised. "Why haven't we heard that then? Interesting. Even if we did get in to see the concert, we'd be followed everywhere."

"If you had some less recognisable faces that could slip into the crowd though, your majesty," Molly added. "Maybe ones that could glamour?"

She couldn't believe she was having an actual conversation with a queen, her gut muscles close to cramping with nerves.

The queen eyed the king consort, who grinned.

"Wouldn't be the first time we've had to muck around with some misdirection. Be worth asking for some of the old gang to join us, those who can move around easily."

The queen nodded. "Good idea, it's been a while."

Molly sagged a little, relieved her outspokenness had gone unpunished and her part was done. Until she realised the queen was staring at her.

"You said your name is Molly, right?"

May had said it but Molly nodded anyway.

"Well, thank you for giving us this information, Molly."

Molly opened her mouth to brush the gratitude aside with some kind of inane babbling, but the woman with the green hair spoke up before she could answer.

"Not that I warrant an introduction apparently, but I also know someone in the citadel, so I'll put some feelers out." She grinned. "I'm Cheryl, by the way, since her queenship is too busy to introduce her friends."

Cheryl that rhymes with Beryl.

Molly froze, but Cheryl looked away before she could make eye contact.

"Sorry. We don't bother with titles here," the queen added. "Especially as most people we know would probably laugh at us if we tried."

Molly hesitated. *Is this some kind of test?*

"It's not a test or anything," the king consort added, his smile kind. "If you call me anything other than Taz, people will think you've been dropped on your head."

Molly nodded obediently. She wasn't likely to see them often, but if she could call the princess of Faerie May, she could be obedient and call the queen and king consort Demi and Taz.

"Well, I'm going. I'm a huge KC fan," May announced.

Taz snorted. "As if mother dearest would let you."

"You underestimate the power of my tantrums, dear brother. I'm the only one she's got left."

"So?"

May grinned. "So, I'll do what you always do and threaten to abdicate."

Molly let the sibling banter slide over her, drifting inward as she realised what exactly her suggestion would mean, and what she would have to tell Ru.

Leading the royal family into the citadel was one thing, but if Marcus knew they were snooping he'd have all the ammunition he needed to be proven right about them interfering. He feared the Oak Queen was focused on the citadel, but the Holly Queen seemed eager to get inside too.

No mention of war had been given yet, but Molly glanced down at May. Time would tell if May proved to be a good mistress, one who might give Molly the chance to find a place outside the citadel to settle. Even if she didn't, Molly wasn't sure she'd stomach a fight between two sides.

If it weren't for Marcus and Celeste knowing the history of how my guardians died and hiding it from me, it would be a simple choice.

A few years in the Menagerie's service against one month in the oak queen's, but now she couldn't trust either side not to use her as a pawn.

CHAPTER TWENTY THREE

"Absolutely not! I forbid it."

The Oak Queen's not-so-dulcet tones screeched through the hall, and likely the entire palace to Faerie and beyond.

Molly hovered outside the throne room waiting for May, who had insisted she would find a way to get them to the Kayla Crane concert the moment they realm-skipped back to the court. May had declined Demi's offer of tea much to Molly's disappointment, as she was more used to serving royalty than dining with them. Staying for tea in yet another royal court, especially an infinitely more relaxed one like Arcanium, would have been amazing.

"What are you doing?"

Molly jumped like a jitter-kneed toad as Ru crept up beside her. She pressed a hand to her chest and huffed an irritable breath.

"We went to Dem- Queen Demerara's court as planned and it's like nothing I've ever seen. They definitely don't behave like Fae royalty there. But the queen is worried about the citadel just like the rest."

She waved a hand at the throne room doors.

Ru grimaced. "Not great news. What else?"

Molly considered telling him about the constipated statue and the relaxed vibe, but that wasn't what he was after. Inside the throne room, furious voices buzzed at lower tones, so she lowered her own to match.

"They don't sound like they want to take over," she admitted. "More like they want to make sure the citadel aren't planning the same thing. They do want to gain access though for a less chaperoned type of visit."

Ru glanced back and forth before stepping closer. Molly froze, her insides somersaulting.

"Anything else?" he asked, his tone turning husky.

"They know about the Kayla Crane concert."

Ru sighed. "How on earth did they find out about that? News really must be leaking out through cracks in the glass these days. Citadel nobles are under strict rules to keep certain privileges secret."

Molly kept her lips pinned tight and shrugged, hoping he'd take her silence as worry, or indifference, she didn't care which as long as he didn't ask how they found out.

Then again, how does he know these rules about citadel nobles all of a sudden?

Instead of asking her more questions, Ru lifted a hand. She tensed as it wisped past her cheek and her hair tumbled around her face seconds later.

He held up her purple hair ribbon with a soft smile. It had acorns on it, her favourite out of the neatly wrapped bundle of ribbons Marthe had provided her with.

"It's a thing apparently," Ru explained. "Everyone's wearing their girl's hair ribbon."

Her somersaulting gut crash landed.

He thinks I'm his girl?

He'd mentioned her being his girlfriend before in passing to others, and he held her hand and kissed her like she was, but the easy way he said it despite them not having actually discussed it made her uneasy. She wiped a hand over her face, using the act of tucking her hair behind her ears to give her a second to think it through.

"We haven't really had that conversation," she muttered.

He chuckled. "I know, but you can't blame me for hoping."

He tied the ribbon around his wrist, the fabric bright against his skin.

"I'LL ABDICATE!"

Molly winced as the petulant scream ricocheted through the palace. Ru might have her hair ribbon as some kind of random claiming, but May clearly had every intention of stealing the moment.

Ru pressed a finger to his lips, one hand to the wall as he leaned closer to the doors still ajar.

"It's too dangerous, Mayflower," the queen insisted. "If you threaten to abdicate again, I'll forbid you from seeing your brother. He's clearly a bad influence on you."

"*Mother,* be serious. I will be with Demi and Taz. Who better to protect me than them? They'll have an army of FDPs floating around incognito as well."

"Even if I were to let you go, I'd need several of our own with you and I can't spare them."

May huffed. "And draw so much attention? I only need to take my maid with me. Besides, you're apparently intent on me ruling this court after you."

"You will be ruling in my stead, yes, but that-"

"So what's the point of me ruling after you if I don't know anything? If I've never even seen most of Faerie? The nobles would assassinate me in two moments flat."

Molly sank into the responding silence. May had a serious point, even if it was only to get her own way.

"Do you not think Kayla Crane will have even bigger security than us?" May added. "The whole of Faerie adores her. That arena, venue, wherever it is, will be full of nobles and protected better than any court."

Again, silence. Molly bit her lip, hoping.

It's madness to even think about going back. What if someone recognises me in front of May?

She doubted they'd be anywhere near the kind of citadel levels where someone might recognise her, but the nerves kicked up a notch all the same.

Sammy will never talk to me again if she finds out I went to a Kayla Crane concert without her.

She tamped down on the urge to smile as a wearily parental sigh echoed out from the throne room, and the rumble of a storm answered somewhere outside.

"I want constant communication open at all times," the queen insisted. "You will keep your orb on you and respond immediately whenever I call."

"Message, not call."

"No," the queen snapped.

"It's going to look pathetic if I'm constantly answering face calls with my mother! Is that what you want? The whole of Faerie to think I'm weak? Is it?!"

Silence.

More silence.

Molly inched ever so slightly sideways to check for signs of shadows approaching the doors. The last thing either she or Ru needed was to be found eavesdropping.

"Fine. Whenever I message you, Mayflower, you answer me. Otherwise I will invite myself to join you."

"Thank you, mother!"

Excitable footsteps tapped over the marble floor and Molly shoved Ru away. He slipped through a side door and left her just enough time to flee a respectable distance before May hurried out.

"Come on," May insisted while powering past. "The performance is tomorrow and we need to plan."

Molly broke into a jog to keep up with the princess powering toward the main stairs.

"Do you really think she'll let you go alone?" she asked.

May snorted loudly. "Of course not, but I've been evading my mother's guards most of my life. I've had to up my game since my brother and sisters fled the nest, but I'm smart."

Recalling the argument between mother and daughter, Molly couldn't disagree with that.

"What we need now is clothes," May added, sweeping into her bedroom.

Molly grimaced. "My uniform is probably the smartest thing I own."

"Oh, honey." May eyed her up and down. "Your uniform is a disaster, no offence. Marthe!"

Molly glanced down at the pale peach shirt and plain

black trousers. She wasn't doing manual labour any longer so her boots were now indoor slippers, and it still amazed her that the shirt and shoes changed colour depending on what hue the queen chose for the court each day. She had the clothes that Marthe had given her for the out-of-court visits, but her uniform was still mandatory inside the court boundaries.

"I don't really have…um, I won't have made enough yet for new clothes," she said.

She thought of the beautiful dress Beryl had lent her for the ball, the briefest glimpse into what it would be like to dress as a proper lady.

Proper ladies probably wouldn't be allowed to have scars and scrapes on their hands from hard work though.

She worried at the skin around her thumbnail as May's laughter boomed through the room.

"I'm forcing you to go with me, so technically I should be paying for them. I have so many it's ridiculous. I tried asking Marthe to donate some once, or at least have them cut up and resewn into something sensible, but mother threw a fit, like she couldn't magic up a hundred more pointless dresses."

Molly couldn't stop her smile creeping up.

"You don't like dresses?"

"I love dresses, but honestly having over a thousand of them is just vulgar. I envy Taz so badly. If I'd been allowed to go to Arcanium instead, I'd have caught me a queen and been allowed to slouch around in ripped jeans and hoodies all day."

Molly choked over a laugh as Marthe realm-skipped

into being in front of them.

"We're going to Kayla Crane's concert tomorrow at the Faerie citadel," May announced.

Marthe nodded. "I know. Your mother has been pacing ever since. Up and down, up and down she goes, muttering things and threatening to overthrow places."

"Excellent." May's wicked grin was terrifying. "We need clothes. Not dresses, orbs please not dresses. Maybe skirts and something suitably noble but casual. I don't think we need to match though."

Marthe's lips thinned. "No, definitely no matching. You must still make a statement as the Crown Princess of Faerie."

"Don't say that! I hate being the only one left."

Marthe only smiled before disappearing, presumably to source suitable outfits.

Molly eyed the sky now whirling up a storm outside, a sure sign the queen wasn't taking May's win over her lightly. She didn't notice May advancing until she heard the telltale click of her tongue.

Molly flinched, shrinking into herself as a large, white bird with dark green under-feathers cannoned down to land on May's shoulder.

"I've been very remiss in our deal," May announced.

"That's fine," Molly squeaked. "I'm fine, forget about it, *please*."

May lifted her arm and the bird hopped onto the side of her forefinger, using her hand as a perch.

"Relax, I'm not going to torture you. Just look at her. She's a Greater Spotted Hump Warbler."

Molly blinked, eying the bird as doubtfully as the bird was eying her.

"But… she's not spotted."

"Well, no…"

"She's not got a hump."

"No, but-"

"Who names these creatures?" Molly huffed, flinching as the bird clicked its beak at her.

May grinned. "I know, traumatic isn't it. Poor thing. She's such a noble bird and she has a really silly name."

"I know what you're doing."

May blinked innocently. "I have no idea what you mean."

"You're hoping if I feel sorry for her, I'll start seeing her as less scary than she really is. You know those talons on your finger could claw your throat clean off, right?"

"Technically, yes, but birds form deep attachments and they have keen instincts. If you mean her no harm, she won't harm you."

"It sounds so simple when you say it like that," Molly grumbled.

"Because it is. No touching, but come stand beside her. The most she'll do is watch you or ruffle her wings a bit."

Molly hesitated. "Is that an order?"

"Yup."

Stupid royal protocol.

She sidled step by agonising step toward the bird, the wide inky eyes tracking each micro movement.

It's fine. It's fine. It's just a bird that can peck your eyes out before you can even take a breath.

"Does she have a name?" she whispered.

May shook her head. "She's new. Usually I say names until the birds respond, but we've been busy. Oooh!"

Molly cringed just beyond pecking distance, knowing what was coming.

"Why don't you try naming her?" May's eyes gleamed at the thought.

Molly had no idea what to name a bird. Scratch that, she knew enough not to name an entire species of bird the Greater Spotted Hump Warbler, but she drew a blank at individual bird names.

"Feather," she suggested.

"That's pathetic."

"Well I don't know, I'm too busy silently panicking about losing my eyeballs!"

She risked a glance at the bird and forced herself to keep looking. There was definitely intelligence in the inky eyes alongside the constant vigilant stare. The wings were hunched and powerful, gracefully so.

"If I don't look at the beak or the talons, I can almost convince myself she's not going to eat me."

"Keep going." May's tone turned gentle. "She needs a name."

"I'm hopeless at names. There was a mouse in my workshop once and I called it Mousie. I don't think this one will want to be called Birdie."

Molly flinched as the enormous beak clicked. She couldn't tell if that was approval, disgust or just a random noise.

"That was definitely a no." May chuckled. "She's

talking to you. It's just up to you whether you learn to listen, to understand her language."

Beak clicks mean no, great.

Molly dug deeper into her memories, trying to think of any stories she might have read about birds. She couldn't think of a single one, couldn't even imagine trying to name the bird after anyone she knew either.

"I can't think, I'm sorry."

She took a shuffling step away, failure curling tight in her chest. Before she could get away, the air gusted as the great wings stretched out and the bird landed. She stood frozen, tension tearing through her muscles.

"The bird is on me. May, the bird is on me, get her off."

May grinned. "No."

"Please get the bird off me."

"No, she likes you. Maybe don't name her straight away then, have a think."

"How do I get her off?"

Molly had no idea how her quaking body wasn't sending the bird fleeing up to the ceiling, or pecking her ear off, but if anything the bird seemed to be enjoying the vibrations. She squeaked as the bird nudged the enormous head against her temple.

"Raise your hand in front of you," May instructed.

Molly did as she was told, anything to get space. The bird hopped onto the side of her hand, the size of a small cat and yet somehow maintaining balance despite Molly's arm shaking like a branch in a hurricane.

From the front-on angle, Molly noticed a flash of electric sky among the darker green feathers under the wings.

"Aurora."

The name slipped out, a mere whisper, but the bird made a strange crooning noise and took flight. Molly ducked away, turning her head to make sure she hadn't somehow caused a great enough insult to get dive-bombed and pecked to death.

Before she could work out what was going on, Aurora wheeled under the ceiling and out of the enormous open window.

"Did I scare her off?" Molly asked, her heart pounding.

May grinned. "Nope. That little purring noise is positive. She'll likely be back with some kind of tiny gift for you. Might be a pebble, might be a frog. She's chosen you and you've named her so she's basically yours now. I'll get you some treats to keep in your pocket for her."

Molly stared in horror as May headed toward the bathroom and shut the door, the words tumbling from her lips instead of echoing in her head.

"I can't have a pet bird!"

CHAPTER TWENTY FOUR

Molly had somehow collected herself a pet bird. She didn't see Aurora again for the rest of the day, and managed to avoid Ru by feigning a stomach ache. She hid instead in the ridiculously opulent bedroom she now had next to May's, joined by an interconnecting door.

Worries raged as she struggled to sleep, about returning to the citadel, Ru's sudden cosy behaviour and the occasional slip into wondering what Sammy might be doing. She wanted to message Sammy and say she was going to the concert but she couldn't risk it. Nobody could know she was from the citadel, or even had any links there. As far as anyone could tell through her orb, she and Sammy had met through the Kayla Crane fan-site, and she needed to keep it that way.

Sleep finally showed up for duty somewhere in the deepest hours of the night, and she woke with the creeping notion that someone was watching her. Cracking one eye open, she managed to strangle the scream in her throat.

Aurora clicked her beak, the sound muffled. Molly inched her body upright and tried to shuffle back against the pillows without making any sudden movements, her gaze fixed on the beak, full of something that she couldn't make out.

"How did you get in?" she muttered, even as she risked a glance over her shoulder at the open window to find early morning light outside.

The queen's temper storm had settled and May wouldn't be up for hours yet, which left Molly with the morning to herself.

Aurora chirped something far too cheerful for the early hour and opened her beak. An acorn fell onto the bedcovers, the shell cracked enough to free a tiny, curling green shoot. When Molly didn't reach for it, Aurora lowered her head and nudged it forward with her beak.

"Is this for me? I can't believe I'm talking to a bird. Okay, please don't eat my fingers."

She inched her hand forward, ready for the bird to pounce. With a click of her beak, Aurora spread her wings and sailed out of the window.

Molly bit her lip, free to pick up the acorn but hesitating. May had mentioned Aurora bringing her a gift which meant Aurora had claimed her, whatever that meant.

If I accept this, does that mean I'm accepting her? Can I even refuse without her getting angry and eating me?

She nudged the acorn with the tip of her forefinger. It would be a shame to let it die, but she could take it down and plant it in one of the many pots of earth Alfie had outside the kitchen door.

She might get bored if I don't do anything entertaining with her.

Molly left the acorn on the bed as she washed and dressed for the day, her uniform taking on subtle hues of lilac. With the acorn in hand, she ambled along the hall and down the main staircase, keeping an eye out for Ru. May had insisted on taking Molly's orb details since the promotion and that she'd message when she was ready for her breakfast, so Molly took that as an order and wouldn't question her morning of freedom any deeper.

She slipped into the kitchen, breathing in the fresh bread scent and the overall warmth from both the cavernous ovens on the far wall and the sunlight shining in through the open back door. A clang near the ovens caught her attention and she smiled to see Alfie's hands whizzing back and forth between bubbling pans.

"Morning, *offke*'s on," Alfie announced without looking.

Molly grinned. "Thank Faerie for that. Can I use one of your dirt pots?"

Alfie gasped, spinning with one hand to his broad chest.

"My *special* pots of dirt? Of course you can." His keen gaze dropped to her hand. "Oh, an acorn, very fitting for the court."

Molly nodded and headed toward the open back door. Several pots of dirt were lined up along the wall outside, but she had no idea what Alfie actually kept them for.

She picked a terracotta pot and crouched down to push her acorn into the earth. With no clue if it would even grow, she wrote '*Molly's acorn*' on one of the little wooden sticks Alfie used for labels and pressed it into the dirt. It might grow and she could take it back to the workshop one day, or plant it in the park for everyone to enjoy. She used the wall to steady herself to her feet and went inside to the butler sink in the far corner to wash her hands.

A cup of *offke* thudded beside her, Alfie grinning above it.

"I'll have the pot taken up to your fancy new lodgings," he said with a wink. "Climbing the social ladder has its perks."

Molly pulled a face. "I don't know about that. The room is nice but it's almost too big. The shadows reach a long way out of the corners even though there's hardly any furniture. Then Ma- the princess has me in some kind of aversion therapy program to get over my fear of birds."

Alfie chortled, sipping from his own mug. It amazed her that he was only a few years older than her, mid-twenties at the most, yet in charge of an entire palace kitchen.

"She's a good soul, mostly, as much as Fae royalty can be. She hasn't done anything to overtly torment you either, which is somewhat astonishing."

"Maybe so, but now one of her confounded animals has 'chosen' me apparently."

"Ah, that'd be the acorn as a gift, would it?"

She nodded. "I figured accepting it would stop me from having my eyes pecked out."

"What kind of bird?"

"Umm… a hump spotted something? Warbler?"

Alfie frowned. "A Greater Spotted Hump Warbler?"

Molly choked over a laugh and took a huge gulp of her drink instead. She wanted to access the library and find out the name of the Fae who had come up with such a mad choice.

"That's the one. Her highness forced me to hold her, then to name her, and next thing I'm waking up with her dropping an acorn on my bed. The bird, not the princess."

Alfie left her side and she drained her mug, conscious she was keeping him from his work. She half expected Ru to appear the moment Alfie was out of sight in some storage room nearby, but when he didn't she went to wash her mug and leave it on the side.

"Here." Alfie reappeared with a clothbound blue book in hand. "Some birds are birds and others are, well, *other* birds. Borrow it, but I'd like it back please."

Molly took the book with both hands. "Thank you, I'll take good care of it."

Alfie patted her arm softly and moved off to clang some pots and pans at the other end of the kitchen, but Molly hovered in the kitchen, flipping open the cover of the book. She could read the section on Great Warbling Humped Spotter or whatever it was called, then give the book straight back to him.

A soft burn against her thigh had her reaching into her pocket and pulling out her orb. It was the highlight of her day often to get a message. She smiled to see Sammy's name flash up, then a message to scroll across the surface from the Kayla Crane fan site forum.

Sammy: *I'm going to escape while Talie is out tomorrow and see if I can get near the stage entrance to see Kayla! It's right down the bottom of the levels apparently, but how far can forty or so levels really be?*

Molly grinned, fully able to imagine it. It wasn't exactly forty levels from what she'd heard, but Sammy would need to grab a passing cart or it probably would take her all night just to get down there. Lifting the orb to her lips, she murmured her reply.

"Because Talie wouldn't go totally mad and threaten to tie you in your room for the rest of your life if she found out."

She barely even had to wait before the reply appeared.

Sammy: *How would she find out? I'm so sulky you can't be here to sneak in with me.*

Molly smiled. She wouldn't have done it anyway, mainly because it might put her situation with the Menagerie in danger and, much like Talie, she often had work to do during the night.

"Who's Sammy?"

Molly flinched and almost dropped her orb. Shoving it into her pocket, she lifted her head with panic thundering through her.

"I- you- you're supposed to tell me when you're awake!"

May grinned, folding her arms across her chest. The hints of tattoo were visible under her body glamour, suggesting she had no real fear of having to mask in front of Alfie or his staff.

"No point, I was up already. Who's Sammy?"

Molly's insides froze over. "Um, a friend. If you want me to get your breakfast and bring-"

"How is she getting in to see Kayla?"

Molly raced mentally through her messages, realising that May must have been hovering right after Alfie gave her the book.

Unless she can make herself invisible, which would be really inconvenient for passing information to Ru.

She wasn't even sure how Ru was reporting back to Marcus without getting caught, but the less she knew the safer she was.

"She… I talk to her through the Kayla Crane fan-site. I don't know how she's getting there but I don't think she has an actual ticket. She just wants to get a glimpse of her I think."

Avoiding lies wasn't something she usually had to worry about. Working for the Menagerie at night, all she had to do was watch and report back, at least until recently. Working in her workshop during the day, her skill did most of the talking for her.

I talk to her through the site because right now I do. I don't know how she's getting there, because for all I know she might hop a lift on a passing cart or walk. I don't think she has an actual ticket, that one's true enough.

May's nose wrinkled. "But she's your friend?"

"I… yeah, we're both Kayla Crane fans."

"That's settled then." May's expression brightened instantly. "If I bring back information from someone in the citadel itself, Mother may actually start taking me seriously. Invite your friend to accompany us."

Molly's jaw dropped. She couldn't think of a single reason not to, but having May and Sammy anywhere near each other was going to cause absolute chaos.

She couldn't refuse either, the demand clear in May's tone and the sharp gaze still fixed on her expectantly. Lifting her orb closer to her face, she sought for the best way to explain without actually explaining. Knowing her luck, Sammy would orb her screaming.

"Hi Sammy, I'm actually going to the Kayla Crane concert tonight in the Faerie citadel, and the person I'm going with asked if I wanted to invite you. I know you'll need to check with Talie, and she probably won't agree to you going, but let me know either way."

Determination rising, Molly shoved her orb back in her pocket without waiting for an answer. She eyed May with a firm look instead, ignoring the burn of the instant reply against her thigh.

"Right, breakfast while we wait," she said, keeping everything vague. "Alfie!"

He reappeared like magic with a tray laden full of food for May and an apologetic glance for her.

"Breakfast fit for a princess. Molly, Ru was looking for you."

Molly gleaned his attempt to help her in the vagueness of his wording, because at some point since they had arrived Ru would have been looking for her, even if it was days and days ago. She shot him a grateful smile as he set the tray down at a chair and flourished a napkin, waiting for May to sit.

"Go see what he wants," May said grudgingly. "Then come straight back. We need to get our outfits sorted."

Molly held in her groan, nodding instead and hurrying

out of the room. She would make a half-arsed attempt to find Ru, then circle back to May.

Before she could pull out her orb to check Sammy's no doubt ecstatic message, Alfie caught up to her.

"Figured you'd be safest taking a few minutes," he said. "I still can't guarantee the food if you share it either, although I won't say any more."

He held up an enormous pastry with oozing purple jam. Molly grabbed it from him and took a grateful bite, closing her eyes happily.

"Thank you," she mumbled through her mouthful. "If I survive this, I owe you one."

He grinned. "You'll survive this, if only so I can hold you to that."

CHAPTER TWENTY FIVE

Molly did her best not to hyperventilate as they stepped into Lavender's rickshaw to realm-skip right into the citadel. She dug her fingernails into her palms, tense beneath the long black skirt with a slit up the side and a sparkly purple top that showed off her bare arms. Suitably understated yet elegant, coordinated to show off May as the real star of the show in her shorter purple skirt and floaty-sleeved shirt, her golden hair braided into a crown. Molly kept glancing at her wrist, but the Menagerie tattoo was still firmly glamoured out of sight.

"Your friend is meeting us at the entrance, yes?" May asked.

Molly nodded. "Once you're with your brother and the queen, I'll run out with the tickets and fetch her. Thank you again for letting her come. She's an even bigger fan than I am."

"I can't imagine not being able to access these things, but there have been occasions where mother hasn't let me go. I know what it's like to miss out."

Molly kept her lips buttoned about how woefully unimpressive May's misfortunes would seem compared to Sammy's as Lavender started forward and the purple-grey swirl of the nether folded around them.

"Here we are," Lavender announced as the rickshaw slid to a smooth halt.

With the swirl of nether still wisping away, Molly shuffled out of the rickshaw and looked around at the citadel arena, amazed at the sheer size of the place. They were inside already, no doubt due to May's status, the stone floor underfoot laid with dark red runners. Flames blazed in brackets on the walls, and servants in fancy suits stood at regular intervals, holding bottles of water and wine with trays of glasses ready.

A soft breeze drifted down from above and Molly stared through the nearest open archway in awe. Even though the citadel was vast in width and length on each level, the enormous open-air arena actually looked out onto the realm itself, to the forest and the sun still setting on the horizon beyond.

I'm on the most prestigious level of the entire citadel. It doesn't get lower than this.

Dropping her head back, she stared up at the citadel itself, the towering structure of glass disappearing into the clouds.

"Does your friend have far to come?" May asked.

Molly didn't want to think about how many levels Sammy would have to descend to get this far down, or how many she'd have to run back up to get home before Talie found out, because of course Sammy likely wouldn't have told her.

Unable to answer without being too honest, Molly shrugged and glanced toward the circular stands above that were now filling with Fae. The covered ground level boxes were in front of them, the only block between where they stood and the stage itself.

"Let me go and get her," she said.

May nodded, holding out two sturdy card tickets hooked onto lanyards woven with threads of gold. Molly slipped one over her head, clutching the other tight in her hand as Demi and Taz approached.

"Hiya." Demi grinned. "We have a box right up front. Shocker."

May laughed but Molly was too busy processing that the Holly Queen of Faerie was in smart jeans, a glimmering red and silver off-the-shoulder sweatshirt and a shining pair of heavy duty boots.

Catching Molly staring, Taz laughed.

"Start ruling as you mean to go on," he explained.

Molly's cheeks burned but she managed a shy smile before giving May a hesitant look.

"Go." May waved her hand in the air, a flicker of tattoos visible on her forearm. "I'm beyond boringly safe now."

Molly hurried toward the entrance, wondering how much time she'd have to warn Sammy of the particulars. She didn't dare send messages via orb in case the Menagerie really did have the ability to monitor orb-waves inside the glass, and May had refused to let her out of sight after she returned at breakfast.

"Molly!"

Sammy didn't wave as she approached, although her bright purple dress would have been visible enough from the very top of the citadel on a clear day.

Molly tensed, bracing herself as Sammy cannoned into her instead and hugged her to death.

"Cnt brth!" Molly gasped.

Sammy laughed. "Sorry. It feels like forever. I had to wait until Talie was out and catch the edge of a cart coming down. My feet are killing me already."

Molly eyed the uneven splash of purple on Sammy's shoes, the fabric parts painted stiff and the canvas parts already flaking.

"Before we go in, I need to ask you something."

Sammy slid her arm through Molly's, clutching tight.

"Say no more. You and Talie dancing around each other before taught me one thing, and that's that you're as involved in dark corners as she is. I don't ask. I don't tell. I can word-tangle quickly enough with the best of them. I'm going to owe you for the rest of my life for tonight, so don't worry."

Touched, Molly risked a smile.

"Okay, but the people we're with are really high profile. They can't know I've ever been here. They think we met on the fan-site."

"Not a word." Sammy tapped her lips with her finger. "I can be high profile when I want to be."

Molly grimaced. "Hold that thought then."

She steered Sammy through the nobles milling about, not comforted by the goggling Sammy did as they passed. By the time they reached May, already seated with Demi and Taz, Sammy's arm had gone rigid around hers.

Two new faces turned to look their way, a handsome brown-haired man in artfully torn black jeans and a leather jacket, and an even more beautiful blonde woman sitting beside him. The woman straightened her Kayla Crane t-shirt with a smile as Demi waved a hand in their direction.

"Kainen and Reyan, Lord and Lady of the Illusion Court, friends of ours."

Molly dipped her head in their direction, unlike Sammy who almost hauled her to the floor as she bowed low.

"Hi, you must be Molly's friend," May said. "Come and sit down."

Sammy froze for several moments. Then she bobbed a low curtsey and sidled into the closest chair, all but forcing Molly down between her and the others.

"This is Sammy," Molly said. "I'm sure their majesties and her highness need no introduction."

Demi pulled a face. "Orbs, drop the honorifics, please. Don't make me force you. Tonight we're just people. I'm Demi, this is Taz, and that's May."

Sammy nodded, her eyes wide and her jaw slack.

"So, is this how you know Molly, Sammy?" May asked.

Molly sought for a suitable answer but Sammy cleared her throat first.

"On the Kayla Crane fan-site? We talk on there all the time. I never imagined I'd have the chance to see her live though. I can't thank you enough."

May smiled. "It's no trouble for a friend of Molly's. Do you live in the citadel?"

"Yes, not as far down as some, but further up than others. I'm still in school for another thirty-five days, but I plan to perform when I leave. I had my first show at our school a few days ago and I think it went well."

"You said they begged you to come back," Molly said loyally.

Sammy smiled. "Maybe one day you'll be able to come and see."

Molly nodded, glad for Sammy's arm wound firmly around hers still. She gave it a squeeze, flinching when May leaned over and linked with her free arm, a firm smile fixed on her face. Stuck between the two of them, Molly looked at the stage instead, perplexed that May seemed to be possessive over her now that she had a friend.

"Ooh, try some oia berry sweets." Demi stood up and approached with a large bowl in hand. "Take a couple of handfuls."

As May reached out, her arm slid from Molly's. Sammy did the same, her eyes lighting up, and Molly couldn't smother a smile as Demi caught her eye and winked. Nothing was said about Sammy not so discreetly slipping a couple of handfuls into the pockets of her dress either.

"Finally," Taz grumbled as the lights dimmed. "Enjoy this, everyone."

Molly's quiet thank-you was lost in the sudden swell of music, everyone leaping to their feet as the lights flashed on the stage and Kayla Crane strode out, hollering a greeting.

She launched into *Strike It Lucky* and Molly forgot who she was with, and the wider truth of where she was, grinning with both May and Sammy as they sang along together.

"We'll be able to meet her after the performance," May shouted above the music. "She's meant to be genuinely nice."

For some reason, being suitably obedient around royalty was one thing but meeting a star like Kayla Crane was another level entirely. Given the wide-eyed shock on Sammy's face, she was feeling the same.

By the time Kayla moved onto *Shine Something Sunny*, her first hit song that won her *Siren-Sing-Along* season one, Molly's mind wandered upwards. Several levels above was her workshop, the familiar lanes she'd grown up on, and the faces she was used to passing daily. She missed it, able to pass off the occasional ache in her chest at the thought when she was busy at the Oak Queen's court.

Maybe May will let me come back to visit Sammy. I could sneak back to the workshop.

She almost missed a jarring note in the song, but May stiffened beside her. Turning her head, she noticed the queen and king consort already alert, twisting back and forth. On their far side, the Lord and Lady of Illusions were on their feet.

A scream echoed in the crowd and the music faltered, the musicians on stage tailing off mid-song. Figures in dark hoods swarmed the crowds on all levels, the flash and spark of gifts hitting wardings lighting up the darkness.

Burly figures burst on stage toward Kayla and the band flocked from their instruments to stand with her as security swept them out of sight.

"What's the plan?" Taz asked, his expression grim.

Demi shrugged. "Defend. You take everyone home."

"I'm not leaving you, don't even try it."

"*So* not the time right now."

May rolled her eyes, her lips twisting over words that Molly couldn't make out. She reached for her, determined not to let May disappear without her and torn at the thought of leaving Sammy behind.

Then May vanished.

"Whoa, cool!" Sammy breathed, already holding onto Molly's arm again.

Taz cursed under his breath.

"Typical. Right, give me two seconds and I'll get someone to take you home, Sammy. Then Molly, we'll drop you back at court."

Molly bit her lip. It was well-known that realm-skipping in and out of the citadel was impossible without using a monitored skip-way, so May was either all-powerful, or she was invisible somewhere nearby.

A figure burst onto the stage, the crackle and whine of the microphone in his hand echoing over the chaos.

"My friends!" The voice was masculine, strident and full of amusement. "I doubt any of you will be well-travelled enough outside the confines of your vast wealth to know the reality of those around you. We have come to disabuse you of that arrogance, which is the product of your gross entitlement."

Even Demi and Taz were watching the man speak, their attention utterly diverted. Molly inched her arm away from Sammy's. She didn't have her usual spying coat with the big hood to hide her, but nobody twitched a single muscle in her direction as she tiptoed out of the royal box and toward the stage.

She kept to the shadows and crept closer. Marcus

wouldn't like a scandal to reach the wider realms of Faerie and draw attention on the citadel, so he would have many minions trained to de-escalate any situation bursting in any moment now.

"There are Fae starving on the higher levels," the man crowed. "Yet you sit here in excess. Watch your backs, ladies and lords."

Even as she reached the stage, she could see the spot of solid darkness amid the gloom off to the far side, a figure in hiding ready to strike. Whoever they were raised their arm, a sliver of glinting metal that caught the light pinched between their fingers.

Molly's chest twisted tight as she recognised the type of dart pipe. She'd seen a couple of people from the Menagerie practicing with them once. Crashing a concert and causing chaos might be against the order of things, but the dart the assassin was holding likely wouldn't be coated with something to tranquilise.

Death isn't right.

She bit her lip and continued along the edge of the stage, obscured from view as the man still speaking stared upward instead of down. Unsure of what she could even do without risking the Menagerie's wrath or the potential anger of whoever the assassin was, she got close enough to see the outline of the legs and the boots, the rest obscured by a hooded cloak.

All except for the arm, a length of bare skin covered only by a ribbon.

A purple hair-ribbon with what looked like acorns on it.

CHAPTER TWENTY SIX

Molly's insides rippled with icy fear as she stared at the ribbon around the assassin's wrist. Ru had promised her long ago that he didn't kill. Even as his arm lifted, ready to blow the dart, she couldn't let herself believe it.

The dart left the pipe. Molly watched it, stunned into inaction even as her pulse pounded and her thoughts raged at her to do something, anything.

The man flinched as the dart found its mark, lifting one hand to his neck. He pulled his fingers to his face next, sniffing until his eyes widened.

"I need to… be quick," he choked. "I've been pois-pois-hit with- *goberia*."

His voice faltered, his face contorting as he spluttered over the bubbles of foam flecking his lips. Molly watched, helpless. No sense turning her head either; Ru would be long gone.

Chaos regained control, nobles rushing like untamed beasts for their carriages, a melee of swishing skirts and sharp elbows, their gifts splaying out to clear their path indiscriminately.

The royal box was empty, no sign of the queen, the king consort or even Sammy.

Molly broke into a run, dodging through the crowds. She had to trust they would get Sammy home safe as promised, and that May really was smart enough to wander around invisibly unchaperoned.

How do I get back to the queen's court from here?

She dashed out of the arena and toward the lanes leading up, reaching out to grab the corner of a cart rumbling past. Securing her foot against the axle spoke, she clung on, her mind racing even faster than the nobles rushing around them.

Sammy would be safe, but May was most likely wandering around the citadel completely invisible. If the royals left without her, May might end up becoming a spoil of war, some kind of hostage. After what had happened with Marcus wanting to make an example of Talie a few months ago, then Ru turning out to be-

Maybe there's something I'm missing. She grimaced. *There has to be something I'm missing. Ru can't be a killer.*

She dropped to the ground with the thud jarring up her legs and through her hips as the cart slowed, intending to sprint on a bit further and catch another. The Menagerie would have given the royals access to realm-skip in directly but the moment the commotion started, they would have locked down the entire citadel to traffic in or out. Whether Demi had strings she could pull with Faerie itself, Molly didn't know, but she was going to reach the nearest skip-way as soon as she stopped off at her workshop.

She eyed a passing cart going up and lifted her hand to catch the side. Rough wood skimmed her fingertips but tightness banded around her wrist before she could grab hold. She struggled as someone pulled her hand away, an arm coming around her chest to pin her from fighting back.

"Easy now, it's only me."

Molly stopped struggling but stayed tense, her senses firing. She twisted slowly until the arms let go of her and she came face to face with Celeste.

"We must talk quickly," Celeste murmured, her voice almost lost in the rattle of passing carts. "What news?"

Molly hesitated. "I don't know what Ru's already told you."

"Next to nothing of use, save what you found in the book. Are there any signs of the queens planning to invade?"

"No." Molly shook her head, glancing around out of habit. "They're worried the citadel is going to attack first. The queen and king consort were here to make sure there were no rumblings of dissent against them."

It was true enough, at least that she knew of. Celeste sighed, her shoulders lowering.

"And the Oak Queen? Ru's reports say she is stewing and doing not much at all."

Molly shrugged. "I haven't seen much of her."

"But you have been spending time with the young princess?" Celeste's lips lifted. "A worthy promotion from bin duty."

Molly didn't have to ask how Celeste knew, her mind swirling instead back to Ru and the inescapable matter of her hair ribbon on the assassin's wrist. Even though there could be many like it in Faerie, a sixth sense told her there were unlikely to be many among the Menagerie assassins considering most never even left the citadel.

"The Oak Queen clearly has less of her former strength than anyone could have assumed," Celeste continued, pursing her lips. "Perhaps your skills would be better set by returning to the citadel. We have the information from the book but now we need all eyes on the enemy, and you already know one of them."

"Talie and I aren't exactly best mates though. She isn't going to tell me anything."

Celeste glanced around at the crowds still heaving past them.

"It's still an access point we need to keep open," she insisted. "They hide in shadowed corners under plain names and menial jobs, and there are far too many scurrying about to track them all. We have limited resources as it is, but a few leads have still led us back to your friend."

"I doubt she'd be mad enough to keep..." Molly couldn't finish without lying.

Celeste's face lit up with amusement. "You and I both know she went right back to her little tricks the moment you left for court. None we could trace, but nights out, disappearances seemingly into nothing."

"You're having her followed?"

"Of course, but she's illusive. I don't expect you to infiltrate them, don't worry. It would be far too dangerous."

As dangerous as turning Ru into a killer? Molly shuddered.

"They will make a mistake eventually," Celeste continued. "Arrogance will drive them to underestimate us eventually, and when that time comes we'll see exactly what they're capable of. Their little stunt at the concert tonight proved that."

How did she know so quickly, unless she was there?

"You think the man tonight on the stage was one of them?" she clarified.

"Yes, and it shows they're finally getting bolder, but we need to see their full strength so we can best it and bring an end to their disturbances."

Molly glanced around again, for all the realm looking like a vigilant spy when all she could think about was making more frantic moments to think clearly.

"The queen and her entourage have already left the citadel," Celeste added. "You've obtained the information from the book, so it would be pointless now to spend time sending you back."

Molly froze. She had expected the royals to leave her behind if they couldn't find her, but she had no idea if May was still wandering around invisible or safely back at court. She couldn't guarantee they'd been able to see Sammy safely home either, and her chest twisted at the thought of Sammy being taken with them away from Talie, or worse. She looked at Celeste and calculated how likely it was that she could get away with a quick burst of her compulsion gift, just this once.

"It might be best for you to turn in your orb as well, for your own safety," Celeste added. "Now it's been used at the queen's court, it could have picked things up or been targeted.”

Molly lowered her hand to her pocket instinctively but forced it to still at her side, her skin flushing with anger. The Menagerie wouldn’t find anything on her orb that could upset them, but it was hers. She’d worked hard to earn it too and they weren’t cheap to come by.

“I don’t think leaving me without any means of communication is a good idea,” she tried, pulling every essence of her charm gift to the fore. “I’ll be ever so careful and only use it for emergencies.”

Celeste tilted her head and Molly focused on the strands of her compulsion gift. She didn’t want to use it, but if Celeste took her orb, she wouldn’t have any way of letting May know she was safe, or that she wasn’t coming back.

At least if I don’t go back, I won’t have to be on bird duty anymore.

The hysterical thought didn’t give her the comfort she expected, the image of Aurora fluttering around her room and the little acorn growing outside Alfie’s kitchen filling her head.

“What about Ru?” she asked instead.

Celeste frowned. “Ru? I suppose there’s little sense him staying either.”

“Will you call him back then?” Molly asked, keeping her voice level. “He was still there when I left with the princess earlier.”

If Celeste heard the subtle distrust in her tone, she didn’t let on.

“Never mind Ru now,” she said. “Marcus will handle his duties. Take tonight to rest and come see me in the morning. You've gained our trust, and I think it's only fair that you're given an increase in your salary."

Molly bit her lip. She couldn't lie that more money would be cool, but she would probably skim by on her workshop efforts alone. The mention of a salary was purely code, a reminder that she was already in debt to the Menagerie for what had happened in her past. Their taking her in when her guardians died was still shrouded in mystery that they wouldn't reveal to her, but one thing everyone had agreed on was that she owed them.

Staying here means I can keep an eye on what's happening though. Maybe if I hound her enough, Talie will tell me what's going on instead.

She ignored the subtle flutter in her gut at the thought and wiped a hand over her face.

"Maybe that's sensible," she muttered. "If May and the others are back in their courts, and I don't have any way back, then I have no choice."

Celeste sighed. "We always have a choice, my dear. Make sure yours is the right one. Give me your hand."

Molly extended her hand automatically, and Celeste passed her fingers over Molly's wrist. In that simple movement, she removed the glamour on Molly's Menagerie tattoo.

And now I can't return to the queen's court without risking them knowing who I am.

Celeste stepped back and walked off down the lane without another word, leaving Molly to stare out at the passing carts without seeing them. Any one of them would have taken her upwards, but she stood at the side of the lane instead, stuck.

She was once again at the mercy of her own effort and had nobody to rely on but herself, as it always had been.

Except for Ru. I used to be able to rely on him.

Questions that had been infuriatingly absent when she had Celeste in front of her whirled in her mind, like how Celeste had been able to send them into the queen's court in the first place, and why Ru was sent to kill the man instead of hauling him in for interrogation.

She said to go and see her tomorrow. If I play it softly enough, I can at least ask.

She lifted her head and reached out a hand, snagging the edge of a passing cart. With a grunt against the speed of it, she hauled herself onto the side, her feet settling on the edge of the base.

Ru would find her, she was sure of it. If he couldn't find her in the arena or among the royals, he would go to her workshop next. She had questions for him, and it was that sudden simmering fire inside her that kept her moving from cart to cart until she stood in the middle of a familiar lane, her heart aching with relief at being home.

She walked down the lane, keeping to the shadows. Tomorrow she would say hi to Beryl and Harvey, see if Beryl had had the baby yet, but tonight she couldn't deal with their dramatics. With her key around her neck, she slid it into the lock and eased the door open. The scent of dust tickled her nose, but she shut the door behind her before turning on the lamp and squishing her nose between finger and thumb to ward off a loud sneeze.

She strode to the back of the workshop, the

overwhelming swell of being home making her queasy, and rifled through the detritus on the kitchen counter for some leftover *offke*.

"It's here somewhere," she muttered.

A loud creak of the hinges had her freezing in place. Steeling herself, even though her anger was laced with fear, she straightened up and faced the doorway with her arms folded.

"Thank Faerie you're okay." Ru hurried forward but stopped in front of her as he caught sight of her expression. "Molly?"

Her gaze flickered down to the purple ribbon adorned with acorns, still very much telling on him from its place around his wrist.

"Just got here, did you?" she asked.

He hesitated. "This evening? Of course."

"No. Right now. Right this second. Tell me that you haven't been anywhere near the base level arena tonight."

He grimaced and she had her answer. Trepidation pounded like drums in her head as she whirled away from him, her mind racing.

If I keep being angry, I can get to the door.

In having her fears confirmed, the sinking realisation that Ru had killed someone, no doubt on the Menagerie's orders, made him someone she couldn't trust.

"We said no killing," she mumbled.

He rubbed a hand over his face with a loud sigh.

"It was just the once," he insisted. "Marcus said so. That man was too dangerous to be kept alive and he had ways of hiding himself. We'd never have found him again until he chose to pop up to spill more vitriol."

"And you believed Marcus won't ask you to do it again? How long before he changes his mind? It's… it doesn't matter if it's one or one hundred people!"

Ru nodded. "I know, I know, but I had to. You don't understand-"

"I understand plenty. I can't even look at you right now."

"Molly-"

"Get out."

She refused to turn her head toward him, pointing to the open doorway even as she prepared to sprint toward it. Beryl might be able to scare him off, or she could disappear into the upper levels quicker than he could follow.

"This doesn't change anything," he pleaded.

"It changes *everything*." She finally lifted her gaze to his, torn, broken by the truth. "After what happened with my guardians? After you promised me that was one line we'd never cross? Leave me alone, Ru."

He took a sharp breath and a step toward her. She flinched around her desk, ready to flee.

"I heard raised voices."

Molly squeaked in alarm as May materialised inside the doorway. Unsure of how much she'd heard, Molly dodged toward her. In that moment of chaos, Ru's eyes narrowed and Molly made her choice.

"You should be back at court with your brother!" she insisted.

May rolled her eyes. "Oh that? I sent a decoy of myself home with them. They can glamour as me well enough until I'm ready to go home."

She pulled off a fine silver cloak, her bare arms merrily displaying more swirls and images than Molly had ever seen. But despite her relaxed stance, May's eyes were full of cold malice.

Molly sighed. "So, you're probably wondering, um…"

She had no idea what to say and warded herself on instinct as Ru took a step toward her. He brushed the edge of it and backed off, hurt filtering over his face.

"Why not tell me the truth?" May suggested.

Molly nodded. "I'm from the citadel. I can't really tell you much more than that, although I wish I could, believe me. I really did like my role at court though, and I definitely don't want anything bad to happen to anyone there, or your family."

May eyed her for a long moment before shrugging.

"All sorts end up at mother's court with stories they choose not to tell." She snorted, leaning over to pick up one of the orb chains Molly made from the basket near the door. "I figured there was something 'other' about you when you both arrived at the same time with odd stories."

Molly had no idea what story had been given, and while the queen had interrogated them both on arrival, nobody had mentioned her background or her past since.

May's face lit up with devilish amusement, her gaze flicking to Ru next.

"I tend to wander around incognito a lot, so I've seen you muttering into your orb at all intervals." She nodded in his direction. "I admit I take a tragic amount of interest in court gossip though, and I thought you might be playing away on Molly at first. Sadly, none of the conversations were remotely amorous, all in some kind of weird conversational code."

Molly hoped May had the sense to ward herself as Ru's eyes flashed with anger.

"You listened to all my conversations then, Princess?" he asked, the title dripping from his lips with uncharacteristic venom.

Orbs, if he tries to hurt her, or turn her in to Marcus...

She couldn't even bear to finish the thought, moving to May's side with her warding tight around her.

"Do you know how you're getting back?" she asked, glancing desperately around her workshop. "I doubt you'll be wanting to bunk here with me."

May frowned. "You're staying behind then?"

"I... don't know yet."

It was as honest an answer as she could give. Whatever the Menagerie were up to, she wouldn't find out at the queen's court.

"This is my home," she added. "If people are making chaos, I want to find out who and why, and make it stop."

She expected some kind of derision but despite Ru's weary huff, May nodded.

"I get that. Don't worry about me though. I have my ways home, and I can send you confirmation that I've made it safely if you like."

Molly nodded, a faint smile making it through the panic burning through her gut.

"It's been great working for you. You're the coolest of princesses."

May laughed. "Thank you. It's like that rhyme Demi once told me that she always thinks of about us, something about us being like some old human king's wives, estranged, defected, died, estranged, defected, and still trying desperately to run away."

"Which one are you then?"

"The last one sadly." May pulled a face. "My eldest sister abdicated and we haven't heard from her since. My sister Belladonna is in the forever mountains as a traitor. Blossom died. Rose refuses to talk to anyone so she's basically might as well be estranged, very obsessed with animals. Taz married Demi and defected to her court. Then there's me."

"Your mo- the queen hasn't taken any of that well I'm guessing."

May grinned. "Does it look like she has? You've met her. That's why I want to escape. Being her last chance at phony redemption is exhausting."

Before Molly could reply, Ru stalked toward them. She slid out of the way but May made a point of blocking the doorway and locking eyes with him for several charged seconds before moving aside.

Molly noted the fierce clench of Ru's jaw as he powered out. He only made it two paces before staggering back, his face a picture of fury.

"Molly!"

Sammy threw herself past May and Ru, arms outstretched. Molly almost didn't brace her balance in time and stumbled several steps backwards as Sammy's arms wrapped around her neck.

"I… er…"

She looked past Sammy and her insides… she wasn't sure what they did but it was extremely unnerving, something between a squelch and a flare of sparks that giggled right through to her bones.

Talie stared back at her, and she definitely did not look like any part of her was even remotely giggling.

CHAPTER TWENTY SEVEN

Talie's radiating gaze left Molly's insides churning as she eyed May up and down next, probably without the faintest idea who she was, unless Sammy had been given a chance to babble on their way to the workshop. Then she flicked a dismissive glance at Ru before meeting Molly's eyes again.

Molly wished her cheeks wouldn't burn so obviously, but she couldn't help that as Sammy let her go.

"I was so worried when you ran off!" Sammy huffed. "Don't do it again."

Molly had the strange urge to laugh, but Ru turned to face her before it could bubble free.

"Don't leave the workshop until I get back," he warned.

Talie snorted. "What are you, her keeper?"

Molly brushed a cold hand over her burning cheeks. She hadn't heard Talie's voice for months, no less soft and low for the harsh or glib words she always said.

Ru scowled. "No, I'm her-"

"Friend." The word leapt from Molly's lips, embarrassment searing through her as she announced it so bluntly in front of everyone else. "And I'll be quite happy not having any of those if people keep barging in unannounced."

She grabbed the first thing on her desk in one hand, a miniature clock stand, and the completely wrong screwdriver in the other. She couldn't look at Ru, even though he stood there in the excruciating silence for several moments before storming out and slamming the workshop door behind him.

"Well." Even Sammy seemed to struggle. "That no friends thing doesn't apply to me, I take it."

"Or me," May added, giving Sammy a bratty look.

Talie shifted her feet. "I'd have very little interest in friendship."

Molly bit her lip. She already knew deep down she wasn't going back to the court with May. As much as she'd have enjoyed longer there, her place was in the citadel, defending her home. If the Menagerie were the ones causing trouble, she'd find out. If they were the ones defending the place, she'd do her best to help them.

Ru I can't decide on so easily.

"It's been a long day," she said eventually.

May nodded. "It has. Great fun. I'll let you know when I've got home safely, Molly. If you do ever get a chance to leave the fortress of glass, come back to court. You won't have to serve or anything."

"Oh, you can't." Molly grimaced. "I… my orb… you won't be able to reach it."

She couldn't explain that staying meant she would have to turn it into Celeste, but she didn't want May giving the Menagerie any accidental fuel if they were the ones setting the citadel's chaos fires.

May shrugged. "No problem, I have my ways. You're on my radar now, honey."

Talie's eyebrows lifted the tiniest amount, her expression clouding as she looked at Sammy, who busied herself far too studiously with a random pile of screws Molly had left on her desk.

Amused, Molly let May hug her much more elegantly than Sammy had, then stood at the door to see her disappear halfway down the lane, then disappear entirely.

"Wotcha, Molly!"

Harvey strolled past with his hands in his pockets before she could shut the door, tired rings around his eyes.

"Hi, Harvey. Any sign of baby yet?"

He shook his head. "Nope. Beryl and her sisters are threatening to smoke it out. I'm off to buy some *offke* in the hope it will wash the poor kid out."

Poor Beryl. Poor Harvey.

Molly smothered a hysterical bark of laughter and stepped back into her workshop.

She'd chased off Ru and seen off May. Now she just had to get rid of Talie and Sammy without being rude. Given the fury massing on Talie's face, it wasn't going to be easy.

"Talk," Talie barked. "You wanted to come and find Molly before telling me anything and there she is, so start talking. Now."

Sammy hesitated. "Well… I told you already. Molly and I have been messaging. You knew that. She said she had a spare ticket for the concert and I can't not go. *It's Kayla Crane.*"

Still jittery from all the panic and mayhem, Molly settled her shaking hands on her desk and focused on fighting the urge to smile. Something about Sammy and Talie's behaviour seemed so familiar somehow that it was the exact comfort she needed.

"You snuck out without telling me." Talie raised a hand and ticked off on her fingers. "You went all the way down to the base level of all places, by cart with Faerie knows who. You went into a concert, with royalty, wearing *that*."

"What's wrong with this?!"

"It's practically neon. And short, way too short."

"It's fashion, actually, and if you paid attention when I talk to you-"

"Don't try to distract me," Talie demanded. "I come home to find the place empty, then the freaking queen of Faerie is walking into our room to drop you home. How do you think that looks?"

Sammy shrugged. "Like she's probably someone who hasn't been raised with a silver spoon shoved in her gob. I like her. She let me call her Demi."

"Do not go around calling the queen by her name."

"You can't tell me what to do."

Molly pressed her forefinger and thumb either side of her eyes and squeezed tight.

"Is this something you two could do at home? I have stuff I need to think about."

Sammy glanced between her and Talie, craftiness lighting in her eyes. Molly groaned quietly in anticipation before Sammy even got a word out.

"It's not that late and Molly's barely eaten. I'm going

for food. You two stay and chat."

Talie opened her mouth to argue but Sammy shot past her and out of the workshop, the yell about having enough pesanas drifting in her wake.

Silence descended and Molly's nerves began to knot.

"We don't have to chat," she offered.

Talie frowned. "What did you end up doing at the court with the princess then?"

On anyone else, it would have sounded like jealousy. From Talie it was curiosity veiled as suspicion drowning in scathing dismissiveness.

"Working. Taking the bins out for a long while, then as Princess Mayflower's personal maid. Well, for all of about two weeks."

Talie's lips twitched. "That bad at it, were you?"

"Probably. We came to the concert and chaos broke out, then I decided to stay here rather than go back to the court."

"Because of your 'friend'?" Talie couldn't hide the subtle sneer in her tone.

"No. I get the feeling you know why I might, but like you said, you and I aren't friends so that's the end of it. I'm about done with friends anyway. They all let you down and lie to you. Sammy not included."

Celeste's words ran through her mind, but she had to trust her instincts and hope that pushing Talie aside would tug at the girl's curiosity enough to have her open up, or let something slip.

All I need is a name, someone I can go to and ask about this so-called resistance.

Remembering Ru's arm raised, the poisoned dart and

the way Celeste had spoken about the citadel's people with such unexpected disdain, she wasn't even sure it would be a ruse if she did join them.

Talie tilted her head, consideration quirking her lips.

"Still running around after your masters then?" she asked. "Or has that gotten old now?"

Molly picked up a small block of wood and a strip of sandpaper, more for something to do with her hands.

Honesty might not hurt here.

"Not sure. There's a lot unsaid and even more to uncover. Not sure if they're the best people to give me what I need."

"And what is that?"

Molly shrugged. "Answers. I've loved growing up here, even though it comes with strings. But I don't like all the chaos that's been happening, the dying artificers and the huge difference in resources between the lower and upper levels."

She abandoned the sanding project in her hands and moved around the desk to pull a couple of chairs closer. Talie would probably choose to stand by the door and collar Sammy the moment she returned, but if she wanted a seat then Molly wouldn't be rude.

"Some say those who oppose the Menagerie are thugs who want chaos," Talie said. "Others insist that there's a secret organisation out there that runs the citadel from the bottom up."

The Menagerie runs the citadel, but not many people know they exist.

Molly held her tongue as Talie paused, then sighed and

crossed the room to take a seat, inching onto it like it might bite.

"What do you believe?" she asked.

Talie frowned. "What do you believe?"

"Do you answer every question with a question?"

"Sometimes."

Molly tried not to smile. "Well, it's infuriating. I don't know how Sammy puts up with it."

"Sammy's Sammy." Talie chuckled, the sound unexpected like she didn't do it often. "I tell her what to do. She ignores me. I ask her questions, she dodges them."

"You have that in common. Fine, no specific details. No sharing."

She fiddled with random items on her desk, aiming for unruffled and failing.

"You're not going to ask me about…" Talie hesitated. "About before you left?"

She shook her head. "No point, right? You're not going to be able to tell me anything. I doubt you're going to ask about why I was there that day in the first place, or you would have done so already. I don't like wasting my time."

She waited for some glib comment, a retort about her pursuits or her life so far, anything. Instead, silence swelled as Talie cocked her head.

"You've got your hair down."

Molly's hands stilled. "So?"

Talie shrugged. "I've never seen you with it down before."

"You're not going to throw a compliment and change the habit of a lifetime, are you?" Molly joked. Talie said nothing. "Someone took my hair ribbon and I didn't think to get another."

Her mind realm-skipped back to the huge pile of clothing May had insisted Marthe source for her, including a whole bundle of neatly folded hair ribbons.

I'll never use them now.

She hoped May was finding her way back to the queen's court easily enough, although instinct told her the hard-headed princess would be absolutely fine.

Without a single thing in her mind she could use for conversation, Molly almost cried with relief when Sammy burst through the doorway a second later, laden down with enough bags to feed an army.

"Sorry, I got chatting!"

CHAPTER TWENTY EIGHT

"Molly!"

The sound ricocheted through the otherwise sleepy morning lane. Molly froze in the workshop doorway. She'd crept out to buy some groceries and put the bag onto the floor by the door before turning around.

Don't comment on the bump. Do not comment on the bump.

"Hi, Beryl!"

Beryl huffed to a stop in front of her, a small package wrapped with festively red and green paper in her hands. The colours reminded Molly of the Holly Queen's court and she wondered wildly in that moment if the queen had sent her a summons to the wrong address or something.

"I know, I'm huge," Beryl grumbled. "Here."

Molly fumbled the package as Beryl shoved it into her hands, gripping onto the soft, squishiness inside to avoid dropping it.

"What is it?" she asked warily.

Beryl blinked. "What do you mean, what is it? Yuletide is two days away."

"Oh *ORBS*." Molly slammed a hand to her forehead.

She'd given Ru his gift already while they were at court,

wanting to be prepared. He likely wouldn't have it with him now, but then she was basically not on speaking terms with him so that hardly mattered. She didn't have a way to get a Yuletide gift to May either, but Sammy deserved one and she always did some for her neighbours.

"You forgot?" Beryl asked. "You wandered off to Faerie knows where for weeks, then you don't even remember Yuletide. Are you okay?"

Her eyes narrowed and Molly gripped the parcel, socks if she was any judge, tighter.

"It's been…" she hesitated. "I had to go somewhere on a job for a bit, but I'm back now. I've been busy so Yuletide completely slipped my mind. Thank you for this though. You'll have yours in time, don't worry!"

Beryl stared at her for several long moments, until Molly's panic started to kick in.

"Don't fuss about us," Beryl said eventually. "Although, if you wanted to give this absolute lump something, I wouldn't say no. It's going to cry, a lot."

Molly nodded. "I'd think so. Babies do."

Beryl's eyes lit up with fiendishly Fae wickedness.

"Have a lot of experience with babies, do you?"

"No! Um… no, none. Sorry. Probably hopeless with them. But thank you for reminding me about the holidays."

She held up the parcel and shuffled backwards into the workshop, grimacing a smile until Beryl nodded and ambled off toward her own home.

Molly shut the workshop door and sagged against it. She hadn't even noticed the Yuletide boughs being out when she went to the shop, although they would be further up a level and Ru usually fetched hers for her.

Ru. I still haven't decided how to handle him yet.

She heaved the groceries into her little kitchenette and cleared a spot on the warped wooden sideboard. She'd get her own bough later and dig out her decorations, then her parcel from Beryl could go under it.

She packed the groceries away and turned to survey her workshop, critical assessment settling over her. The baby would need a crib and she had the perfect wood for it. Worst case they could donate it if they already had one. For Beryl, she'd repurpose the old rocking chair she had in the corner gathering dust. For Harvey, perhaps a tin of *offke* to get him through.

Smiling at the idea, she avoided all thought of Celeste and the Menagerie.

For Sammy, perhaps I'll ask Simone at The Level if she can hold an open performance evening so Sammy can sing.

Simone had owed her a favour for a long while and now it was time to finally collect.

Molly bit her lip as she continued to search for odd items that might become good presents. She had no clue what Talie might need.

Something to attack people with. Her lips lifted. *Not a totally awful idea.*

She guessed Talie didn't need to attack people given that she was supposedly part of some underground resistance movement rather than an outright fighting force, but the memory surfaced of her pinned in Marcus' office, defiant to the last.

Molly grabbed a length of leather she'd not found a use

for yet and a sharp blade. Sinking into her chair, she sliced a thin strip off the length, found her stiffest needle and set to work.

Everyone who knew her knew the one rule: if the workshop door was shut, don't disturb her. She sank into her work, dipping between sanding and varnishing the rocking chair, painting it first with streaks of muted purple, and making sure Talie's gift was perfect.

The day passed in a whirl of activity, her back aching and her joints clicking when she stretched. She had forgotten about eating breakfast after returning with the supplies, and missed all thought of lunch entirely. Her stomach growled several hours later and finally she had to concede. Grabbing her favourite bag over one shoulder, she swirled her coat on top and peeked both ways before stepping out and locking the door behind her.

Several people smiled at her as she passed, nodding or saying a quick hello. It was home, but she couldn't help thinking of May, of Alfie down in the court kitchens, her little acorn plant she'd never see grow, Aurora fluttering around the ceilings.

Irritable suddenly, she turned down a side-lane and vaulted onto a wooden packing box, leaping to a window-sill and up further to the wood-panelled girder of the level above. These lengths she'd paced for the last few years of her life and they were as much home to her as the workshop or her neighbours.

I miss the air though. She sighed, walking along. *Actual fresh air, the wind and rain and volatile changeability.*

She passed one of the metal vents that pumped out the

refiltered air, a simulation of a breeze brushing past her face.

Would the Oak Queen give her courtiers snow for Yuletide? She had no idea. Demi probably would for hers. She shook her head sadly. All her focus needed to be on the future, and hers was firmly tied to the chaos of the citadel.

Celeste would expect promises, but Molly couldn't declare undying loyalty to the Menagerie anymore, not without lying.

Usually it was something she would have taken to Ru, and he would have talked the issue through with her to settle her doubts.

Ru wasn't a killer back then though.

By the time she reached the window that would drop her into the Menagerie, any hint of positivity had faded away on the synthetic breeze, replaced by gut-churning doubt.

Molly slid in through the window, landing noiselessly on the plush carpet. She glanced toward the double doors at the end, but it wasn't Marcus who'd given her the new orders. She turned the other way instead and headed down the hall to Celeste's office, taking a deep breath before knocking on the door.

The door swung open a moment later and she stepped inside to find Celeste seated behind her desk with a soft smile.

"Shut the door behind you, dearest."

Molly did as she was told, walking to the chair in front of the desk and putting her hands on the back. Celeste gave her a disapproving look.

"Take a seat."

Sliding onto the chair, Molly forced herself to stay calm. She wasn't going to lie to Celeste. She had her doubts and they were valid, especially if the Menagerie was on the side of the citadel's people. If they weren't, she'd have to tread carefully.

"How are you this morning?" Celeste asked.

Molly shrugged. "Confused, if I'm honest. I know we're not meant to ask too many questions, but I have some serious doubts."

Celeste smiled, leaning back in her chair, elbows on the armrests and fingers steepled before her.

"The Menagerie operates in secret for the good of the citadel. We all know this. The resistance operates in secret because they want to undermine the work we've strived to create."

"There's too much going on in secret though," Molly countered. "I don't want to be the reason people get hurt. Marcus was ready to sacrifice Talie, and you were happy enough to trade her right to freedom in exchange for getting someone into the queen's court."

She let her protection warding creep around her as she spoke, cloaking herself in a thin veil of safety. She had no idea if Celeste was strong enough to get through a warding, but she clearly had social power enough to orchestrate things and that could be just as dangerous.

"Marcus is zealous about protecting our family here. He wouldn't have agreed with me sending you out of the citadel in any normal situation. You've always wanted to see the wider realms of Faerie, isn't that right?"

"Yes, but-"

"And your friend could have taken a lot of information about us back to the enemy as well. By trading your service for her freedom, everyone got what they wanted."

"It's not about wants, her freedom was never his to barter with!"

Celeste sighed and picked up the sweet bowl. Molly shook her head as it landed in front of her, but Celeste left it there.

"Fae don't always get the luxury of their own freedom, my dear. It's a lesson best learned earlier rather than later. Still, you're home now, and she has another opportunity to prove herself obedient to the citadel's laws."

"But you want me to befriend her, right? Spy on her?"

"If you have the chance, yes. We can consider removing the eyes we currently have on her too, as she's not given us much we can follow as yet."

"She knows you'll be watching her. I'm not sure what you expect me to do either. I can't exactly ask her 'hey, are you part of any secret resistance?' She wouldn't tell me even if she was."

Celeste chuckled and took a sweet, toying with the edges of the wrapper.

"Of course not, but she may open up to you given time. Whatever the fluff around the edges, there are deaths mounting up and no way to successfully track every labyrinthine route through the citadel. The enemy spawn as quickly as we can track them."

Molly pressed her lips together to hide her disgust. Even

though the resistance were the ones supposedly causing the trouble, Celeste clearly had no intention of seeing them as anything more than pests to be crushed.

"I can't promise she'll tell me anything," she warned. "I also… I'm almost scared to ask but I have to. Do the Menagerie have anything to do with the artificers going missing?"

She didn't mention gift extraction, even though both she and Celeste knew she'd seen the contents of the book at the queen's court. Ru would have no doubt reported back what she'd told him about the star-eye symbol on the bracelet she'd found, as well as the paper Talie had dropped with the wording on it.

As Celeste's expression turned grave, Molly pushed the thought of the book's full paragraph, and the extra part of about the coalbane that she'd not disclosed to anyone, to the very back of her mind.

"I did say before that sometimes we need to keep secrets for the greater good of the citadel." Celeste's tone carried a hint of warning. "That means it's sometimes necessary to investigate or use a less ethical method to keep control."

That's not a no.

Her insides burned and her warding reacted to the rising emotion, tightening over her limbs.

"Don't worry yourself too much about the complexities, Molly," Celeste added, her expression clearing like sunshine after rain. "I can sense you're conflicted."

Molly wiped a hand over her mouth, swallowing to quash the nausea rising to her throat.

"I'm not ashamed of that."

"Neither should you be." Celeste got up from her chair and walked to the wide open windows overlooking the lane outside. "A stout heart can be a blessing and a burden. What you need to be above all else is clever. Smart. Devious if you must. The histories of Faerie are plagued with nonsense about 'good' and 'evil', but it's rarely ever that simple."

"And how far do you expect me to go?" Molly hesitated before landing the final ugly truth. "I'm not killing, not for anyone. I don't want to have to hurt anyone either."

Celeste chuckled, her gaze still fixed on the lane.

"Nobody would ask that of you. Nobody here anyway, I forbid it. There are those that will do what must be done and take both the praise and the penance accordingly, but not you. Stout hearts shrivel under the weight of such wickedness."

Molly sagged, relief pounding through her. Even though Celeste had all but promised her she merely had to tail Talie and report back, Celeste had also technically admitted there were those in the Menagerie willing to kill if needed. She hadn't outrightly denied Molly's fears about their involvement with the missing artificers and others either.

"What about Ru?" The words were out before she could stop them.

Celeste turned with a frown. "What about him? Is he causing you trouble as your liaison?"

If I tell her he crossed the line romantically, it'll make trouble. Liaisons aren't supposed to have relationships with anyone reporting to them.

She grimaced. "No, he's not, but… I might be… I think he's doing something for the Menagerie that he promised me he'd never do."

"Ah." Celeste reclaimed her seat. "That's his affair. Probably Marcus's too, but we can't interfere. Fae must walk their own paths and make their own choices, for better or worse. If you'd rather I replace him…"

"No, it's fine. So, if I do learn anything from Talie, I report it back to him?"

Celeste sighed. "Thinking about it, best come direct to me. Marcus has a lot to cope with at the moment and he does have rather a soft spot for Ru, so chances you'll be able to see much of each other are slim. Different schedules and all that."

Unsure whether to be glad or upset, Molly nodded. Space would let their argument settle and give her time to process what she now knew about him. If she was attempting to hang out with Talie as well, probably against Talie's wishes at least to start with, she'd get to see more of Sammy too.

"So keep an eye on Talie and report back anything I think you should know, got it."

Celeste nodded. "We need to know what their plans are, who they are, names, locations, resources, anything and everything. Even if it doesn't seem important, I need to know."

Celeste bent sideways and slid open a drawer. Molly breathed a tiny sigh of relief that she wasn't going to have to promise, or say that she would do her best. She still had the underlying gut instinct that until she knew which side was the right one, she wasn't tying herself to anything binding.

"Here, this is for you."

Celeste passed a small gift bag across the table. Molly stared at it.

"What is it?" she asked.

"It's a Yuletide gift, one I think you'll want." She held up a hand as Molly opened her mouth to argue. "In exchange, you'll need to relinquish your orb. We can't risk any orb-waves, new or old, being traced back to us."

Molly took a deep breath.

"My orb in exchange for whatever's in this bag?" she asked. "What is it?"

"Consider it a sign of trust, yours in us. I promise nothing in that bag will harm or inconvenience you. Quite the opposite."

A show of trust. Molly's gut twisted with nerves, her hand shaking as she retrieved her orb from her pocket. In addition to being hers, Ru had obtained some illicit extra permissions be allowed on it through favours he owed various people in the Menagerie. If Celeste found out, and asked, she would have to refuse to answer.

But if I refuse to hand my orb over, prove I don't trust them, Celeste will have me watched forever.

Molly dropped her orb onto the desk, waiting for Celeste to take it before she took the gold gift bag. Beneath a rustle of bough-green tissue paper was a small glass jar, stoppered with a cork. She picked it up between finger and thumb.

"It's a jar."

"Well, technically yes-"

"It's an empty jar."

Celeste laughed. "No, it absolutely is not. Put the vial beside your head, then remove the cork and press the opening to your forehead, but be quick about it."

Feeling like the realm's biggest idiot, Molly did as she was told, yanking the cork out and almost impaling the neck of the vial into her forehead in her hurry.

For a moment, nothing.

Then her Fae connection giggled awake, warmth shooting from her forehead across her skin, skating through her muscles right down to the bone until her entire body felt fluttery.

"What's happening?" she asked.

Celeste smiled, leaning back in her chair.

"That, my dear, was a gift."

CHAPTER TWENTY NINE

"A gift?"

Molly didn't dare remove the vial from her forehead, just in case. Only nobles could gift others, and her own charm gift had come from a passing one years ago at great expense to her guardians.

"The Menagerie has various contacts on many levels," Celeste announced, her tone drenched with amusement. "Sometimes we trade in gifts as well as favours. When I obtained this one, you came to mind immediately."

"Wow. Thank you. I don't know what to say. Thank you. Um…"

Celeste chuckled. "Don't babble, dearest. Two thank you's are more than enough."

Worrying thoughts filled Molly's head as her gut plummeted.

"This isn't… I thought a kiss from a noble was the only way to get a gift."

"Oh no, dearest. A kiss sealed in a bottle will work just as well. This one is stealth. I hear you're very good at hiding in shadows, but this should allow you to pass unnoticed by most. Practice it in front of a mirror first. You should see yourself go semi-translucent."

Molly nodded, astonished. Celeste was essentially her employer, the right-hand woman of the man who paid Molly's pitiful wages garnished by the debt they held over her head after her guardians died.

I still haven't figured out what happened with them, if their deaths weren't due to a cart accident after all.

Talie had been unable or unwilling to tell her anything, although she'd intimated before not everything was as it seemed. The Menagerie held all the strings governing her past and her future while she owed them, so she couldn't push too hard for answers there either.

But a Fae gift was a huge thing to receive, and she bit her lip as more gratitude bubbled up to her lips.

"Go," Celeste insisted. "Take the Yuletide time to relax and rest yourself. Once the festive season is over, we need to be chasing that information. Oh, and you can let the vial go now. Keep it if you like. Maybe you can find some extra use for it."

Molly lowered her arm with the bottle clenched tight in her fist.

"Um… can I keep the bag too?" she asked.

Celeste nodded. "Of course. Merry Yuletide, Molly."

"Merry Yuletide."

Molly left the room and shut the door behind her, unable to move with her usual purposeful stride while the new gift was still whizzing through her. It tingled and zinged randomly in different parts of her body, so different to the subtle cool of her charm gift that she usually felt as an easiness in the set of her shoulders, or her compulsion gift that was most often like a tug in her chest.

It'll settle, she reassured herself, moving to the window and clambering out onto the girders. *It has too, or I'll be jittering all over the place.*

She traversed up two levels until she could drop down in front of The Level, a rambling inn with clusters of mismatched tables, chairs and tat collected over the years, and followed the scent of wine and the kitchens inside.

It was still early but she found Simone sweeping under the tables, preparing for the late afternoon rush, her fizzy brown hair twisted around a corkscrew.

"Hiya, Molly." Simone grinned. "Am I in trouble?"

Molly shook her head. "I need to call in that favour."

Simone seethed through her teeth and set her broom against the nearest table, running a hand over her face.

"I knew this day would come." She sighed. "Alright, out with it."

"I need you to hold an open performance. Sometime soon. I've got a friend who wants to be a singer, so ideally have her do the last performance of the night."

Simone stared. "That… wasn't what I was expecting. Can she sing?"

"Oh yeah. Well, according to others she can, at least that's what she says."

"You going to tell her or am I expected to materialise like some genie and invite her to sing?" Simone asked, a broad smile breaking across her face.

"It's her Yuletide present from me, so I'll tell her."

"That it? I feel I've gotten off lightly."

Molly nodded. "Yep, that's it. Let her have top billing, maybe even do a bit of advertising, something on paper she can keep. Who knows, maybe she's so good you'll have her back every week."

"Don't go promising that." Simone laughed. "One night, but as you say, who knows. Want a drink?"

"Can't stop, but I will come by for the lunch rush soon, when I can. It's difficult at the moment what with the workshop and stuff."

Simone grinned. "Busy?"

"Fits and starts, and yes, if you've got something that needs doing, bring it by. I need all the pesanas I can get."

"Fair enough, will do, and come back for that drink when you get a chance." Her expression turned wicked. "Bring that lovely specimen with you that can lift all the barrels next time as well."

Simone grabbed her broom, chortling to herself. Molly ignored the sinking in her gut at the mention of Ru. She was home with time for Yuletide and she had a brand new gift with a few days free to test it out.

She walked up two levels the normal way through the lanes until she reached the workshop, so deep in thought that she almost missed something on her doorstep. The moment her gaze swept down, her insides plummeted.

"Oh, no," she muttered. "No no no."

Aurora tilted her head, ruffling her hefty white wings as if in answer.

"What are you doing here?" Molly asked. "Why am I talking to a bird? It's not like you can answer me. Okay, I'm going to open the door and step around you. Please don't peck my face off."

Wishing to high heaven that she'd found somewhere to

practice her stealth gift before coming home, although she wasn't sure if gifts like that worked on animals with more honed instincts than Fae had, Molly reached out inch by agonising inch.

Aurora watched the progress of her hand as it moved quakingly above her head, key clenched between finger and thumb. Molly had no idea how she could start sweating so fast, but her face was burning and her body shaking from the awkward angle.

The key clicked in the lock and she forced herself to take a shuffling step closer.

If I swing the door open and leap, I can get in before she attacks. She put her hand on the handle. *One, two, LEAP.*

She jammed the handle down, threw the door open and leapt. A rush of air ruffled her hair and she dropped to her knees with a squeal, rolling out of the way.

Seconds passed and she lifted her head.

Not only was she back outside on the doorstep thanks to panic-fuelled disorientation, but Aurora had settled on top of her mirror right at the back of the workshop.

"You can't stay there," Molly insisted.

She took a step inside the shop, reminding herself of the scant knowledge May had told her. No sudden movements. Birds don't attack unless they feel threatened.

None of it helped.

Before she could contemplate the idea of going to find Sammy to ask for help, or even Ru, or Talie, or Beryl at a push, Aurora opened her beak and something dropped with a hefty, clinking thud.

Molly inched closer.

"No pecking at me. If you brought it, and dropped it, I'm going to pick it up," she said.

Aurora clicked her beak once, dismissively almost, and tucked her head against her wing.

"You can't just go to sleep there!" Molly hissed.

Aurora ignored her. Taking advantage of the situation, Molly crept forward and snatched the bundle of fabric, which turned out to be a small cloth bag.

Undoing the drawstring, she found a tiny letter in a thick cream envelope with scalloped edges, and at the bottom of the pouch were more pesanas than she could remember seeing in one go.

Stepping cautiously away from Aurora, Molly slowly lowered herself onto the chair nearest the door, keeping the bird in sight at all times as she opened the letter, the pouch resting on her lap.

Molly,

I promised I'd let you know I got home safely, and here I am letting you know. Mother didn't even have any idea so all the better. I did ask about visiting the citadel again but she'd heard about the attack on the concert and it was an unyielding 'never again'. I have no idea what brought you to the court, or what convinces you to stay behind, but I won't message your orb unless you message me first just in case. If you ever do get a chance to leave again, as long as you mean us no harm or ill-will, visit me as my guest anytime.

The pesanas are your up-to-date wages by the way. We'll see each other again someday. I'll make sure of it.

May.

P.S. Aurora will not peck your face off, don't worry.

Molly pressed the letter to her chest, touched that May had gone to the lengths of sending Aurora to bring a message.

I doubt I can get Aurora to take a message back, assuming she knows how to get out again.

Considering she'd got in somehow, Molly had no doubt Aurora could go wherever she pleased. She would leave the door open and the bird would inevitably find her own way out.

CHAPTER THIRTY

Aurora didn't fly out that day, or the next. Molly woke up two days after her arrival with the covers over her head, under the impression that if Aurora dive-bombed her during the night, she could use the blankets to wrap the bird up and throw her out of the door.

Aurora didn't dive-bomb her. She chirped and ruffled her feathers, occasionally took a lap of the workshop and left an unavoidable mess at the base of Molly's mirror. Molly had grudgingly put out a bowl of water for her, then conceded to sharing some bits of each meal which Aurora picked through daintily, but mostly Molly worked on her Yuletide gifts.

Sitting up in bed, Molly realised Aurora had no intention of leaving until she was ready, but now that the festive morning had dawned, Molly had to venture out and deliver her gifts.

"Are you going to fly out then," she asked grouchily. "Or do I lock you inside?"

Aurora eyed her, answering with an indecipherable chirp. It didn't sound like 'thank you for having me, I'm off home now' either.

Molly risked leaving the door open while getting herself

washed and dressed, but Aurora made no move to leave. Mumbling under her breath, Molly shunted the newly varnished rocking chair with its purple streaks toward the door, the baby's cot piled on top. Her bag rested underneath the cot containing Harvey's tin of *offke*, a card for Sammy explaining her gift and Talie's more physical present.

"What the bloody hell is that noi- Molly, what are you doing?"

Beryl's voice all but shattered the windows. Molly winced at the loud noise bouncing around the lane and peered over the top of the chair with a hopeful smile.

"It's your Yuletide gift. A rocking chair for you, cot for the baby and a huge tin of *offke* for Harvey. I tend to make things for people rather than buy them, so I hope they're okay."

Beryl stared at the pile, her eyes wide and her hands flying to her belly.

"Harvey!" she bellowed.

Molly gasped, a stab of panic gripping her. Thoughts of her gifts somehow shocking the baby out filled her head as Harvey thundered out of their front door with a t-shirt stuck over his head and only one sock on.

"What, what's happened? Is it time? I have the bag, the other bag, the smaller bag, the pillow-"

"No, you idiot. Presents, look."

Harvey emerged blinking and red-faced from the neck of his t-shirt.

"Don't do that!" He huffed. "I thought it was baby time. Wow, those are cool."

Beryl rolled her eyes. "Get them inside then. This is too much, honestly."

Molly managed a weak smile, her heart still pounding as Harvey ambled up and took the arms of the rocking chair. She rescued her bag and stepped back as he hefted the chair and cot easily.

"Cool, flavoured *offke*! Cheers, Molly."

He grinned at her before carrying the rocking chair toward their door.

"I have to get going," Molly said, sidling backwards.

Beryl's gaze sharpened. "Leave your door open, yeah?"

"Er… what? Why?"

"Because." She scowled. "It's not like I'm going to take anything!"

Molly held both hands up in pre-emptive defence.

"I never said you would. Merry Yuletide."

She escaped before Beryl could tell her off. The moment she was safe inside the workshop, she hovered by the door and peered out until Beryl retreated into her home, slamming the door behind her.

Molly slid out and shut her door, locking it disobediently.

If she wants in, she can wait for me to get back.

She turned, took two paces toward the main lane, and slowed immediately to a halt. At the entrance to the alley, leaning against the side of the wall as though she had all the time in the world, was Talie.

Smirking.

At her.

"Come with me," she said.

Molly frowned. "Why?"

"Do you still want to fix the citadel, Princess?"

Always a question for a question.

"Of course."

Talie pushed away from the wall, glancing over her shoulder.

"I won't make any promises, but I'll take you to someone you might be interested to meet. All you have to do is tell the truth."

Molly huffed. "I'm Fae, It's not like I can lie."

"Tell the truth, that's all I'm saying. You coming?"

Molly shoved her bag firmly up her shoulder and walked forward.

It can't be this easy. Talie knows who I'm affiliated with, so why would she let me anywhere near the resistance?

"Is this some kind of trap?" she asked. "If it is, nobody's going to come get me, if you're trying to draw anyone out."

Talie snorted. "No worry of that. Nobody's going to harm you, not unless you start a fight. You want answers so bad? I'll take you to someone who has them. Whether they'll answer any, that's up to them."

Molly let that filter through her. Talie couldn't lie, but not lying wasn't the same as telling the truth. For all she knew, Talie might believe she was safe enough but whoever she was leading them to could have an entirely different motive.

I didn't have much chance to practice my stealth gift either.

She'd tried a few times, managing to locate the

sensation of it lurking somewhere near her belly, and almost woke Aurora into a flapping fit when she squeaked as her body started to fade.

Invisibility was impossible, she wasn't royalty like May, but to be able to make herself opaque as a ghost, like a soft outline of light and matter against shadow, it was unnerving and awesome at the same time.

Compulsion may still be my safest defence.

She dredged a warding around her, glad she'd had the last two days to rest and eat properly.

"How far up is it?" she asked.

Talie shrugged. "Four levels. Tired already? You can turn back anytime you know."

"No thanks, Sunshine. I've never felt more ready."

She caught Talie's tiny smile out of the corner of her eye while smothering her own. They weren't friends but assuming she survived wherever Talie was taking her, she would deliver Sammy's gift in person or die trying. She shuddered at the thought, hunching her shoulders to bring her coat closer around her.

"Here we are." Talie strode up to the front door of a gym. "After you."

Molly ignored the mock civility in Talie's tone and glanced around before walking inside. It was a vast warehouse space, three square platforms roped off for training rings and a collection of weights and mats in the far corner.

A couple were already sparring in one of the rings, but Talie walked toward the back of the room like she owned the place. She pushed open a door marked 'Toilets' and waved her arm impatiently at it when Molly hesitated.

The narrow hall on the other side had peeling wallpaper and a scent of dust lingering, but Molly kept walking with Talie breathing down her neck.

"Hatch above your head, up you go," Talie announced.

Molly looked up, eying the conveniently placed table beneath the mostly closed hatch. Pulling her protection warding as tight around her as she could, she vaulted onto the table and slid her fingers in the gap to prise the hatch open. She hauled herself up into the dark space, legs swinging and cheeks flushed.

Even if they have me up here, there are ways out. There are always ways out.

She'd learned the various building structures that made up the levels of the citadel, where the bolts would be that could remove a metal panel. In the lining of her bag and her coat she had spare lock-picks and a few lightweight keys and screwdriver heads.

Even so, her pulse thudded as Talie appeared beside her.

"Come on, Princess. Not far now."

Molly followed her through the gloom toward a dim flicker of light ahead.

"Does whoever I'm meeting have a name then?" she asked, her tone steadier than she felt.

"He'll tell you if he wants to. Mind the hole in the floor there."

Molly looked down to see a gaping rubbish chute and dodged accordingly. A door loomed up ahead, lit by a single bare bulb hanging above. She sucked in a shaky breath and straightened her shoulders as Talie knocked loudly then threw open the door without waiting.

"In you go."

Molly wanted to ask if Talie was going in with her, but she wouldn't give her the satisfaction. She stalked past her through the doorway without a thank you and scanned the tiny room as Talie shut the door between them.

Large wooden filing cabinets with chips and nicks all over cluttered up every corner, and a large barrel with a bunch of paper piled on top claimed the centre of the cramped space. A couple of crates made seats around the barrel, but Molly's attention stuck on the man standing on the other side of it.

His face was more youthful than she'd expected, definitely a fully grown man but without being actually old. Despite the lithe body and handsome pale face, with a sheet of silver-blonde hair falling loose over his shoulders, Molly skated right past his looks and settled on the shrewd grey eyes narrowed in her direction. She recognised him as the man from the warehouse the day she and Talie got stuck in the rubbish tunnel, and she firmed her warding around her.

"Talie says you have questions," he said.

No sense of accusation in his tone, not even any real wariness or curiosity, but it was still there in his eyes.

"I do, but who are you?"

He sank onto one of the crates, indicating she should take the one opposite him. She glanced back at the door and sat with her back rigid, ready to run.

"I'm Phoenix, like the bird." His lips lifted.

Molly grimaced. "Always orbing birds."

"Huh?"

"Never mind. I've had odd run-ins with birds recently. Perhaps it's an omen. I do have questions, and Talie seems to think you can answer them."

"I might."

Molly bit her lip, unsure where to even start.

"It's no secret that the citadel is descending into chaos. Artificers going missing, some murdered, resources sparse on some levels but not others. Nobody knows where the artificers end up but some don't make it back. Those that do don't remember anything. Why? Why take them? What are they being used for? Why wipe their memories, and how? Who's responsible?"

The questions thundered out and Phoenix started laughing. He stood up, grabbed a tin of *offke* from the top of one of the filing cabinets and held it up.

"I'll let you serve us both if you're twitchy accepting drinks?" he offered.

Molly shook her head. "I'm fine thanks, but you go ahead. I get it if you can't answer, or won't. You don't know me or owe me anything."

"Tell me this then." He paused to shovel *offke* into a grubby mug and flick on a kettle. "Talie seems to think you'd join the resistance. By her reckoning, you might already be spoken for by their enemy. Are you here hoping to find a way to spy on them?"

"Tell the truth."

Talie's words circled in her mind. The worst Phoenix could do was try to attack her, but her warding was still strong. He wasn't anywhere near the door to block or lock it quick enough either. If she had to, she'd compel him to stand down.

It would be so easy to compel him to tell her what she needed to know. She hesitated, her previous promise to herself at the forefront.

How long before I'm using it for every little thing? Or someone finds out and starts using me for their own ends?

She wouldn't risk going down that road. Emergencies only.

"I am, and I'm not." She sighed. "The… There are people who claim the resistance are their enemy, and they hold a debt over my head. Until recently, I thought it was legitimate. Now I'm not so sure. They want me to spy on the resistance, and I imagine if I were to get anywhere near the resistance, they'd want me to do the same but going the other way. I don't know."

Phoenix sipped his *offke* and tilted his head, his gaze radiating over her. She forced herself to stare back, the temptation to shrink away from his assessment clawing at her insides.

"Do you have any gifts?" he asked.

"Yes, charm."

"Any others?"

She hesitated. "Stealth, but I'm not very good at it."

Yet. She would practice daily from now on.

Phoenix set his mug down on the barrel and sat again, his forearms resting on his rangy knees.

"If you wanted to join the resistance, they would probably send tests for you first. Chances to prove you're genuine about the cause."

Molly tensed, her chest swooping.

"How would they even know I was looking?"

Phoenix grinned. "How does anyone know anything about anything? How do the Menagerie find out their secrets? Word gets around one way or another."

"So you know who the Menagerie really are, which is more than most in the citadel do. What if this resistance ask me to do tests, but I say no?"

He shrugged. "If you were to keep quiet, nothing would happen. If you blabbed, everything could happen. If they asked, and you joined them, they'd likely train you to fight, maybe even find more suitable gifts for you to wield in time."

Molly ignored the mention of extra gifts, fixing on the promise of training instead. Doubt still swirled in her head but that wouldn't be leaving her anytime soon no matter what Phoenix promised.

"Do you know the truth about who's targeting the artificers?" she asked, bold despite her nerves.

Phoenix leaned forward, both hands cupping around his mug as he looked her dead in the eyes.

"Ask yourself this: what crime have they committed? According to all reports, none. It's a mystery. So what would an organisation like the Menagerie want artificers for?"

For the experimentation of gift extraction.

She shrugged instead.

"To do their dirty work I'd imagine."

"Exactly. If the powers that be want something hidden, you can conclude it's not in the service of the people they're supposed to serve, or they'd be shouting it from the rooftops."

Molly nodded. "There's logic to that, I guess. So what would the resistance say is happening to the missing Fae then, or the dead artificers?"

Phoenix smiled as he shifted his weight, hooking one ankle over the other leg and balancing his mug on his knee as if they were friends having a chat.

"The artificers are a bloviated guild full of pompous Fae," he said. "Many of them are nobles too dabbling in keeping a hobby. Ask yourself why a seat of power like the Menagerie would want to target them."

"Control."

"Exactly. The resistance has no reason to kidnap or kill artificers. If they were going to target anyone, it would be the Menagerie themselves."

He has a point, and Celeste didn't exactly deny the Menagerie's involvement in the disappearances.

Behaviours spoke more than words often could, and through Phoenix she might have a chance to find people who could give her proper answers in time.

"I get the theory behind that." She hesitated. "But I still can't see the connection. There was that cobbler who went missing, and one of the boots, then a couple of artificers."

She waited as Phoenix eyed her, his stare unflinching until she had the urge to retreat from the room.

"Ask yourself why Lady Carrington died," he suggested.

Molly frowned. "Well, she supported more liberal freedom from noble rule."

"So do many Fae that don't get murdered."

"She annoyed someone perhaps, caused a feud or something."

"Maybe."

As Phoenix smiled, she let her theory tumble out.

"Or it's a distraction. Lady Carrington doesn't fit the same type as the previous missing Fae. The cobbler, the man from the boots, they were regular. Then the artificers, they might have relevance to whatever's going on."

"What links them then?" Phoenix leaned forward to brace his forearms on the barrel. "If the artificers are being taken for what they know, why take normal people as well?"

"Because they had something useful, obviously, but I've not got a clue what that might be. Her death has been waved away as a noble vendetta."

He nodded. "Which spins us what story?"

Molly wiped a hand over her face.

"The man from the boots would have stumbled on something he shouldn't. The cobbler maybe knew too much. The artificers would have been on Lady Carrington's payroll, and a rival noble killed her for it."

"And there you have it." He sat back. "You have no concrete proof of anything but you've made up what happened, dismissed it and life in the citadel goes on."

"I haven't dismissed anything-"

"But most others will have."

Molly hesitated. "Oh."

"Yeah, oh." He sighed. "So the Menagerie will likely lie low a while now, and blame what happened down at that stadium as an assassination attempt on the queen, who I heard was in the audience."

He doesn't know who did the killing though.

"People will think whatever suits them," she said. "So, now that I'm here, you're going to expect something in return I take it? Or your mysteriously hypothetical resistance will?"

Phoenix laughed. "No, the resistance aren't in the habit of forcing answers from teenage girls, or anything else. They'd admire loyalty, but a time will come one day for everyone to choose a side."

Molly stood up. He'd as good as told her the resistance would send tests for her, and he likely wouldn't tell her much more with his veiled chatter. He didn't move as she walked toward the door and stopped with her hand on the handle.

"Whichever side stops the killing and supports the people of the citadel, that's the side I want to be on."

She didn't wait for him to reply as she opened the door and stepped out. Talie stood waiting for her, scuffing her shoe across the dusty floorboards.

"Molly."

She turned back before realising she hadn't given Phoenix her name, although Talie no doubt would have.

Phoenix lifted a hand and something small sailed out of it. Instead of retreating like she should have done, Molly reached out on instinct to catch it.

A small, cool sphere settled on her palm, glinting cornflower blue and flecked with gold, a keychain drilled into it.

When she looked up, Phoenix gave her a teasing bow of his head.

"Welcome to the resistance. Shut the door on your way out."

Molly clamped her fingers tight around the orb and closed the door behind her with a shaking hand. Questions poured around her bewildered mind like soup, but Talie's pursed lips and furrowed brow didn't invite any conversation.

She followed Talie wordlessly along to the hatch, shoving the orb into her jeans pocket so she had her hands free to drop through onto the table. She slid down and stepped aside to give Talie room, still baffled.

"Not a word," Talie muttered.

Molly nodded, not sure she even had any words left.

The resistance had apparently taken her on just like that. Phoenix would have known she was part of the Menagerie from Talie and yet he'd still accepted her, unless it was some kind of cruel joke. Phoenix seemed like he might be the kind for pranks, but maybe not cruel ones. Talie most definitely wasn't.

Given the irate twist of Talie's face as they left the gym, she hadn't expected Molly to get anywhere.

"You're angry?" She had to ask.

Talie shrugged. "Yeah. I had to do several boring errands before I was welcomed in. You chat to him for all of five minutes and he's all arms open."

Molly fought the urge to grin. She ducked her head, guessing annoying Talie wasn't the best way to go about getting on the right side of someone she was apparently now affiliated with instead of pitted against.

"I must have had something he wanted."

Talie's chin lifted. "Like what?"

"You know who I know, now so does he. Guess he thinks it could be useful."

"You told him you're part of… you know?" she asked.

Molly nodded. "Not directly. He talks in circles. I didn't see your resistance symbol anywhere though."

"Resistance symbol?"

"Yeah, the bracelet you wear, I've seen it on others. Always the same insignia."

Talie's expression didn't falter. "Oh, really."

"And I saw you in the library once. You dropped a piece of paper with the same symbol scribbled on it."

Talie's lips lifted. "Ah. I wondered where that went. As for the bracelet, the symbol isn't for any specific resistance, it represents freedom."

"Oh."

"Yeah. It's an ancient sigil the citadel was built on, and it's also the physical outline of the citadel itself, how the internal structure is laid out. Learn a lot if you know where to look, Princess."

Molly rolled her eyes. "I know where to look for what matters, Sunshine."

The taunt reminded her she still had Yuletide gifts in her bag.

"Can I come by yours for a moment?" she asked.

Talie frowned and her folded her arms over her chest.

"Why? If I invited you in, it wouldn't make us best friends or anything."

It shouldn't have hurt as much as it did. A flicker of memory filled Molly's head, of them dancing close and pretending they weren't who they were for a night.

She shrugged, forcing her expression to remain neutral.

"I wouldn't dream of assuming you want to be anyone's friend. I'm only asking because I have a Yuletide gift for Sammy. I'd rather give it to her in person. Is she home?"

Talie's brow lifted. They stared at each other for several seconds, neither backing down. Then Talie's lips pulled thin and she turned to walk up a level without a word.

Molly followed her, awfulness roiling in the pit of her stomach.

I'll give Sammy her present then leave. Talie may have gotten me into the resistance, but I saved her from the Menagerie before so we're quits.

Talie opened her door and stomped inside, leaving Molly hovering in the doorway.

"Molly!" Sammy scrambled to her feet and hurried over. "What are you doing here? I wanted to come down and see you, bring you a Yuletide gift. It's nothing much at all but the thought's there."

Molly smiled. "I came to bring you yours. Here."

She pulled out Sammy's card, her fingers hesitating over Talie's wrapped present. She gave Sammy both, but tapped her finger on Talie's name scrawled on the wrapping, mouthing 'shhhh'.

"Thank you! We don't open them until later. Here's yours."

Molly clung onto their gifts in one hand as she took the small wrapped parcel Sammy handed her and slipped it into her bag. She didn't want Talie seeing she had one until the last second so she could avoid the inevitable awkwardness.

"Thanks, I open mine later too. I gave my neighbour hers and I swear she was about to give birth out of shock."

Sammy grinned. "She's scary awesome. Did you get one from your princess friend?"

Molly nodded, thinking of Aurora and the pouch of far more pesanas than she could have earned.

"Yeah, I will need to think of something to send her though somehow."

"She's actually sort of interesting, you know, for someone so disgustingly privileged."

"I won't disagree with that." Molly laughed. "Right, I only came to drop these off. Here, and Merry Yuletide."

She handed the presents over and Sammy grabbed them with a wicked grin.

"You didn't get me anything, did you?" Talie muttered.

Molly froze, her mind whirring. If Talie wanted to stalk about with an attitude, she could match it.

"Like you said, it doesn't make us friends, right? See you, Sammy. Pop by the workshop sometime soon."

She walked out before Sammy could even say goodbye, knowing Talie would be getting an earful immediately for being grouchy.

Walking down the levels to the workshop, she let her mind wander. She had no guarantee the resistance weren't the enemy, or the Menagerie, but she had to hope one or the other would reveal their evils in time. Or both. Until then, she would hone her gifts and play both sides to find out the truth.

She let herself into the workshop, stepping high over several wrapped parcels identical to the one Beryl had given her before. Beneath those was a bough, something she still hadn't managed to get. With a grunt, she swept the lot into her arms and ferried them to her table.

The bough had a small envelope on it, and her heart sank as she recognised Ru's handwriting.

They always spent Yuletide together, watching old shows on the orb and making too much food.

Not this year, not yet.

She left the card on the bough and took it to the usual place on the wooden sideboard. As she placed her presents around it, she eyed Aurora warily.

The bird eyed her in return, head tilting back and forth. She hadn't attacked yet, not once. Sometimes, Molly wondered if Aurora sensed she was nervous around her and was keeping her distance.

"You can't understand me, but I'll say it anyway. If you want to stay, you have to poop outside. That," she pointed to the base of the mirror, "is disgusting."

Aurora chirped at being spoken to and Molly checked her water bowl before surveying the pile of gifts. Beryl's were all soft and squishy, no doubt various pieces of clothing for random occasions. Molly bypassed those along with Ru's envelope, and settled her hand on the parcel Sammy had given her.

She pulled off the wrapping, nobody around to tell her she had to wait until after dinner, and smiled.

A rainbow of hair ribbons fluttered out, twirling around

as they fell to the floor. She bent to scoop them up quickly, noticing something sparkle as it hit the ground with a tiny *thunk*.

Beneath the ribbons, she found a tiny silver key charm.

Digging into the wrapping one more time, she found a slip of paper.

The charm is from me, I traded at school for it. You wear a weird collection around your neck so I figured you could add to it so you have something of our friendship always with you. Talie insisted on hair ribbons for some reason, but they're practical I guess.

Molly found a muted emerald green hair ribbon in the midst of the cluster and dropped the rest next to the bough so she could tie her hair back.

She couldn't fathom why Talie, grouchiness personified, had not only noticed her absence of a hair ribbon but also gone to the trouble of buying her several.

As she set to making her Yuletide dinner, she entertained herself with thoughts of how irritated Talie would probably be when she unwrapped the thin dagger all polished up neat alongside a leather wrist strap to secure it with.

I'll start practicing with my stealth gift tomorrow too.

She set her dinner out on her desk, the echo of screaming and shouting coming from Beryl and Harvey's home, and something going bang which suggested it probably wasn't the arrival of the baby.

The thought of her stealth gift and Celeste's generosity

warred with her worry that the Menagerie might not be the ones she trusted now. She also still had the nugget of information about the *coalbane* that both sides would likely kill for lodged in her mind.

"It's weird," she told Aurora, grudgingly because the bird still showed no sign of going outside for the toilet. "Despite all my fears about which side I'm on, I'm now standing on both with no idea who I can trust."

Aurora clicked her beak in reply but Molly couldn't even bring herself to flinch, not even when Aurora left her perch on the mirror and fluttered to land on the edge of the desk, her attention fixed on Molly's spiced and roasted vegetables.

Molly sighed and slid a few bits onto a separate plate.

"If you peck my eyes out, you might be doing me a favour."

Joining the resistance wasn't going to be easy if the mention of fighting training was anything to go by, and she would be pulled thin working with both sides as well as running the workshop.

"Yuletide first," she told Aurora, flinching when the bird chirped happily back. "Let everything settle down until we find out more about which side we need to be on. Then we get to work."

ACKNOWLEDGEMENTS

A huge thank you to every reader who has walked with me through Faerie and is still coming back for another visit! To those who've shared on social media, done ARC reads or just given me compliments about the book to keep me going, thank you!

To my family and also my writing family as always, your support means everything to me – Aerin Apeltun, Katina Wright, Estelle Tudor, Anna Britton, Sally Doherty, Marisa Noelle, Emma Finlayson-Palmer, writing Twitter, the amazing ARC readers (who have caught so many printing blips it's not even funny…), the wider writing community and everyone who joins #ukteenchat, WriteMentor, SCBWI, and especially libraries and schools who've taken a chance on the previous books, shops that are still stocking them and giving this indie author a chance to reach more readers *deep breath* and most importantly to the readers who will find these books in the future:

THANK YOU!

ABOUT THE AUTHOR

While always convinced that there has to be something out there beyond the everyday, Emma focuses on weaving magic realms with words (the real world can wait a while). The idea of other worlds fascinates her and she's determined to find her own entrance to an alternate realm one day.

Raised in London, she now lives on the UK south coast with her husband and a very lazy black Labrador who occasionally condescends to take her out for a walk.

Aside from creative writing studies, an addiction to cake and spending far too much time procrastinating on social media, Emma is still waiting for the arrival of her unicorn. Or a tank, she's not fussy.

For the latest news and updates, check the website or come say hi on social media:

www.emmaebradley.com
@EmmaEBradley